Sam Carmody is a writer and award-winning songwriter from the town of Geraldton on the central coast of Western Australia. He is also a previous recipient of the Mary Grant Bruce Award as part of the Fellowship of Australian Writers (FAW) National Literary Awards and his short fiction and non-fiction have been published widely online and in print.

Carmody's first novel, *The Windy Season*, was shortlisted for the 2014 *Australian*/Vogel's literary Award. He is currently living in Darwin on Australia's Northern Territory coast lecturing in creative writing at the Batchelor Institute of Indigenous Higher Education.

SAM CARMODY

THE WINDY SEASON

ALLEN&UNWIN
SYDNEY·MELBOURNE·AUCKLAND·LONDON

Shark Fin Blues
Written by G.Liddiard (Mushroom Music)
Reproduced with kind permission

First published in 2016

Allen & Unwin
83 Alexander Street
Crows Nest NSW 2065
Australia
Phone: (61 2) 8425 0100
Email: info@allenandunwin.com
Web: www.allenandunwin.com

Cataloguing-in-Publication details are available
from the National Library of Australia
www.trove.nla.gov.au

ISBN 978 1 76011 156 4

Set in 12.5/16.5 pt Berkeley Oldstyle by Midland Typesetters, Australia
Printed and bound in Australia by Griffin Press
10 9 8 7 6 5 4 3 2 1

MIX
Paper from
responsible sources
FSC® C009448

The paper in this book is FSC® certified.
FSC® promotes environmentally responsible,
socially beneficial and economically viable
management of the world's forests.

In memory of my grandmother, and first reader,
Freda Vines

Standing on the deck watching my shadow stretch
The sun pours my shadow upon the deck
The waters licking round my ankles now
There ain't no sunshine way way down

I see the sharks out in the water like slicks of ink
Well, there's one there bigger than a submarine
As he circles I look in his eye
I see Jonah in his belly by the campfire light

From *Shark Fin Blues*, The Drones

THERE ARE THINGS OUT THERE worse than sharks.

He had been told that so many times. The German enjoyed reminding him. Three months he had said it and Paul never knew what it meant. He suspected he didn't want to know, that it was wiser not to look that hard. After all, there were ten thousand kilometres of coastline, from the Northern Territory border right down to the South Australia border. Most of it unpatrolled. All that ocean to the west, the Indian Ocean. There were bound to be things moving about that you didn't want to come nose to nose with. And Paul never did, not until the twenty-mile crucifix, when Paul saw the body tied to the marker above the old shipwreck. Unrecognisable from weather and sun and birds.

There are things out there worse than sharks. He would know that in the end.

I

Missing

PAUL WAS WORKING HIS SUPERMARKET shift when he first heard Elliot was missing. It was a Wednesday morning. Seven o'clock. The dairy delivery had just come in and his fingers were blue from freezer cold. The floor was empty of customers when he saw his mother, crossing the fruit and vegetable section, tugging at the sleeve of her sweater. He waved to her but she didn't smile when she saw him. She wasn't wearing makeup. It was rare to see her outside of the house without makeup on.

Has Elliot called you? she said before she got to him.

Paul shook his head.

Shit, she said, stepping backwards as though she'd been pushed. Has he said anything to you? Was he going anywhere?

What's wrong?

I don't know where he is, she said. His mother was almost shouting. She looked into the misted glass of the fridges and seemed to catch her reflection. She put a hand to her face and looked back at Paul. He saw the panic in her eyes, how in that moment it changed her completely, made her seem like a teenager. We don't know where he is, she said, quieter. It's not like him.

With that she turned and walked towards the checkouts.

Paul spent the rest of the shift moving between the storeroom freezer and the supermarket floor carrying crates and sodden, frost-covered cardboard boxes. The store manager, Bec, had her word to him in the delivery yard. As usual she made him stand looking west, squinting at the ocean torn by the sea breeze, white with sun. Far out in the sea lane, freighters queued, their black flanks shrunken and blurred in the glare. He watched the ships as she recited some new complaint about him. He had been getting that speech most days, Bec's hands jammed in the back pockets of her black pants, belly out towards him. She told him that he wouldn't get checkout duties again until he looked customers in the eye, like a man. He needed to speak up. He needed to know that everyone thought he was a pervert. He could think about sucking clit in his own time, she said. He apologised. Paul didn't tell her about Elliot, didn't mention to anyone what his mother had told him.

The shift finished at midday and when he reached home on his bicycle his father was already back from the university and his grandmother had arrived and installed herself in the kitchen, fussing over the few dishes at the sink and preparing food for no clear reason. She cornered Paul when she saw him and filled him in.

Elliot hadn't been seen for days. He was last seen in Stark, the fishing town where he worked. His phone was going straight to messages, as though it were switched off; or he could be out of range, somewhere even further up the coast. He could be hurt, his grandmother said. Could have got himself into trouble on one of his surfing or fishing trips. Could have crashed his car or been washed off rocks by a king wave. His grandmother clenched his wrist as she said these things, not really looking at him. Then she let him go, returning to her post behind the kitchen counter to scowl into a white plastic mixing bowl.

Paul found his father upstairs in his study, still in his suit jacket.

Paul, his father said, and straightened his glasses. He was standing beside the wall-mounted bookshelf, leaning back on his heels. He held a large ring-bound document. You know, his father said, leafing through it, I met a student's grandfather today. We had a morning tea for our doctoral grads and this very good student of mine had brought along his family including this grandfather. Ninety-two years old. First time I ever saw the man but then I remembered that the same man had died six years ago. Six years ago I gave an assignment extension to this student because one Mr Horsley, his grandfather, had died. But there today at this morning tea sat Mr Horsley definitely alive, and in reasonable health. Paul's father smiled. A miracle, he said, and ran a hand through his clipped blond hair.

As usual, Paul didn't know what to say to his father. He had expected that maybe this one time the Professor might even be angry, having to cancel a lecture, arriving home to bad news and patchy information. He had expected that he might be aggravated by the unproductive fretting of Paul's grandmother, impatient with the whole thing, feeling all the same things Paul did. But the Professor stood there in the study as absentmindedly as a man standing in a park.

And I thought to myself, his father continued, that is dedication. To be willing to do-in your grandfather for a one-week extension.

Elliot, Paul said. The word echoed darkly in the study.

Yes, his father replied. Your mother is making calls.

Paul waited for more, but that was all his father said on it.

Where is Mum? Paul said.

Maybe try his room.

Paul waited a moment longer, watched his father's back, turned to the door.

Paul, his father called after him, removing his reading glasses.

Yeah.

I don't like you going on my computer. You know that. I have a lot of work on here. I can't afford to lose it.

He didn't answer as he left the room.

Paul's mother spent the afternoon in Elliot's bedroom on the phone. She tried to call Tess, Elliot's girlfriend who had first reported him missing, but she didn't answer. She spoke to the police in Stark and the city police. An officer told her they would send someone out to see them.

It wasn't like Elliot. Paul's mother repeated that phrase a number of times on the phone with people—to Elliot's small circle of friends and their parents, in the phone calls from his aunty Ruth, and to the dozens of other concerned or curious people who phoned, some of whom she hadn't seen in years. And she would repeat it to herself. *It's not like him.* And it wasn't. Elliot called regularly. Even when he was on his trips up the coast he had always been clear about when he was coming home. Paul didn't think of Elliot as secretive. He was reclusive, but not shady. But no one knew where he had been for three days.

Paul's grandmother suggested the possibility of an accident, that Elliot might have run off the road somewhere in a place that would conceal the car, hidden behind a wall of trees or deep in desert bush. In the course of the afternoon she became convinced of the scenario and suggested that she set off and begin a search of the country roads. Paul's mother found the idea simultaneously irritating and overwhelming, and ordered her to stay until the police arrived. She said it was unlikely that Elliot could have left the road without a trace. Paul's grandmother went quiet, as if suddenly realising the practical dilemma posed by the theory. Seven hundred kilometres of looking for brake marks on worn highways, of searching the roadside bush north of the city and the infinite maze of four-wheel-drive trails between Perth and Stark and all those barren stretches of coast and beaches that didn't have names. And Paul suddenly understood the power of losing someone, just how big it made the world seem, so impossibly endless and silent and indifferent, and how small it made you feel.

It was evening when the police car pulled into the driveway, the headlights shining through the living-room windows.

They sat at the kitchen table upstairs. His father opened the balcony doors. The night was hot and still. The dog panted at their feet. Paul's mother sat at the head of the table, opposite his father. Paul sat opposite the officer. He was not much older than Elliot, maybe mid-twenties. He smelt of spray deodorant.

He works on boats, right? the officer said, pen poised above a notepad. Crayfish?

Yes, said Paul's mother.

Stark?

He's been up there the last two seasons.

The officer paused to write notes. Paul watched his mother. Her fingers were curled in Ringo's hair. The fox terrier's panting smile looked ridiculous in the seriousness of the moment. For a second Paul had the terrifying sensation of wanting to laugh out loud.

So he'd be making good money? the officer asked, looking up. Could take off any time he wanted? You said on the phone he travels a lot.

But always comes back, Paul's mother said.

She's right, his father said. Always comes back.

Does he go away for long periods?

He'll be gone for a few weeks, sometimes, his mother said. About this time of year, after the season, in the winter. He'll go up the coast.

Alone?

Sometimes he'd take that girl of his, Tess, she said. But he likes his own company.

So he could just be up the coast somewhere? It's only been a few days.

Not without telling Tess, his mother said. He wouldn't just pack up and take off without telling her where he was going.

The girlfriend, the officer said. Tess. She's been in a little bit of trouble with the local police.

What does that mean? she asked.

Drug use, the officer said. Possession.

Elliot's never said much about her, she said. He wouldn't even bring her down with him to meet us.

He's never got into any kind of trouble? Any disagreements you know of, people who might want to hurt him?

His mother shook her head.

The officer paused. And the cousin, he said. The one he works for on the boat?

Jake? his mother said sharply.

I read his file also, the officer explained.

He wouldn't hurt Elliot.

I have to ask, the officer said, eyes down.

Paul's father peered over as if trying to read the officer's notes.

It was a long time ago, his mother said. What happened with Jake, it was a long time ago.

Okay, the officer replied. But you haven't noticed anything strange or different about your son's behaviour?

Elliot's not the sort to disappear, his mother said, the volume of the statement causing the policeman to lift his eyes from his notepad.

Mrs Darling, I know this is difficult, but we see it every other week. Around forty thousand people go missing around the country every year. Ninety-five per cent of them turn up in a matter of months. I'm guessing Elliot's had a gutful of cray bait and wanted some fresh air. He'll be back.

There was silence. Paul looked at his parents. His father stood up and walked towards the kettle on the kitchen counter. His mother was staring at the tablecloth.

He's just an ordinary kid, she said.

The officer nodded.

On that first night after Elliot's disappearance, Paul found himself on the computer in the study long after midnight, unsure of what he was trying to do, what he was looking for. In the hours before dawn he gorged on the cases of missing people, the search results serving up the usual extremes: people who had returned or been found sometimes decades after they had disappeared.

There was the case of the Croatian woman who had been missing for twenty-five years. It had been big news years ago, when he was in primary school: the girl who had vanished as a ten-year-old only to be found in a makeshift enclosure in an inner-city backyard by fire crews responding to a blaze within a house, her now-elderly captor having left the kitchen stove on while he was sleeping.

He read dozens of articles. The Brazilian fisherman who had drifted a thousand kilometres to an island in the West Indies and was found by a BBC film crew who had come to do a story on migratory birds. A girl the same age as Paul, seventeen, who awoke with severe retrograde amnesia in a Los Angeles hospital. She had a Yorkshire accent but carried no identification.

There were more of these kinds of stories than were possible to read. The internet was thick with them. And it left his mind feeling choked and heavy, like a greasy washcloth, dense with information that it didn't need, but couldn't easily let go.

Elliot never did social media, thought the whole online thing was bullshit. Paul figured his brother was suspicious of the virtual world, uncomfortable with the performances of people. And how close you get to the shadowy core of them if you wanted to. It was all there online. And Elliot didn't have Paul's appetite for digging around. There was only one mention of his brother that Paul could find, in the result of a cricket match on the North Metropolitan Cricket Association website. Paul remembered the game. Elliot had filled in reluctantly for a team captained by an old high school friend and he had taken a wicket. E. Darling 1/12. And that was it. No video or photographs. In the infinite landscape of the internet, where Paul could find any mad story, where every wild hypothetical had a real-life, human example and every unfathomable, immaterial thing took shape, Elliot could almost have never existed.

The longer Paul stayed on the computer the harder it was to leave it. It was the illusion of doing something. Typing words into the search engine had the feeling of action. He would be better off sleeping. He knew that. But there was an element to it that he wasn't in command of, hitting search on autopilot, feeling neither fully awake nor tired enough to sleep, feeling nothing much at all. 1994 Pajero Western Australia. Search. Car accident Brand Highway. Search. Young surfer accident Stark. Search. Each failure fuelled the next attempt, and each new search led him deeper. And then he would give in to the undertow of the search engine, its eddying into darkness. He found himself watching Russian dash-cam footage of head-on car accidents, and he saw the grainy CCTV video of a gangland shooting in Portland. He lingered over links to execution videos recorded on mobile phones. Brazilian drug-cartel beheadings. Sniper kills on Middle Eastern battlefields. He didn't click on these but maybe he wanted to. Was it nobility that stopped him or gutlessness? It made him tired of himself, this tiptoeing at the threshold, like a pervert. Or, perhaps worse, a cowardly pervert. It left him feeling like shit and exhausted, but restless too.

He found a satellite image of central Western Australia. Hovered over Stark. Scanned the coast as if he might see a figure walking on some remote beach. Knew it was pointless, but he kept looking anyway.

Out the study window was the fading night. The suburb emerging in colourless, cubist forms. Huge windows opaque in the low light. He heard the flickering of sprinklers, watched them misting over lawns as flat as carpet. At the end of Eileen Street the sea off Cottesloe was still and grey. He saw the weakening flash of the one-mile reef markers. The tourist island beyond them, a thin line on the horizon.

He heard his alarm go down the hallway in his bedroom. Six am. The dairy shift at the supermarket started in an hour. Paul turned back to the screen and the pixelated coast of Stark, the dark ocean to the west and the brownish desert stretching endlessly east and out of view. He switched the computer off.

13

~

The President said to me that a man knows most about himself when he's got his eye through the scope of his rifle. Glassing over the torso of another man at nine hundred metres. The world all distant and shimmering and silent. That's when he learns the things about himself that he is connected to. The things he can live with. The President said he learnt all of his lessons through the scope of a Parker-Hale .308 in Vietnam. And I imagine that big sweating face of his against the stock. Sprawled out with his balls steeped in the jungle mud and his cheeks rippling with each gunshot and I see him learning and I often wonder what. But I don't doubt that he did learn something. You don't become the president of anything without some sort of education. The President said it's a fact this country was born in battle and it's not the first time I've heard that, but no one could tell a war story like him. All wide-eyed fishermen and farm fellas stumbling seasick over tidal flats into Turkish rifle fire. Wading through bloodied trenches in French wheat fields. And I wonder what sort of country is born in all that and I wonder the effect it has on fellas. If it explains anything about the way they are. The things they say and the things they don't. The sounds that come out of them when they sleep. Cos I've held a gun in my hands and I've just shot a man dead. I don't know what all of this has done to me or what I have learnt and it's probably for someone else to judge. So I'll tell you all this from the beginning. The way we came through the heart of everything. Tell you how it got here.

~

Victim or criminal

THE POLICE FILED THE MISSING PERSON'S report a week after the officer came to the house. It didn't make the television news but Paul found a piece in *The West Australian*, a photo and article taken word for word from the press release. The local newspaper also ran an article, again with the same text but this time with a headline in bold type. COTTESLOE MAN MISSING. The word 'man' felt off. Every time it was used, by the police or in the news, it felt like they were getting something wrong, talking about the wrong person. Paul always saw Elliot as older but 'man' seemed inaccurate for a twenty-year-old. It was as if they were all missing an important point, getting further from the truth of what might have happened to him, or that they were never close.

A letter arrived to inform them that Elliot's profile had been uploaded on to the national Missing Persons website, and Paul began to visit the site often. He stared at Elliot's face amid the collection of profile photographs as odd and unrelated as the items that wash up in a storm. Old photographs and new ones. Elderly faces and then younger ones like his brother's. The faces of children. There were photos that had been taken by family or friends, faces smiling warmly back at the camera, children laughing. Others looked like driver's licence photographs, or police mug shots, the expressions in them steely or panicked, as though the person was already lost or in danger, like they could see their future coming.

Elliot's expression in his photograph was typical of him. Smiling politely but as though he was bracing himself, holding out for the camera to leave him. His smile was tight, fading before it had even started. His brow furrowed. Paul knew that the photographer, most likely his mother, would have been laughing while the picture was taken, the laugh of someone revelling in stealing something. Everyone in the room would have enjoyed his discomfort.

When he clicked on Elliot's name a new page opened with a larger photograph of his brother and a short statement.

Elliot Darling. 20. Perth, Western Australia. Mr Darling last seen driving north of Stark, Western Australia, Wednesday, 17 August.

He read those nineteen words over and over, as if staring hard enough at them might jar some secret loose. He was struck by the economy of them, the things they didn't say. On other profiles of missing people, those of young women and children, that short description would conclude with a muted statement that implied the worst. *Concerns are held for Ms Robert's safety.* But his brother's profile didn't say this. Why weren't concerns held for him too? The officer who filed the report, or the administrative employee who added his profile to the database, where did they imagine Elliot might be?

~

In the first month, relatives and family friends visited the house. Paul would sit on the lounge and listen to them wade through conversations with his parents, as if in an interview. He had listened to Brian Guff, an elderly neighbour, assure his father that *the coppers are right, the boy will be fine*.

Father Walsh from the local parish came and spoke to them, invited by their grandmother. The old priest looked pale and shrunken sitting on the electric leather recliner in their living room, his skin grey, eyes dull. Father Walsh told him that if Elliot was lost it was Christ who would find him. If the Bible was about anything, the old priest explained, it was about the lost being found. Jesus, Jonah, Lazarus, they were all thrust into the dark, he said, cast into a desert or the belly of a whale or even to death itself, and then were saved, returned into light. A Catholic must have belief in life after death, Father Walsh said. Of being lost and then found.

Paul had watched his grandmother cry and had seen his mother's face hardening at the sound of it. He charted that anger in her face, how it grew like bad weather, settling in. His mother's eyes had become permanently widened, alert. She had the look of a cat in a moving car, simultaneously vulnerable and dangerous. And it warded people off. They stopped visiting, and before a month was out the only people who called were telemarketers.

Where his mother had hardened, his father just stayed the same as he had always been. He rarely spoke about Elliot, and when he did it seemed forced, as if he understood he needed to make some contribution to the topic. It was the tone that someone used when musing on some minor complication, as if he were talking about the printer in his study running out of ink.

~

Paul often had the feeling he had just missed his brother, as if Elliot had been sitting in the same train car or walking along the same footpath, or had been in the same store, but moments before. Elliot felt close and far away. Alive and dead. Paul knew his mother lived with the same sensation. He could see it in her face when in the shops with her or when they were driving on the freeway together.

At night the three of them would sit around the dinner table in silence, which was not so strange. They had never been big talkers, and Elliot hadn't eaten with them for years. He was away so often. Even when he was home he would choose to stay in his room. After a day of people asking after Elliot, wanting to hear about the latest sighting or theory, there was relief in not talking. He understood that. Still, there were things Paul wanted to ask his parents. There was so much to say. But even if he had the words he knew his father wouldn't have wanted to hear them. It was just the way he was. Maybe it was the way he was, too.

Only once or twice did Paul have the feeling that he had actually seen his brother, and it was never a person who caused the confusion, but the car they were driving. He became aware of just how many four-wheel drives of the same make and model as his brother's were on the road. There were '94 Pajeros everywhere. Wherever he went, he was searching for that car, searching for Elliot.

They were surrounded by him and without him. They lived with a ghost, and people began to treat them warily. At the supermarket Paul gained a temporary celebrity. At the checkout children frowned at him and their parents shuffled them through, like he carried a contagion.

But missing was different to ill. It was different to having cancer, or to being killed in a car accident. There was a kind of queerness to it, he understood that. It was odd. Sordid. One afternoon, Bec called him out to the delivery yard and told him she was there to help. She knew what it was like to be alone, her husband away on the mines. Even with the sun blanching her glasses he could see her glancing at his crotch as she told him this.

He understood how others felt; he found himself making the same sort of judgements when he looked at the faces on the Missing Persons site. Who disappears? It seemed voluntary; or, if something bad had happened, it was as if the person in the photograph had in some way contributed to it. They had chosen to go off the map.

At the beginning of November, after a second month had passed, Paul decided to leave. He could get a job in Stark on the cray boat with his older cousin Jake, his mother's sister's son, in the family business, just as Elliot had done.

He expected some resistance from his parents. He thought it might come off as perverse, like he was ghosting Elliot, treading over the same ground. If he was honest with himself, it was precisely what he was doing. Stark was Elliot's. It was where his girlfriend, Tess, lived. Where he had lived a whole life that Paul knew nothing about; a life that Elliot had been careful not to share. When Paul thought about Stark he had the same precarious feeling as he did when he would sneak into Elliot's bedroom and rummage through his things. A hollowing excitement, like digging around on the internet. The fear of what you might find, the seductive dread of finding more than you might have been searching for.

But what about his parents? How could he leave them? Yet when he told them his intentions, they seemed strangely resigned. His father just nodded obediently and his mother, if anything, thought it would be good for him to leave, to get away from everything. She would arrange for Aunty Ruth to drive down to collect him.

She had said that if there was anything she could do to help I only had to ask, his mother told him one bright afternoon in the backyard while washing the dog, strong wind in her curled dark hair, crouched with a hose to the terrier with one hand in its collar.

I can take the bus, Paul replied.

I'm not putting you on the bus.

You don't need to put me on anything. I'm buying my own ticket.

Ringo trembled under the hose, legs braced as if the ground was moving.

My sister wants to help.

Aunty Ruth hates me.

She's been through a bit, Paul. With Jake. And now your brother.

I'd rather walk.

Well, it'd take you three weeks and you'd probably die.

I'd rather die.

Don't be stagey, Paul.

The dog looked slowly up at him when the hose reached the top of its head, gave Paul an assaulted expression.

Six hours shooting the breeze with Ruth? I would rather die, Mum.

His mother looked up at him once, grimacing with the sun in her eyes. She wiped soap-foam from her cheek with the back of her hand. Just let your aunty help, she said. I'll call this evening.

The dairy manager, Trev, asked Paul on his last shift at the supermarket if Elliot did drugs. Trev cackled with Bec in the storeroom at the idea of Elliot swallowing condoms of ice, and the two of them mused out loud on how stomach acids might cause one to burst. If it would hurt to die that way or if it would feel good. Like being strapped to a rocket. An awesome, overheated trajectory towards death.

A victim or a criminal. Elliot was one or the other, and both titles had darkness about them. He could sense it in the way customers looked at him. Amused more than sympathetic. Disdainful, even. A young man twenty years old. He doesn't get killed, he gets himself killed. He lingers too long around danger, the wrong crowd. Everyone was thinking it.

Or perhaps no one thought that. Perhaps they were his thoughts.

II

The President is asleep when one of the general's phones sets off. Organised Crime Squad hit the North Bondi mansion four suburbs away from our hideout. Not ten kilometres up the coast. Two men shot and one more who gets on the phone gutshot and groaning but spits the words out before the phone is taken off him.

When I take off up the floating staircase and wake the President he doesn't look surprised that his men have been killed or taken or that we have to go. Like he knew it would work out this way.

So we strip the old townhouse in Maroubra in the hours before midnight. Four of us. Me. The President. The two old generals. I load the dirt bikes with auxiliary fuel tanks. Pack the rifle and ammo in the cricket bag.

The generals douse the floorboards and the attic space with petrol while the President and I wait a few streets away with the bikes. Can see the glowing heat in the dark and the smoke. In seconds the fire climbs up off the roof into the jacarandas, flames jumping in the storm-wind. We set off quiet into the freezing night and don't hear sirens. In hours Sydney will be loud with them.

I'd always figured it weird for a bikie group to own a mansion perched on the cliffs over the Pacific. All marine-grade steel and huge windows sparkling each day under the sun like a disco ball. But I see as we weave through the narrow streets and when I look at the President riding with his eyes on the road and not once looking back that the mansion in Bondi was a decoy. A big-arsed Trojan beast that the cops would sniff out first and trip the alarm. It's obvious then.

We stay off Parramatta Road as we go west through the city, suburb by suburb. Surry Hills and Camperdown. Homebush.

I wonder what the President is thinking. He doesn't say a word, but I'm sure at each corner we'll see flashing lights or receive bullets out of the roadside dark and I've no doubt the President is thinking about ambushes too. From the police or anyone else. But there is no ambush or roadblock and no sniper fire and by the time we reach Kurrajong and the foot of the mountains it's almost light.

A spectator enthralled

FROM THE ROADHOUSE WINDOWS PAUL could see the long, crawling line of vehicles. Surfboards on car roofs. Camper trailers. A Greyhound coach sat heavy on its wheels, inching forward in awkward, convulsive movements. He could make out the faces, their listless expressions within each window frame of the bus, a wall of tortured portraits. Paul and his aunty had been going along like that for almost an hour, the traffic slowed by the unknown trouble ahead, before they pulled into the servo south of Dongara. Ruth said she needed to take a piss. Paul was grateful to get out of the car. It had been a long drive.

A man and his daughter stood at the counter in front of him. The girl swivelled impatiently on her ankles, one hand behind her father's knee, forehead creased. The man swung a thick arm around his back and fished in his shorts pocket while the other balanced Kit Kats and iced-coffee cartons on the ledge of his stomach. A wiry man with neat grey hair stood straight-backed at the till. He was staring out at the traffic.

Crash? the customer asked, bending his knees as he lowered his bounty onto the counter.

Head on, the older man said.

That's the diesel too, the customer said.

The girl glared at Paul. She had a pink, shining stain around her lips and on her cheeks and he could smell the cloying scent of sugar and saliva.

Had some people stop in here a moment ago, the man at the till said. They came from the other way, seen the thing not long after it happened. Was a mess, they reckon.

Fatal? the customer wanted to know, plucking two straws from a container on the counter.

The man serving him nodded.

Jesus, he replied.

Paul followed the older man's eyes to the bend where the road disappeared, hidden behind eucalypts and peppermint trees.

Might as well get a bite, Ruth huffed from behind him. She squinted into the hot light of the food cabinet. Be a bloody age till I'm getting home, she said.

They sat in the old LandCruiser with the windows down, the car stationary, listening to the single station Paul could find on the radio. The late-afternoon sun was hot on his legs. Ruth let out a sigh, pushing back into her seat, straightening her fleshy arms on the steering wheel. She smelt of chicken salt and cheese sausage.

Be good for you, this, Ruth said. Get you out of the house, give your parents some space. You'll do some real work, too. Might harden you up a bit.

Paul didn't say anything. Up the road a man emerged from

26

the rear door of a van, rested his beer bottle on the bitumen and hurried, barefoot, into the low grass by the roadside. He squared his hips towards a tree, arching his back and looking skywards in the typical reverie. Paul watched him grin and lift a middle finger back towards the van.

You know, you're damn lucky Jake took you on, Ruth continued. It's been a shocker season. Stormy as shit and he's bringing back fuck-all. If it wasn't for this business with your brother he'd only take one deckhand out with him. Ruth turned to face Paul as if to ensure he was listening. Better pull your fucking weight, she said.

His aunt had talked a lot on the drive but she wasn't one for conversing. She spoke at him and answered her own questions. There was a persistent anger in her talk that had sustained the five hundred kilometres they had driven. Paul had learnt it was better to keep quiet. There wasn't much to say, anyway. He had never liked her and he knew she cared little for him. It was obvious that she figured she was doing him and his parents some kind of grand favour. Easing the burden on them all. Going out of her way. He found it hard to even look at her.

Paul searched for another station but only found static. Ruth knocked his hand aside and clicked the radio off. Outside the bush murmured. Ruth tapped out an agitated beat on the steering wheel with her thumb, and briefly lifted herself in her seat, trying to lengthen her torso to see beyond the cars ahead. She was desperate to see it, whatever it was that waited for them up the road.

I mean, the stress of it all, she continued, the monologue into its second hour. It is making me ill. You do understand this? Thyroid's had it. I'm expanding like a force-fed duck. Shingles on my fucking arse.

Paul sighed.

Think that's a real laugh, do you? she said.

Paul shook his head, turned towards the window.

You do, she said. You think it's funny that I've got these shingles.

No.

I'd crack you one. I swear I would knock you back in time.

I don't think it's funny.

Well it isn't. Hurts like nothing else. It's making me depressed. That's how bad the pain is. Ruth breathed out. God's way of telling you you've got too much on your plate. That's what the doc said. Take it easy, Ruth, he said. If he only knew the half of it. The shit I've got to deal with.

A police car howled by them in the opposite lane, rushing towards where the highway swept left, hidden behind thicker, darker bush. It was followed seconds later by another. The traffic was now at a complete stop. Music pumped from the P-plated hatchback in front of them. There was the low throb of a bass drum and the sharp, repetitive refrain of a synthesiser.

It's weird for a boy to not have his licence. And at your age. What are you? Eighteen?

Seventeen.

It's queer. People will think there's something not right with you.

I wanted to take the bus.

Even queerer, she said. Who takes the fucking bus? Junkies and paedophiles. And you don't look like a junkie. You've got that going for you. Do you want people to think you're a paedophile? They do come as young as you. That is a fact.

The hatchback in front creaked and shuddered with each beat. Paul could just make out a girl in the back seat with straightened hair and large black sunglasses. She was laughing at someone or something out of view.

Ruth shifted in her seat again. God, it's a circus out here, she muttered. The boys are right. A fucking dam has broken.

Paul didn't say it but he too thought it was strange. The dense procession of overloaded cars and trailers had been with them the entire trip north from Perth. It was a Friday afternoon but it wasn't a public holiday or long weekend. Christmas was still nearly two months away. He guessed it might be the university crowd, clearing out of the city post-exams.

I told your mother I didn't have room. I used to have room but I have Jake there now and I told your mother that I don't have room anymore. She said it was good enough of me to drive down to get you. That you didn't need a room.

I called the hostel, Paul said.

The hostel will be closed by the time we get there.

They said they'd leave the door unlocked.

Jake doesn't need any more trouble, Ruth said.

Paul was looking out the window but he felt the look she gave him.

In the side mirror he had noticed a white four-wheel drive that looked a lot like his brother's. There were the same yellowed circles of rust on the bonnet, and the roof was laden with gear, perched high enough that you'd think a strong wind might blow the whole lot over. Elliot would have driven this stretch of the Brand Highway countless times, the Pajero packed heavy like a gypsy caravan. Paul had never gone with him. There had been school or his shifts at the supermarket. Even if he could have gone with his brother, he would have found reasons not to.

Wonder if anyone survived it, Ruth said. She pinched at a pale, freckly patch of skin high up on her arm, clamping the flesh between her thumbnail and forefinger. Could just be cleaning it all up, Ruth said. Wish someone would tell us what the fuck is going on.

Out the driver-side window, looking east and inland, the horizon was a sad, purplish mirage, the ridgeline rendered two-dimensional by distance like the painted horizon of a movie set. Leading to nothingness. Dead-ended. Paul glanced again into his mirror and caught the silhouette of the driver of the Pajero, and for a moment he saw Elliot at the wheel, staring out at those same paddocks. He felt a grim tightness in his stomach.

There was the shuddering drone of a helicopter above them. His aunty fell back again into her seat and exhaled, long and loud.

Elliot had been happy to travel alone. It was probably the thing Paul least understood about his brother, the way that they were most different, that Elliot could withstand that kind of isolation, be all alone in truly remote places. And he did it often, too.

When his brother was away, Paul often found himself entering the bedroom at the end of the hallway with a kind of tourist's nosiness. Ringo had sometimes followed him, becoming more interested in Paul's comings and goings than usual, as if the dog could sense that he was up to no good.

The room had the dank smell of sea things, long dead, and the bubblegum scent of surfboard wax. Paul had more than once rummaged through Elliot's bottom drawer. Amid the thicket of expired cards and broken watches and empty aftershave bottles, there were odd treasures, the stuff of a life that he knew was far more exotic than his own. A shark tooth on a chain that had been given to Elliot by their grandmother. Maps of islands below India called the Sentinels, fingers of land engulfed in the blue of the Indian Ocean. Paul would return to an envelope he had found. In it was a photograph of a short, thin girl: Tess. She was naked, her dark hair falling forward over her angular shoulders and only partially covering her breasts, wearing the halo of a camera flash reflected in the mirror behind her. The collection of things in Elliot's room had always tantalised him, and with each search he had grown more reckless. He'd lit cigarettes and sipped at a miniature bottle of Jack Daniel's. He'd once found a packet of condoms and put one on, felt the starchy powder between his fingers. He knew there was a kind of madness to it. He would often catch his reflection in the long mirror on the cupboard door, see the embarrassment and disappointment on the face staring back at him, and he would wonder who was accusing whom. Ringo gave him that look too, the old dog studying him between naps on the carpeted floor.

Almost an hour passed before they were moving again. A policeman sat against the bonnet of his car, parked across the highway lanes. He waved the traffic towards a fire break that ran parallel to the road. They drove down the narrow overgrown track. Grass brushed underneath the LandCruiser. On one side of them eucalypts lined the road like a curtain. Paul could still see bitumen between the trees, the broad highway eerie in its emptiness. Further up there were lights and the grim cordon of emergency vehicles. Ruth leant so far forward in her seat she was almost up against the windscreen, eyes narrowed, peering through the leaves. Paul caught a glimpse of an ambulance officer on her knees beside a twist of metal and he looked away, stared out his window and into the white light of a field. The paddock was barren apart from a few strange trees. Dwarf trees, bent and bowed, their gnarled grey branches leaning north. Some had grown completely twisted to the ground. The wind, Paul guessed.

Beside him with her eyes still on the highway, a spectator enthralled, Ruth gasped.

~

We set up camp in flat country near Cobar. Dead arse tingling from the day's riding. Hard to sleep in the winter desert. The rocky ground like a freezer block. Feeling like a corpse in your swag. Harder to sleep with what lies ahead. It is impossible this. What the President is wanting us to do. Go from coast to coast, east to west. Six thousand kilometres across the country. So many who would shoot us on sight.

But it feels inevitable too. The President has that way about him. Like there is no stopping what we started.

At sea

PAUL HAD BEEN IN STARK NO MORE than four hours.

Ruth had dropped him at the hostel near midnight, the front of the building unlit when he arrived. There were signs of backpackers, the beach towels and t-shirts on the wooden rail of the veranda twisting and thrashing in the gale, but there was no movement from inside. The reception area was closed when he entered and most of the lights were off. There was no one about except for a girl leaning against the bench in the small kitchen, eating cereal and reading. Paul made a sandwich using bread from a loaf on the bench and a crusted jar of honey he found in the pantry. He then went to the dorm, sat down on the bottom bunk that was left free, tried to eat as quietly as he could by the small light above his bed. Listening to the breaths and snores of strangers behind the curtains that hung across each bunk. For the few hours until his alarm went off he lay on top of the stiff sheets, his bum numb from the seven-hour drive, his mind alive with thoughts, kept awake by the frenzied song of the wind and rain against the window.

Now, standing at the kerb in the predawn, the town was black around him. He barely recognised it. In the dark the place seemed almost shrunken, the inlet smaller, the town flatter. It just wasn't like he remembered it from when he was younger. A terrible, howling wind blew from the inlet, smelling of rotting seaweed. The rain fell in jagged panes. Paul held his damp backpack to his chest, under his jacket.

A ute rounded the corner, headlights tunnelling through the sea mist. It pulled a skiff on a trailer. Paul raised his arm in a wave. The vehicle stopped. Paul had started to walk around the bonnet to the passenger door when there was a whistle from inside. He looked through the windscreen into the gloom of the cabin. Jake peered out at him from under the hood of a jumper.

In the boat, he yelled through the open window. And keep your head down. Don't need a fucking fine.

Paul stepped on the hub of the trailer, dropped his bag in first then clambered over the lip of the dinghy. The walls of the boat were low and he tried to lie as flat as he could but there were things in the hull, lumpy objects with hard edges, and he couldn't make them out. He touched one with his hand and felt its icy damp. He felt around for his backpack and pulled it to him, but found it was soaked, creamy and slick under his fingers. He put his hand to his nose, smelt the stink of fish blood and almost heaved. The ute set off and the boat jolted and bucked on the trailer. Another sheet of rain slapped over him. He leant back into the frozen bed of bait boxes. The sky above was a dense, shapeless dark.

After a few minutes the ute slowed and then stopped. The

engine idled. There was an accented voice and then the closing of a car door. The trailer lurched and they were off again. He felt jittery, lying there. A sort of edginess he couldn't put his finger on. Exhaustion, he figured, or the putrid cold on his skin. Whatever it was, he felt weak and empty, and as though each bump in the road was shaking him loose.

It wasn't long until the drone of bitumen ended and they were on sand. The trailer squeaked and rocked. The boat swayed. Paul raised his head as they slowed again. The ute groaned, revving hard as the load was manoeuvred. The skiff was reversed down towards the water. When the vehicle stopped he climbed out.

The inlet seethed with chop and spray. Jake and the deckhand stood at the water's edge, staring at the clouds dark and knotted above them. Out past the sandy spit of the rivermouth, Paul could see the glow of surf. He could hear it too, a seismic rumbling that he expected to feel in the ground under his feet.

The deckhand, thin-armed and blond, not much older than Paul, signalled as the skiff was backed further down the bank. He shielded a cigarette under the crook of his arm and winced at the sea spray in his eyes. But he was grinning, a proper joyful smile, despite the wind and the mouldering stink of the rivermouth and the thunder of the surf, and Paul assumed he must be drug-fucked. The trailer submerged and as the back wheels of the ute touched the water the deckhand gave a shout and held his palm up. The ute halted. Jake jumped out and threw the keys to the younger man before hauling himself into the boat with a grunt.

Okay, the deckhand yelled to Paul. You with Jake.

Paul stood, unsure what he meant.

Fucking now! Jake shouted. Get in so the German can give it a shove!

Paul scrambled once again over the rim of the skiff, back into the foul wet. The German leant against the nose of the boat and pushed it free of the trailer. Paul watched him scamper up the dark beach as they drifted out. The small boat reared and jerked in the water. Spray whipped over them. Paul hid his head under his jacket arm. The older man swore. On the shore, the ute's headlights streamed over seaweed, pot floats and dune scrub before turning off the beach. Jake tilted the outboard from the water and pulled hard at the cord. The motor gave a startled growl and went silent. In the purple light Paul studied the look on the man's face. The eyes were wide, staring at the outboard with a kind of desperation. Teeth gritted and lips flattened. It was a look somewhere between contempt and repulsion. Anger and fear.

Hi, Paul said.

Right, Jake said, and pulled at the cord again. Fuck this!

The boat dipped and the river cast more water over them.

Paul yelled into the breeze. This is my first time out.

I know. Jake ripped at the cord once more and the motor cried out. You've picked some day . . . The words trailed off under the grunt and sputter of the outboard and the moan of the wind.

They bumped across to the jetty where the German was waiting, holding a packet of tobacco and a red thermos. The deckhand climbed down into the skiff and sat at the bow. He yawned and then smiled out into the dark. The three of them made their way into the inlet where the boats were huddled together in deeper water, hulking silhouettes that wrenched and nodded on their moorings. It was a short stretch from the riverbank but it was miserable going. Jake cringed and swore at each pitch of the bow, at every shower of brackish water.

As they neared the moorings, Paul could see the flicker

of lights on a few of the cray boats and the shadows moving about on their long decks. There were names tattooed on each bow. *Lady Stark. Hell Cat. Nun's Nasty* and *Blue Murder*. Jake cut the outboard when they pulled up against the vast side of *Arcadia*. The German hurried the rope around the brass bollards of the cray boat then gestured for Paul to climb up. The skiff reared and kicked, battering the walls of *Arcadia* like a riled bull. Paul hesitated. Jake grumbled. When the skiff bucked again Paul jumped, scrambling up and over, landing on the carpeted deck on his belly, breathing hard. Jake climbed up behind him. The German stood wide-legged in the skiff and passed up the sagging boxes of bait. At one moment he thumped a hand down on the rim of the small boat, just keeping himself from going in, and grinned wildly.

When the bait was loaded, the German tied the skiff to the moor and clambered onto the deck. Inside the cabin Jake put the kettle on. Paul crouched beside the bait. He pulled back the clear tape from one of the greasy cardboard boxes and again almost vomited at the flash of scales and purple eyes and reeking stench. The German squatted with him under the lights of the deck to quarter the silver bream, slipping the long knife through the fish with such nonchalant ease that he might be slicing oranges. Paul turned away and gulped in the sour air of the inlet. He looked beyond the twisting mouth of the river, past the white boil of the inshore reefs and out to the shadowy scowl of the horizon.

Alright, Jake sighed, stepping out from the cabin. He closed his eyes for a moment before settling a glare on Paul. You listen to the German here. We're not going to have time to fiddle around and show you what's what. You keep your eyes on the job and you work hard. While you're on this boat you're busting your arse. Not here to fluff about.

Yep, Paul said.

Yep, Jake mimicked, unsmiling. Hope your head's screwed on. There's a million and one ways it can all go to shit out there.

Paul nodded.

Jake pointed to the circular steel head of the winch at Paul's back. If the German rips a pot in too hard and it leaps into the boat, and you're pissing about in front of that winch, you're gone.

Paul looked at the taut face of the skipper, at the slight spasm of his jaw, the swollen vein on his temple. He spoke like he was trying to hold his whole body together, so tense he just might fizz over, spitting into oblivion like an aspirin.

It's going to be ugly water, he said. Keep the rope off your legs or you'll go over. Don't fuck about with the winch or I swear to God it will take your arm clean off. You listen to the German. You listen to me. He gave Paul a long stare. Just fucking pay attention.

Yes, Paul replied.

And don't use the shitter, Jake said, flicking a hand towards the white booth on the outside wall of the cabin. It's buggered. If you have to, you piss or dump over the side.

He stepped back inside the cabin and left Paul and the smiling German to the pong of the bait and the hostile company of the breeze. For a moment Paul thought about the broken toilet, trying to imagine how one would keep their balance squatting on the low wall of the cray boat, bum dangling over the sea. He pictured Jake, grim-faced on the gunwale, arse poised above deep water.

On the shore there was still no sign of the sun but it had lightened just enough that Paul could see the caravan parks and bed-and-breakfasts that crowded the banks of the rivermouth. Behind those, spied in glimpses down darkened streets, there was something like suburbia.

Jake climbed up onto the bridge with his coffee flask. The diesels announced themselves with a thought-clearing rumble and the huge deck began to vibrate. Paul felt the tremor of the engines in his body, rattling through the hollowness of his stomach. They taxied out to where the river gave way to the sea through a narrow gap between the sandbank and the churn of a reef. Paul looked back along the broad creamy wake to the paradoxical vision of the town. A mess of new and old. Smooth and rough. Shiny and dull. There were the bright rendered walls of the resort on the headland and then the yellowed brick of the TAB further down the inlet. Ruler-straight tropical palms and twisted dwarf trees. He saw the buttery light from a hotel-room window and wished like hell he was in there. Or even in that musty bed in the hostel.

The cray boat roared as they reached the rivermouth, running the gauntlet of backwash and coral. There was the gnash of water over shallow reef. They hurtled through the gap in a hail of spray and in an instant they were on the sea, the swells long and bloated beneath them. The boat tore impatiently for deeper water, like a jet seeking altitude. The horizon danced about. Paul's mouth was dry. The bow lifted over a swell and then dropped and all the gear on the deck slammed. His stomach tightened.

Pretty rough, eh? Paul yelled to the German, breathless.

The German gave him a sick grin. Out there, he said, tilting his head towards the horizon. Out there it really kicks inside your arse.

The town was now just a grubby white streak. Further south, Paul could see the pale red of the bluff and the sheer face of rock that disappeared down the coast like a great wall. He looked at the cleaved outline of those cliffs and imagined a giant and an axe.

Michael, the deckhand said, introducing himself.

Paul could only nod. His mind was fixed on his stomach. He felt his intestines tighten, withdrawing. He tasted the sourness on the back of his tongue.

I am sorry about your brother, the German said, above the noise.

Before Paul could attempt a word there was the toot of a horn up on the bridge and the German readied himself at the gunwale. Paul stood next to him and could see the pink flash of the floats between grey swells.

I will winch this in, Michael said. You empty it.

What?

The pot. I get it in and you take the crays out and drop them in the box there. Then stack the pot up the back. Easy.

Paul felt lightheaded. The wind was cold on his cheeks. He looked for land but it was hidden behind the roll of water. Michael started the winch. The spindle hummed.

How do I grab them? Paul asked. Where?

By the back or the legs. The dick. Whatever. It is just a lobster. Any other shit in that pot you chuck back over. Seaweed. Octopus. Port Jackson. Just fuck it off.

What's a Port Jackson?

It has got rough skin and sharp teeth. Like my father. The German chuckled to himself. You might want those, he said, pointing to a pair of orange gloves on the deck.

The engines quietened and the boat slowed as the pots brushed the hull. Michael swung the grappling hook down into the water.

I lied, Michael said, grimacing as the rope tightened in his hands. Crayfish do not have dicks. Not that I have seen. Tell me if you see one, yeah?

In one practised movement he hauled the heavy line through the tipper and wrapped it onto the winch head. The rope sang and water spun off it as the line whipped around the capstan and coiled into a bucket. The wooden pot emerged from the sea in a coat of white water. It clattered against the steel of the tipper. Michael pulled the pot up onto the railing. Paul gazed through the ribs of wood, the trap bristling with red feelers and spines and shiny black eyes. He was staring dumbly at the animals when a swell thundered against the hull and over the gunwale and he collected a horrifying mouthful. He gagged. His throat burnt. Michael waited next to him. The skipper sounded the horn again. Paul cringed and threw a gloved hand through the gate and grabbed something prickly and hard as stone. The lobster flapped in his hand, a wet crunching sound. He pulled the crayfish out, met its steely glare and could have sworn it winked at him. Another wave slapped over the hull, tumbling into him, soaking through his t-shirt and jeans and tennis shoes. Paul dropped the lobsters into the tub one by one and then slumped against the gunwale. His body shook with cold. Michael stacked the pot for him, carrying the heavy trap across the tilting deck with an almost comic stagger, legs and arms akimbo, feet splayed like a clown.

They pulled the second and third line. Michael lugged the emptied pots to the stern.

Paul waited for Jake to call it all off, to decide it was too rough, to step down from the bridge and say, Sorry, boys, we should never have come out. But once more the engines quaked beneath them. The deck shuddered. The boat heaved around, turned seawards, and they were gunning out to even deeper water. The bow butted against the swell, bobbing like the head of a racehorse. The swell lines broadened. The ocean grew big and dark and seemed to move in slow motion. Paul looked up at the grey ridges of water, felt his breath go at the sight of each one. His mouth was sour, his jaw tight.

When the horn sounded Michael prepared the hook. Paul struggled to lift his eyes to the water. The sun had broken through the clouds but it brought little relief. Under the hard light the waves looked even bigger, their threat clearer. He could see the arms of kelp strewn across the surface of the sea, torn from the ocean floor. Swells glinted like knives turned to the sun. The danger around him seemed more defined, his fear sharpened.

The tipper banged again and Michael slid the pot over. Paul had a hand on a cray when the boat lurched down so hard that he had the sensation of being parallel to the surface of the sea, levitating inches above. He gripped the gunwale with his free hand, holding himself in the boat, while the pot wrenched at his right forearm. It threatened to take him over. The deck seesawed. The hull levelled out. And then the cray boat rolled again, leaning down so that all Paul could see was ocean, green and clear and bottomless. He yelped at the deadly weight of the pot on his arm, at the thought of it rushing him down to the seabed. Then the boat steadied. The German hooted, laughed. Paul moaned.

He emptied the pot and waited for Michael to stack it for him but the deckhand was already pulling another line. Paul leant back and took the weight of the trap on his thighs. He stepped once towards the stern when the deck reared violently and he was thrown onto his back. The pot clattered on the floor. His limbs stiffened with panic. The deck was alive beneath him, a frightening energy, as if he was lying on quaking earth. He rolled onto his stomach and for a moment he was looking down on the cabin, the boat seemingly vertical, pitched forward on its nose.

He heard terrible music falling out of him, a mad wailing that he didn't recognise as his own voice. He crawled towards the cabin door. The German was shouting something but Paul couldn't hear him. All he could see was the deckhand's mouth moving and the apocalyptic scene of the ocean beyond the walls of the boat, flickering and dancing like fire. Surrounding them. Endless.

The cabin was dark. It smelt of leather and cigarette smoke and bile. The walls buzzed and creaked with every knock of swell. Paul hunched on the floor. He gripped the steel base of the table and closed his eyes.

What do you think you're up to?

Jake was standing in the doorway.

Paul spat into the white shine of vomit. He looked up and groaned. The man glanced down at the spoilt blue nylon carpet and made a long revving sound like a shark alarm.

Out! Get out of here!

He gripped Paul's arm hard, dragging him across the cabin floor, out through the door. The boat battered over another swell. The deck reared and Paul purged over Jake's boots.

Fuck it! Fuck it! Fuck it! the skipper screamed, as though letting off a round of bullets. He grabbed the back of Paul's t-shirt and ripped him to his feet. Paul wanted to apologise, wanted to stop, but all he could manage was a prolonged vomit that went all over his arms and into the winch-rope bucket.

Stop spewing on my fucking boat! the man cried, almost pleading. Over there!

Jake pointed to Michael who was balancing a pot on the boat's edge, pulling at the seaweed tangled inside and flicking it out into the wind. Paul gripped the doorframe and stared big-eyed at the sight in front of him; at the German's legs spread like a cowboy, the violent pitch and roll of the deck.

The water! the skipper cried again. If you're going to chuck, do it in the fucking water!

Paul looked at him, unable to speak. He shook his head and then lifted an arm, gesturing towards the white door at the rear of the deck with the neat black sign with silver lettering. TOILET. Above this, scrawled on a flecked sheet of paper taped to the door, was the word BROKE. Paul staggered towards it, his legs sluggish.

Jesus! Jake groaned. I told you. The toilet's fucked!

Paul ignored him and turned the silver latch. He closed the aluminium door behind him, shutting out the skipper and the stormy sea. His refuge was a rusting toilet box that smelt of month-old shit. He retched into the copper-stained sink.

Jake let go another treble scream. He thumped the cabin wall.

You can clean the fucker out when you're done!

Paul looked up at the pale face in the mirror. His cheeks sunscreen-smudged. Eyes wide with fear. His brown hair was plastered to his forehead. There was something of the child in that face, someone he recognised from another time. It was a strange thing to see him again.

Ghosts in the water

PAUL LOOKS OUT INTO THE GREY DARK; it is like peering into a well. The water in his mask tickles under his eyes. His breath rasps and rattles in his snorkel. He shouts at Elliot in his thoughts. His limbs feel heavy and useless to him. He had followed his brother across the shelf in a panic of arms and flippers, always falling behind, the older boy's kicks long and even. Now he can no longer see the wash of Elliot's fins. It is cold. The ocean in May is dim and colourless, a liquid fog. The fish are also dull and pale. They move without urgency in the seagrass below him. They are stern-looking, those fish. Dead-eyed. There are only a few of them and they swim alone. To Paul the sea looks deserted, the sandy gullies and ditches in the weedy reef below like the bare streets of an abandoned town. He thinks of the empty beach where he and his brother had left their clothes and the red plastic bucket. How the sand was dark and rutted with the night's rain.

A swell passes and for a moment lifts him. The bottom stirs. Sediment rolls upwards from the reef in thin clouds, like reaching arms. The wave leaves him bobbing there, the sea clouded around him. Light drapes through the water in dreary, tattered curtains.

Above the water there are the far-off sounds of traffic on Marine Parade. He can't see far for the swell around him. He pulls his mask up above his eyes, feels the easterly cold on his cheeks, the spit of rain. He thinks of yelling but knows better. No one would hear him. Maybe they would see something; a waiter who happened to look out a restaurant window, or an executive on the balcony of his Cottesloe mansion. From up there they would be able to see everything.

Paul follows the fringe of the ledge. He doesn't dare to kick out from it. He takes short glances. Staring might coax something out from the shadows. He looks again towards the deep and then he sees it. The huge, shimmering flank. Pale grey. An apparition, parting the dark. He lets his legs dangle. His chest throbs. It sails at the edge of his vision, fifteen to twenty metres away, wearing the misting water around it like a cloak. Paul hears the muffled roar come from him. He rips the mask from his face and turns toward the beach, legs and arms wild. He knows it is there behind him. He waits for the sudden heaviness on his legs. The reef below is a green blur and his eyes sting. A gulp of ocean flows hot down his throat and he swings his head to the surface, bleating and retching and trying to draw breath. His arms swing at the water. He only stops when he hears the crackle of seaweed, dry and lifeless underneath him, and when he feels beach sand wedge under his lips, hard and cold against his gums. He hears mad laughter. A shadow falls over him. Elliot.

A stingray, you dumb-arse. Should have seen your face.

~

We are moving before the sun is up and we go further into the flat country. The President says one hundred million years ago all of this out here was a sea. Told me about the bones of a giant fish they call a Cooyoo found in the desert chalk and limestone. I swear as the sun gets on our shoulders that I see them Cooyoo fish rising from the earth. A big old Cooyoo shaking the sand from its back and then weaving through the scrub and I laugh while I'm riding cos I know I am losing my shit. But it makes me smile to see us going on a sea floor. Sky blue. Clouds like rippling wave-foam. Brown kites turning in the warm current whirling over our heads.

We stop near Wilcannia and I head in for fuel and water and the President's jam doughnuts while the big fella and his generals wait in the scrubby cover of desert oak at the edge of town.

Then we ride into the afternoon past burnt-out cars and beat-up sheds. Closer to evening there are mobs of kangaroos and emus at the edge of the track. Wild goats that stare at us like we're lost.

It's strange the mood when that sun starts to go and you feel its warmth go with it and the light turns blue like something in the air itself has died. At the speeds we're going the wheel lines blur in the low light and the sandy track is pale and milky as a river and the riding gets sketchy quick. So we pull off the track some ways and set the bikes down and I get putting on some food while the two generals they watch me quiet as ghosts. They unwrap the cotton bandaging from around their heads that has gone red with dust. The faces of those two old generals they are hard to look at. Skin paper white and dried like the faces of fellas who have had their throats cut. There is no colour in their eyes from what I have ever worked out.

The President stands on a plate of sandstone and looks around at the vanishing light and the desert and the shadows fading into the earth. His boots loud on the rock as he does half-turns. Look on his old bearded face like he can hear something far off. But I listen hard and there's nothing. No sound. Just the thoughts in your head. Loud and strange. After a day of dust and light and screaming dirt bikes the stillness of everything can make you feel weird. Quiet enough that you sense something get turning inside yourself. It is hard to explain but it is there in your gut turning over and over. What it feels like. Like a wheel spinning.

The sun touches down to the west. Where we're heading. Through the guts the President says. Away from the highways that tiptoe around the centre of the continent. We're going right through the heart of everything. To the Indian Ocean and our fortune he says. Fortune beyond imagining. He likes to say this. Beyond imagining.

And the dark sweeps over us and soon the President is saying about as much as those two old generals. And for a fella with the President's reputation you wouldn't think the dark would get to him. But every evening out there when the light turns blue and the heat in your skin disappears the President gets quiet then. Doesn't say hardly a word until he's sleeping.

~

Stark

IT WAS DARK WHEN HE WOKE AND when Paul stepped out from the hostel into the street there was no sound other than the wind in his ears and the far-off shushing of trees and the sea that he couldn't from moment to moment distinguish between. He was unsure of the time and had no way of telling. When he'd got back to the dorm he'd found his phone in the pocket of his sodden jeans, lifeless, and when he had pressed the screen down with his thumb droplets of water had bubbled at its edges.

He was thirsty. His mouth was dry and his nostrils were hot. His knuckles stung when he closed his fists. In the breeze he felt shivery and unsteady. It occurred to him he hadn't had much to eat or drink since the night before.

The roads that intersected the main street were lightless, as though abandoned. There were no cars in the yards and most blocks were concealed by corrugated asbestos fencing. Paul walked in the middle of the road. Before he reached the shops it was clear they were closed, the muted light they gave coming from fridges and other appliances inside. Through a cafe window he read a clock on a microwave behind the counter: 9.20.

There were lights on further around the inlet, the orange fuzz of the lamps above the jetty, and the lights from the building beside it which he remembered was the tavern. Aside from the tavern car park the jetty was the only other landmark in town that had something like a streetlight near it. There were a few figures at the jetty's end, rods backlit, legs dangling from the edge. He crossed the road and walked across the small park to the cycle path that fringed the river. In the flat darkness of the path he let out a deliberate sigh and then laughed when the sound startled him. He laughed once more at the sound of his laughter, at how abrasive and mad it seemed in the quiet. Welcome to Stark, he said out loud, the words swallowed by the wind almost before they had left his throat, in an instant leaving him alone.

The day had collapsed into hazy memory, the long hours of the afternoon merging into a collection of moments. The bucking deck. Sea spray. Diesel fumes. And sleep. A guilty, nervous, claustrophobic sleep. Paul had retched until long after his gut was empty and when the purging subsided and tiredness overtook him he had staggered from the toilet and away from the open deck to the gloom of the cabin. In the dark he drifted off repeatedly, face scratching against the cracked leather of the seats, before the weightlessness of a swell passing beneath the boat would open his eyes and halt his breath. He had watched the droplets gather on the white metal rims of the doorframe. And he had watched the ocean beyond it turning like a green, apocalyptic sky, towering above Michael, who was left to work the deck alone. In patches of consciousness, Paul watched Michael pull, empty, carry and stack each heavy trap.

Paul woke at one point to see the deck full, the pots stacked three high and dancing like a miniature wooden cityscape in an earthquake. He had woken again later to see half the traps gone and thought for a moment they had been washed overboard. But he stayed lucid long enough to watch the deckhand carry the fifty or so pots that remained, place shining fillets of bream in the bait baskets, and heave each trap overboard with their coil of rope flicking behind them like tails. Paul watched him repeat the process until the deck was clear. Michael had occasionally glanced towards him, sympathy diminishing with each haul. When the last run was complete the German sat slumped on the gunwale, ocean huge behind him, his hair wet and his face blank with exhaustion.

They arrived at the inlet sometime mid-afternoon. Once the boat was tethered Jake had cut the engines and in an instant was down the ladder and in the cabin. He put his nose to Paul's while the German stood quiet behind. In the fog of seasickness the moment had been terrifying and surreal, the skipper's face weird with anger, shaking, and Paul could smell the meaty, bourbon stink of his breath. He had thought for sure Jake would hit him but he didn't.

The tavern car park was almost empty with only a few four-wheel drives parked close to the unlit back steps. Laughter drifted from the doors.

Inside there was no music playing, just the percussion of loud talk, and the trebly call of dog racing coming from the bar televisions. At a far counter, sitting under the glow of the televisions, there were men who looked scarcely alive. Their skin was a dark, patchy red. Their eyes were red too, and all settled on the woman behind the bar. They hadn't noticed Paul.

Jules, said one of the men, I've got an itch that needs scratching.

You better get that looked at, Anvil, the woman said.

The man grunted, smiled. A couple of the others snickered. He was huge, much bigger than the rest of them.

You look tired, Jules, he said. Let me take you home. Give you a back rub.

Christmas is it? I thought that was still a couple weeks away?

Nah, just your lucky day. We can fuck too, if you want.

The other men laughed.

What are you feeding this one, Arthur? she said. He's got a horrible look in his eye.

The woman saw Paul and made her way over, collecting empties on the bar. She was pretty, but looked overtired. There were deep creases around her eyes and at the sides of her mouth, puckered like old scars. Her black top was pulled down over the small paunch of her stomach.

What you having? she said to him.

Paul looked for a menu along the counter. He sensed the group become aware of his presence, backing themselves away from the bar to sit upright. They fell silent.

You look like shit, kiddo, she said to him, grinning. You alright?

He nodded. Hoping I could still get some food?

Jules shook her head. Kitchen is shut. Jolix has gone home. Got chips. Burger Rings. That's it.

Can I have some Burger Rings? And a bottle of Coke?

Only cans, darling. Vending machine is behind you. I'll get your chips. Three bucks.

She reached up to the shelf of chip packets behind her. Paul looked back across to the group at the bar and saw one of them watching him, gazing blankly through long hair, such an odd, clownish expression that Paul thought for a moment that he was joking. He looked the youngest of the group. He was the smallest by a long way, and he had a dying man's skinniness, the skin of his face tight against the skull underneath, squared bones of his elbow and wrist clearly visible. There was no white at all to his eyes, and in the way he stared, hunched low over the bar with his eyes locked on Paul's, he had all the menace of a dog leering through a gate.

You want a bowl? Jules said to Paul.

No thank you, Paul replied.

He looked back across the bar. The skeleton's gaze remained on him. His head was drooped forward and his mouth hung in a sort of grin, nostrils flared as though he was trying to smell him.

I can give you a glass, Jules said. Some ice.

I'm okay, Paul replied, looking back to her and trying his best to smile.

Suit yourself. You go have a lie-down somewhere.

Paul walked to the door and heard the laughter at his back.

The concrete floor of the phone booth was dusted with white sand. There were names scratched into its Perspex walls and short, hard-won statements that had been etched with the edge of a coin or a knife. The plastic of the phone was cold against his cheek. It smelt of cigarettes and perfume.

Dad.

Paul? You calling from a pay phone?

Yeah. My phone's not working. You asleep?

Um, no, his father said softly. Not really. Was watching something. He yawned. Must have gone under. What's the time?

Around ten, I think.

His father yawned again. I should put myself to bed. Everything alright up there?

Yeah, good, Paul said. Just letting you know I got up here.

Oh, okay.

How are you, Dad?

Tired. Ringo's been keeping me up. Got that thing with his ears again. Your mum is going to take him to the vet tomorrow, get more of those drops.

Haven't heard anything?

About what?

Elliot.

No, his father replied. I have not heard anything.

What about Elliot's birthday? Paul said.

Yes, it is his birthday this month, he said.

Paul had known the weakness of his question, how it reached for an answer that his father couldn't provide. His brother's birthday was in three weeks, but what about it? What would his birthday mean? Could they celebrate it? Would they wait for him to call, on that one day, as if that was what he had been waiting for? It made no sense. The idea seemed laughable, almost cruel. But still Paul could feel a kind of hope in him that he couldn't control, the belief that maybe Elliot's birthday might deliver them something. He wondered if his father hoped for that too.

Anyway, mate, his father said, you should be in bed. Won't make Jake too happy if you're late tomorrow.

Yeah. Okay.

Goodnight, Paul, his father said.

Paul hung up the phone and stood listening to the wind, looking through the scarred Perspex to the splintered image of the main street.

In the hostel lounge Paul went on a computer, lights off around him, enveloped by the light of the screen.

He searched his brother's name. He was good at digging through databases. Combing forums and chatrooms. He had been like that for years, long before Elliot went missing. It was just the way he was. It wasn't something to be proud of, but it had become something of a skill.

It was on the blog of a retired naval officer that Paul once found a record of his father from the first gulf war. A photograph taken on the black deck of an aircraft carrier. The image was overexposed, hard sunlight fuzzing the figure standing proudly at its centre. But it was clearly his father. Thin-faced and smiling, in a green jumpsuit and black boots. A clear blue sky behind him. Sandy fringe in a breeze. In his right hand he was holding a small novelty American flag. Paul had read the caption beneath the photograph enough times that he could recite it word perfect. Thomas Darling. Combat Systems officer. Operation Desert Storm. Persian Gulf. January 1991. Two years before Elliot was born.

The Professor of Statistical Science had been to war and he'd never said a word. There was not a physical record of the tour in the house, for all of Paul's searching over the years. But the internet had delivered the secret to him.

And a secret like that was hard to take on. Because he knew when he found it, when his heart was beating with it all settling in his mind, that it was something that Paul would never be able to speak of. He'd die with it.

In the dorm most of the curtains were pulled on the beds. He drew the thin bedsheet over himself and thought about the girl he'd seen in the kitchen the night before, the sun-darkened skin of her legs and shoulders. He wondered if she was behind any of those curtains, then he fell asleep.

55

Shadow

PAUL.

He felt the hand on his shoulder.

Paul, the voice repeated.

He looked up into the gloom and saw brown eyes, and such a look of terror that Paul sat up in his bed. Through the dorm window it was almost light.

You are Paul? the man said, the words rolling at the tip of his tongue, gentle but urgent.

Paul nodded.

Someone has come for you.

Paul leapt from the bunk. He peered into his bag, swore into the black of it.

You know this person? the man asked.

Yes, Paul said. He sat back on the low bed, pulling on his jeans.

He has been yelling in the street, a girl said above him, accusation clear in her South American husk. She rubbed her eyes. He has been hitting the doors. How did you not hear this?

Paul stood up without answering and ran through the corridor with his boots in his hand. Some backpackers stood in the doorways of their dorms, all boxer shorts and harem pyjama pants, foot stink and yeasty breath, blinking at him as he dashed past.

Out in the half-light a shadow paced the front lawn, lurching back and forth. Jake's arms were braced by his side and he was bent forward, as if there were a great pain in his stomach. When he saw Paul he came at him. Four steps and Jake had a hand underneath Paul's face, fingertips pressed hard into his jaw like he was trying to break it. Paul heard the strange note come from his mouth. Jake let him go and leant onto his heels, and Paul could see the man considering coming again, contemplating sending his knuckles across Paul's face. But instead he turned and, after a breathless moment, Paul followed him to the waiting ute and climbed into the dinghy.

He lay in the same cold damp, wondering what was wrong with him. He should have run. Had never seen such a look in a person's eyes. Even in the tray Paul heard his older cousin's muffled screams from within the cabin. He palmed his throbbing jaw, could feel the trembling in every part of him.

He didn't see Jake for the rest of the day. The skipper rarely came down the ladder. Paul did his best to keep up with Michael. And the day went as an uncomfortable dream, unhinged from time, unending. Wind and light. The perpetual slamming of the hull against sea swell. The sound of the horn, a pause over a float. And then the cry of the engines as *Arcadia* raged onwards, like a tortured horse. Pot pull after pot pull. Hard bodies clicking and crunching in his gloved hand. Carrying traps to the stern. Kicking the deadly rope from his feet. Retching into the windy sea. And those shadows flitting underneath the hull, their movements short, direct bursts.

In the misting water deep beneath *Arcadia* he sometimes thought he saw someone, sure for a moment he had caught the pale outline of a figure in a shaft of sunlight, or seen a face materialise in the eddies of silt, looking yearningly up at him. Doomed at mid-water, imprisoned.

Out on the horizon he sometimes saw figures standing on the water, thin and skeletal, shimmery. They were reef markers, he guessed, but he couldn't take his eyes off them when he got thinking of them that way.

Like most thoughts Paul had, there was no resisting them when they came.

He saw Elliot's four-wheel drive rolled, hidden by scrub. He smelt fuel in those moments. Felt weight on his limbs and on his chest.

He imagined his brother dead. A leathery, dark heap on the fringe of a desert track. Ribs exposed, eye sockets empty and rimmed by soldier ants. Or he would see a slick body, melting into the car seat, hear the energetic song of the flies, deafening. And there would be Elliot's face, black.

In another version, his brother fought to stay afloat in a windy sea, heavy in his fishing boots and flannelette, gloves on his reaching hands. Paul heard the drawing and breathing of swell, the foaming water white as teeth. He would feel short of breath for several minutes, the image lingering on him like a scent.

He wondered how much of these visions he controlled, and if he was choosing them. He didn't think of them as premonitions, but the violence in them was real.

Elliot could be dead. That was true. The police had told them as much. Be prepared for the worst. Whatever that meant. He was there when the constable delivered those words to his mother at the front door all those weeks after his brother had disappeared, returning the box of letters and photos the unit had taken. Prepare for the worst. He hated the man for saying it, how useful he might have felt offering those words. It was like telling someone to be prepared for a bullet to the head. There was no preparing for it.

When *Arcadia* reached the inlet Paul felt as if his limbs were hollow, the wind cutting through him as if he were only a phantom. Mouth bitter with bile, his legs weak.

Inside the deli it smelt of bait and cigarettes. The icy breeze of the air con on his sunburnt arms. He walked quickly to the soft drink fridges, the orange linoleum cold under his bare feet.

At the counter the clerk was talking to an older customer about the afternoon's wind, guessing the speed of it. She held out her palm to Paul without breaking the conversation and Paul levered the coins into it.

He stood out front of the deli under the sun, warming himself. The Coke made his eyes water.

Hey.

Behind him a man in a black hooded jumper stepped out from under the shade of the shopfront, head down, and closed in on him in a burst of energetic steps. Paul backed away a few metres, braced himself. The man looked up as he neared, grinning without any teeth that Paul could see.

Don't normally ask this but I need a few groceries mate and the missus would kill me if she knew I was asking but it's tough this time of year with Christmas lurking around the corner like a

59

bloody thief and we got kids and all that and there's no work and you know how it is. Think you could spare some coin?

Sure, Paul said, hearing the feebleness of his voice. He could not have guessed the man's age. There was a disconnect between the man's head and the clothes that surrounded it. The worn face peering out from under a baseball cap, his skin pale and potholed in the hard light. The hoodie and tracksuit pants and skate shoes, the body underneath thin and formless. It had a strange dress-up effect, like an old man in teenager's clothing. But he could have been eighteen.

Paul reached for his wallet.

Anything you've got, my friend.

Don't think I have many coins.

Anything at all.

Paul peered into the leather laggings of his wallet.

You a deckie? the man asked.

Yeah.

Oh cool. Yeah, fucking knew it. You look strong, hey. No shit. Can see it in your arms.

Paul looked up at him, tried to smile.

I used to work boats too, he continued. Good work if you can get it. But I'm no fisherman. Skipper said I'd be better as bait. The man laughed.

Paul had used the last of his change on the can of Coke. There was only a twenty dollar note. He handed it to him.

Fuck, you're a saint. Really, man. You're a fucking saint, hey.

Paul shook his head and turned for the hostel.

When he was some distance away he glanced back to see the man walking quickly down the main street, a fast stumbling walk as if he was being blown along with the wind.

~

Back at the hostel he saw the backpacker who had woken him that morning sitting with others, shirtless, on the front steps, soccer ball gripped in one large hand. He straightened up to face Paul when he saw him, causing the group to turn and consider him too. They were all older. Mid-twenties, maybe thirties. A girl lay on a beach towel on the lawn in a green bikini, Brazilian flag printed on the rear of her bather bottoms, the starry blue dome over the scarp of her bum. Paul stepped around her. The group was silent as he took the steps to the front door. He heard their laughter through the hollow walls of the hostel. Listened to it as he lay back on the bunk, alone in the dorm.

Sometime later, when it was dark, a girl entered the room. Through a gap in the curtain he watched the outline of her, partially backlit by the lights on the hostel balcony. He was close enough to feel the shower-heat from her.

As he watched, she looped her underwear over her legs, pulled on jeans, a dark t-shirt. When she left he smelt her perfume.

~

The generals are brothers from the northern beaches in Sydney. Twin brothers each as ugly as the other. Like they are in some terrible contest at who might be the ugliest. They are even uglier with the bad looks they've always got. Those two are uneasy out here and you can tell they are dying for saltwater. Grumpy when they look on the desert like they are looking at their own coffins. I think about the sea while we go through the hot sand. Think about how I don't know if city people love the sea or just love looking at it. I know they spend all their money trying to get close to it and on it cos I've seen the boats and jetskis on the TV and I know about the holiday houses and the whole lot. It's all gazing out to sea and it doesn't make much sense to me why anyone would want to be always looking at the horizon like something good is going to come over it. The whole country is crammed above the beaches like they are banging on a gate and I sometimes wonder if they are waiting for someone to come rescue them.

But the sea is where we are headed.

The President calls it a clean-up, this thing we're doing. There are big things happening on the west coast, developments that will make fellas like him and me more money than we'll know what to do with. We have opened up a vein bigger than anyone could ever imagine.

But there is cleaning up to do. Too many people know things they shouldn't and the President doesn't like that. He doesn't like anything that isn't clean. He says you watch the smartest fellas, they know how to keep things clean. Like surgeons. A surgeon is an expert at washing his hands and arms and tools and spraying down his operating table, and the President says if it is good enough for the smartest fellas then it is good enough for him.

~

Hidden

THEY WERE THE LAST OUT OF THE INLET. Paul had waited an hour on the kerb and it was light by the time his cousin's ute turned into the street with the skiff on the trailer. Paul caught sight of his expression, unsmiling. When they arrived at the beach Jake didn't explain why he was late, and he said nothing at all as they crossed the inlet to *Arcadia*, the only cray boat still on its moorings. He looked like he hadn't slept and he had the powerful scent of alcohol on him. The skipper was up the bridge ladder even before Michael had climbed aboard.

Paul knew there were problems with Jake. Everyone in the family did. There wasn't much detail, or not that Paul knew anyway. But for as long he could remember he had been aware of the trouble on his mother's side of the family. He had sensed it, as kids do, noticing the adults exchanging looks whenever Jake's name came up, or the way his parents never really spoke about him when they thought the children were in earshot. Paul had once overheard his father mention that Jake had been to jail. His parents had talked of it while they worked in the front yard, unaware that he could hear them as he lay on his bed. Paul had shared the news with Elliot, who seemed unimpressed and didn't want to participate in guessing what crime their older cousin had committed. Paul had always imagined some kind of robbery. Pictured his cousin's stormy glare through the eyes of a balaclava. Maybe Elliot had known what Jake did. If so, he never let on.

The swell had dropped from the previous days but a gusting wind still blew over the sea from the west. The water was a cloudy green, the surface speckled with kelp and cuttlebone and flecks of foam from shattered pot floats and other things that the storm had washed in and swept out from the beaches. They pulled the pots on the inside reefs, two and three miles out, always within sight of land. The sun was warm on Paul's skin and the swells that surged and foamed on the shoals no longer held the same threat, but there was still that dullness in his ears and his stomach still wrenched with each tilt of the deck. By mid-morning he was dizzy from purging.

You shall disappear if you keep that up, Michael said as he returned from the back of the boat to the cabin. You will look like a supermodel. Just teeth and knees, that is all.

Paul attempted a smile.

Michael watched him, as if waiting for him to speak, before returning his eyes to the sea.

You don't get seasick? Paul said.

Not me, Michael said, looking back at him. My mother, she was in the circus. She used to do trapeze when she was pregnant with me. This big tummy, flipping through the air.

Really?

Michael laughed.

Paul watched the older boy's face, trying to read him.

If you are hungry, I have some food. My girl Shivani made me lunch. You are welcome to it.

I don't think I could keep anything down.

Michael scoffed. With the lunches my Shivani makes that is the problem. Are you staying at the backpackers still?

Paul nodded.

Michael groaned. Hot girls, yeah? The German sighed at the thought, almost mournful. Paul didn't know how to respond.

I thought you would be staying with the skipper, Michael said.

What? Jake?

He and Ruth, they are not family?

They are, Paul said. But I don't really know them. They've always lived up here. We never really had much to do with them. And I guess all that stuff with Jake . . .

He left the words suspended and glanced at Michael. If he knew any more than Paul did, he hid it well. The smile on his face was as inscrutable as ever.

Ruth hates me, anyway, Paul said.

Michael leant down to the deck and picked up one of the crystal crabs he'd earlier removed from a pot, the animal pale from its life at depth without sunlight, twice as big as a lobster. The German held it by its rear legs, away from its pincers, and dropped it overboard.

So, how long you been doing this? Paul asked.

Two months. I found the job in September. Jake needed a deckhand. You know.

Paul nodded.

I was on the east coast before this. I have not seen Stuttgart in four years, Michael said with a proud smile.

Four years is a long time, Paul replied.

It is a long time if you are not moving, if you are just still, in the one place. I have been elsewhere too, not just here. Did the traveller thing, you know.

You like it here?

Working on a boat? Michael shrugged. I could make more money in a mine, he mused. But I would not want that. Life is too short to go digging around in some billionaire's sandpit, you know? And what a way to die, buried in a mine. Take me to the sea bottom any day. Feed me to the fishes.

Ruth told me the season isn't going well.

Shit this year, they say.

Why?

Michael reached for the rollie papers in the pocket of his cargo shorts. They are calling this year the windy season. Something about the wind doing strange things. Winter storms still blowing in summer. I don't know. No fucking fish, anyway. They do not allow many pots. He took off a glove and looked at it, turned it over in his hands. Maybe that is why I enjoy this, he said. The way I see all of this, we will not be doing it forever. People, I mean. One day there will not be this. We will wake up from our dream and there will be no fishing boats in the sea.

Michael rolled a cigarette, turned towards the cabin wall, out of the wind. He lit it, then held the bag of tobacco out. Paul shook his head.

Is Jake worried? Paul asked.

The German let the smoke go from his lips and frowned at the sea, like Paul imagined an old man might frown at the sea. Maybe, he said. But, you know, every man is worried about something.

Paul looked at him, again trying to figure out if the deckhand was being serious or not.

So, Michael said, eyes widening again. You getting pussy?

Paul smiled and shook his head.

My god. The girls that come and stay in that place. I would live there myself.

Don't you have a girlfriend?

Girlfriend? Michael replied.

Shivani? Who made you lunch?

Shivani? Michael repeated, and paused to think on it. Well, yes. I guess I do.

Paul scoffed. Michael grinned.

She is always packing me lunches, Michael said mournfully. Every day. It is hell.

Why is that hell?

Shivani is Sri Lankan, Michael said. Her parents, they run that Tamil place. You understand? He looked at Paul sternly. They run a fucking restaurant. But Shivani? When Shivani is in a kitchen she is lost. She always has a cookbook like this. Michael held a palm close in front of his eyes. It is like watching a tourist, Michael said. Her head in a map, totally lost. Like one of those tourists in a big city who gets confused and steps out in front of a bus. They do not know which way the traffic runs, which way to look, and everything goes to shit. That is what it is like. I see her in a kitchen and I just want to shout, Shivani, get the fuck out of there before you kill yourself!

Paul listened for Jake, concerned about Michael's volume.

And she is always packing me lunches, Michael said. I mean, what are the possibilities of that? How is my luck? I find myself a Sri Lankan in this tiny place and she speaks more Aussie than the rest of you, and she cooks like an old man who has lost his mind. Fuck me.

Paul grimaced to hide his smile.

Amazing butt, though, he said, and gave Paul a serious look. My goodness.

Paul laughed at the earnestness in his eyes, couldn't help it.

Michael smiled. No, no, he said. I love that girl. Very much. Michael stretched. I need coffee, he declared. You?

Don't think I should risk it, Paul said. It had been almost an hour since he had last been sick.

Michael walked away up the deck, pausing to take his gloves off. You know, he said over his shoulder, we have got a spare room, me and Shivani. Piece of shit, our place, but cheaper than that backpacker joint. No good you wasting all your money there, even if it is full of girls.

Paul opened his mouth to thank him, but the deckhand had already entered the cabin.

There were long hours during which the deckhands said nothing to each other, when there wasn't a word said anywhere on the boat. Michael smiling into the breeze; Jake lurking on the bridge, like Quasimodo in his tower, unseen. It was something like calm. You could retreat into yourself and it was acceptable. Expected. The work was good for that, Paul thought. Still had your thoughts to deal with, but at least you didn't have to share them, or hide them. You didn't have to communicate at all.

By five o'clock *Arcadia* had completed six runs and the deck was empty of pots. They were heading back to Stark, and Paul was relieved at the relaxed pace Jake was going. It was a rare thing. Paul was sitting in the cabin, his eye locked on land to manage the seasickness, when he felt the engines kick under the deck, heard the rumble of them. The boat lifted in the water as it gained speed, the deck slanted upwards towards the sky.

Michael jumped down from the bridge ladder and stepped into the cabin.

More pots? Paul asked.

No, no, Michael said hurriedly, one arm in his backpack. Something is out there. Jake wants a look.

How far?

Michael either didn't hear him or chose to ignore the question. Got it, he said to himself, and pulled his camera from the bag.

They headed north-west for twenty minutes, away from town. Paul felt the nausea descend on him again, a heaviness that swept through his limbs. Michael paced the deck. At last the boat slowed and the German roared with excitement. Paul stumbled out from the cabin.

Michael was leaning over the gunwale, talking to himself, eyes wide. Paul didn't know what they were seeing, and he struggled to focus his eyes on the water. It looked at first as though something had been spilt over the sea, like the fuel from a wreck. But he saw the thickness of whatever it was, like a giant bluish rug that had been dumped into the ocean, laid out and floating, inexplicably, on the surface, its edges torn.

What is that? he muttered.

Moby Dick! the German announced theatrically.

What? Paul asked.

Not much left of him, though, he said, grinning.

As the boat neared the whale carcass, the smell flooded Paul's nostrils and he instantly retched. Michael bellowed.

Jake cut the engine when they were alongside. He heard the German exhale.

Paul gazed into the thick, ruffled carpet of white tissue. The stench seemed to warm and thicken the air, like the smothering fumes of petrol.

And then he saw the flesh tighten, drawn flat by some great force at its far side.

See that? Michael gasped, his voice a high-pitched wheeze, as though someone had him by the throat. Up on the bridge Jake hooted.

Big fish down there, the deckhand muttered. Jesus.

Paul could sense movement in the water but all he could make out were shadows. His vision flickered.

Fuck, eh?! Jake yelled down, head over the railing. Get up here, Michael. Think there's two big sharks. Fucking whites, too.

Paul turned towards Michael. He thought he might pass out. Michael gave him an almost crazed look, tongue out, eyes huge, and laughed. Should throw over the handline, he shouted to no one in particular and then hurried up the ladder to the bridge.

The boat bobbed and danced in the water, and Paul settled his hands on the gunwale, head over the sea, waiting to purge. And he could hear the sharks, moving their huge bodies around the carcass. He expected the sound of ripping and tearing, like knives through upholstery. But there was only the shushing of water. Muffled. Benign. He could hear Jake and Michael above him, delirious. And he forced himself to open his eyes, shuffling along the gunwale, trying to get a clear sight of them, the shadows sweeping underneath.

Circus

MICHAEL ATE WITHOUT SPEAKING. Paul still felt the hollowness in his gut that was with him all day on the boat and he was suspicious of it. He dismantled his burger slowly and picked at his chips.

Men from another crew filed into the tavern and sat on the bar stools next to them.

German, a red-haired deckhand said to Michael, sitting down next to him.

Noddy, Michael said matter-of-factly, and shook the man's hand. He returned to his pizza, his eyes on his food.

You boys saw a white? Noddy asked.

Yep, Michael replied through a mouthful. We saw two.

Two? Noddy turned to the men next to him. Hear that? Two white sharks.

There was a pause, the crew silent as they considered Jules, the barmaid marshalling the beer taps.

That's not normal, declared someone up the end of the bar, a smoker's voice growling each word. Not this far north, and so many of them. Fucking sharks have been hanging around all year. It's like they're homeless.

It was a dead humpback, eh? Noddy asked, turning back to Michael.

He nodded.

There you go, Richard, Noddy said, looking down the bar again. Rotten whale. What do you expect?

That's not the only rotten thing down there, the man growled. Whole coast is a corpse.

Paul looked at the quarter-eaten burger on his plate and knew another bite would make him sick. He closed his eyes and felt the room move around him, as though his chair was being lifted off the floor, drawn perpetually to the ceiling. He pressed his palms hard against his eyelids. The voices swum around him.

Was it that freak show? someone asked.

Circus, another voice said, confirming the name. That fucker still loitering around?

Yeah, Circus, said another. The retard. We saw him last week, didn't we, Robbo? His big, lazy mouth all over the hull like he's got dementia. Swear he looks like my pop.

Was it him? Noddy asked, turning back to Michael. The bar quietened.

Different sharks, Michael replied, uninterested in the conversation. We just saw two regular, able-bodied great white sharks.

The group gave a tired laugh and went quiet as Jules put the orders on the counter. Paul could smell the reheated chicken. His gut recoiled.

That shark, whatever you call it—Circus—isn't retarded, the older man grumbled. There's nothing dumb about it. It's hungry, that's what it is.

Circus is retarded, Richard, Noddy said. No doubt about it. Taking a propeller like that. It's got a hole the size of a laundry bucket where its eye should be.

Won't last long like that, said a deckhand that Paul had heard the men call Elmo. Paul could guess why. The deckhand's face was permanently flushed red, bloated and shining as if he had been hanging upside down

The men fell silent again as Paul heard the shuffle of boots coming from the doorway. He removed his hands from his eyes and recognised the men he had seen on his first night in Stark. They took the stools underneath the televisions.

Paul nudged Michael with his elbow. Who are they? he whispered.

Arthur's boat, Michael replied without taking his eyes from his pizza. *Deadman*.

Deadman? Paul repeated. I haven't seen it.

You probably would not.

Why?

They moor it further up the inlet, upriver.

Why?

Michael returned a slice of pizza to his plate and breathed out impatient. I have not asked them, he said.

Paul glanced towards the crew, careful not to be seen staring.

Roo Dog, Michael said, anticipating the incoming question. He looked at Paul. And Anvil, Michael continued. Those are their names. It is best to stay far from them.

Which is which?

Roo Dog is the one like a skeleton, the one who looks sick. His brain is not well. Anvil is the big one. Not so smart, not so nice either.

Elmo overheard Michael's words and grimly nodded in agreement, eyes wide.

There was something magnetic about the *Deadman's* crew. They had everyone on alert, all eyes inexorably drawn to them. The old captain sat in the middle like a ringmaster.

Arthur, Jules greeted him. Good day?

The old man shrugged. Things stay like this I'm gonna have to start prostituting myself.

Anvil grunted.

Give them my lovely arse, Arthur added, and sculled his beer, pleased with himself.

Oh yeah, Jules said. Real gold mine.

Arthur cackled. A girl walked out from the doorway behind the bar and immediately the gallery went quiet in a kind of perverted reverence. Kasia. Paul recognised her. It was the girl who had been in the hostel kitchen the night he had first arrived in Stark. He had seen her there again the night before, pouring milk from a carton with her name written in black.

She pushed a mop and bucket across the concrete towards him. He didn't look, but Paul could sense the men were watching them. Kasia looked up, her eyes square on his as she drew the mop from the water, wringing it out against the wire arms of the bucket. The bleach drifted hot from the floor and bit deep in his nostrils. He noticed the lightness of her blue eyes. They were almost fluorescent against her dark hair and the brown of her skin. The girl raised her eyebrows comically at his staring, and he willed himself to say something to her.

Hey, fuckwit, take a photo, a voice boomed from the other end of the room.

Kasia looked down at the mop head and he saw her smile.

I said hey fuckwit, the voice came again, louder.

Paul looked searchingly up at Michael.

The German winked at him. You should be going, he said.

Deadman

ON MONDAY AFTERNOON HE SAW *DEADMAN* moored in the inlet. It was where Michael had said it would be, away from the other boats, where the inlet hooked into the cover of the rivergums and sandstone gorge.

Paul went there alone, as soon as he and Michael had loaded the crays into the freezer truck on the jetty. He didn't tell Michael where he was going. He knew it wouldn't make much sense. He walked along the beach of the inlet, below the tavern beer garden. Beyond the town the beach narrowed to a thin bank, and the beach sand gave way to firmly packed clay. He felt the breeze, confused in the mouth of the gorge, as if trying to turn back towards the sea.

The boat was moored in shallow water, the river dark red with tannin. *Deadman* flew two Stark Vikings football club flags, the black cotton stressed and frayed. A sheep's horned skull was tied to the bow rail, sun-yellowed.

He stood there for fifteen minutes, boots in the river mud, just watching.

Three afternoons in a row, when *Arcadia* had returned to Stark, Paul did the same thing. Walked into the shadow of the river, watched *Deadman*. There was no sign it had left its mooring. Nothing had been moved on deck.

On the fourth day, *Deadman* was gone.

~

Every night out in that desert I listen to the President while he has those bad dreams. The big fella grunts like he is dying, makes sounds like he is crying. When I say his name he doesn't wake but he stops for a while.

He kicks about when he sleeps too. Kicks his sleeping bag right off him every night so it is just his big tattooed body lying there with the desert air on him. Somehow it doesn't ever wake the two old generals he brought with him. They both sleep heavy after a day's riding but I can't sleep a second with him doing all that kicking and crying business. Out in this flat country in the dark before morning it is below zero and could kill even a fella as big as the President and sometimes I get up and lay the sleeping bag back on him. His face is all scrunched up like a white-bearded baby under the moonlight. Shivering and grunting. It is a weird thing to see an old fella looking like that and I don't know how it makes me feel.

One thing I do know is that it is hard to sleep easy when you are as heavy as the President. I tell him that he is an unhealthy man and he just says, Swiss, you mind your own business.

I tell him it is a miracle how fat he is when out here nothing much is moving around more than bone and tendons and fur except for the President. I tell him he is the exception to every rule out in the flat country. I can tell him these things and he seems to take it okay and plus he knows it's true. We been in the desert five days but the President can sniff out a jam doughnut from two hundred kilometres. Anytime we get near enough to a town or a roadhouse he sends me in to get fuel and food and water and I know if I want to keep the peace I won't forget those jam doughnuts. Half a dozen of them. He likes Wagon Wheels too if they got them. He drinks chocolate milk like it is keeping him alive and I reckon he has got chocolate milk running through his veins. I get that mean look in every shop with all the stuff there in bags on the counter. I know they look at my skinny arse and wonder where I'm putting it all.

An hour out of Innamincka the big fella has to ditch his bike. Steering head bearings gone and he can hardly turn it, so I have him on the back of mine, feel him killing the suspension. Imagine the bike exploding out on every drop in the track. Bolts and spokes and pistons rifling out into the brush in so many million shining pieces like space junk.

The President is heavier in more ways than just the guts.

I think it is the worry that makes him eat like he does. Like a hole in him that he cannot fill and I swear to God he tries real hard to plug it right up but there's no way of plugging a hole that big.

And every night he is grunting away and whimpering like a dying man. I listen to it and think it is all the dead speaking through him. God knows there are enough dead fellas who would have something to say.

I tell the President he has a hole in him that he cannot fill and he just says to me, Swiss, you mind your own business.

~

Jester

THAT NIGHT, IN THE SPARE ROOM MICHAEL had prepared for him, Paul lay uselessly alert in the heat, the skin of his back stuck to the bedsheets. He lay on his right side, turned where he couldn't feel the throb of his heart against the bed. Measuring time between pulses. He listened to the wind outside and studied the bedroom that was still new to him. The room was empty of furniture and the walls were blank. There was just the mattress he was lying on and his suitcase in the corner of the room with his clothes spilling out the top of it.

There was the familiar grip in his stomach, the ache from a day of purging but also of worrying. Paul had never talked to his parents about it, but for a long time, since he and Elliot were kids, he had worried about his brother. There were times when his brother's listlessness had drifted into something worse, darker; something that scared the shit out of Paul.

When he saw Elliot like that he had capered around him like a jester, as though it was his duty to resuscitate his brother's mood. In those times, Elliot looked at all things, living or inanimate, as though waiting for them to perform. A television show. Food. Paul could sense the pressure he applied to each experience and he took it on, urging them to please his brother, yet they invariably disappointed.

Occasionally Paul could persuade him down to the ocean. He'd talk up the conditions, the likelihood of finding octopus or groper, the evangelising speech coming out of his mouth almost involuntarily, and if he went on long enough he could get Elliot moving. He'd pull the gear from the shed then herd Elliot into his bedroom, waiting outside as his older brother languidly put on his wetsuit.

On the short walk up to Swanbourne Beach, at the edge of the Cottesloe marine reserve, Elliot would state what Paul had known all along. That the time of day was all wrong. The ocean was too warm, the sandy bottom barren and exposed. That they'd be unlikely to find anything. Paul willed there to be fish. He could physically feel the urging in his skin, like he was trying to summon the elements. In the water he wouldn't even be afraid. All he wanted was for Elliot to find something. His brother's spear became his own. But there would be no fish. The sea would go quiet on them, as if it could sense their desperation. And Paul would feel all the emptiness his brother felt. He cursed the sea under his breath. The sea that had all the potential to make things better would feign lifelessness. The brothers would walk home together in silence, Paul feeling the full weight of failure, and a creeping worry that wouldn't leave him until night came and he knew his brother was asleep.

Torpedo

ON SUNDAY PAUL WOKE AT MIDDAY. Fingers stiff. The pillow smelt of shampoo and salt and fish blood. After three weeks he had almost grown used to it. The wind was going outside. He could hear the German's voice, deepened and muffled by the plasterboard separating their bedrooms. Paul couldn't make out what he was saying but there was an odd pattern to his talk. He spoke in short, careful sentences that no one responded to. Then he heard Shivani moaning. It began as a gentle calling out, as though Shivani was trying to keep quiet, maybe aware that he could hear them. He closed his eyes and pictured Kasia, the barmaid from the tavern. Imagined her naked body on top of him, her belly against his. Calling out for him. But the sound beyond the wall grew. Something somewhere between pleasure and pleading, a contradictory call for help, before it opened up further into a big, whooping exhalation that repeated itself over and over like an alarm.

Within what seemed less than a minute the noise had grown almost violent and it stirred Paul again into wakefulness. He opened his eyes and withdrew his hand from his cock like he might get sprung, as if the neighbours would wonder what the hell was going on in their house and press their faces up to his bedroom window, peer at him through the blinds. But Michael and Shivani continued, the volume impossibly escalating. Paul snorted. He felt his heart gallop. He knew he had listened to them for too long and when at last he had decided he should sneak out of the house he had only put one foot on the carpet when the girl let go a scream that seemed endless and that made him freeze where he was. He listened to her call trail off, replaced by the finishing grunts of the German. Paul sat on the edge of the mattress, silent, not wanting to move in case the bedsprings gave him away. He waited until they were in the shower before he grabbed the beach towel from the couch and stepped out the front door.

Paul cut through the caravan park, the buffalo grass coarse underfoot and a bore-water-fed, supercharged green. The park was full with tents and vehicles, beach towels drying on bonnets. He didn't see many of the campers on the grounds. Most would be down at the inlet, he figured, or in town, or surfing further along the back beach or up at the point. He saw a few locals from the permanent lots drifting about, eyes down, carrying washing and cleaning up their caravans. Above a lot of the annexes, along-side large aerials, flew Australian flags, the cheap cotton faded and shredded by the weather.

At the back beach the nor'-easter was hot against his skin. Far around the bay he could see a herd of four-wheel drives parked adjacent to the surf breaks. The section of the beach where Paul entered the water was just enough in the shadow of the outer reefs to be waveless, but it was still open water. It was of course preferable to swim in the ocean rather than a pool, but a shark barrier or sea bath seemed a more reasonable management of risk. Open water always gave him that feeling of entertaining unnecessary danger. It was going to sleep with the doors unlocked, a window left open.

He walked until the water was waist deep then sank into the warm sea, felt the sting of it on the fine cuts on his palms and a graze on his shin. The sun was now above the dunes but it glanced over the water in a way that rendered the surface a dull, impenetrable green. Paul had once heard Elliot say that a great white shark begins its attack from up to eighty metres away, driving itself like a torpedo at its target in one smooth, unerring trajectory. Elliot had always been full of this kind of information. He always smiled when he said things like that.

Paul lay belly up, feet free of the water. He looked beyond his feet to deeper water. Out of the cover of the dunes, where the water went dark with the reef below it, the surface prickled by the breeze. He imagined the torpedo, hurtling over the weed and reef and then across the sand, charging at the wrinkled soles of his feet. He shook his head, annoyed at himself, trying to dislodge the image. He knew that few of the stories Elliot told him were accurate; they had been manufactured to feed his fears. It was unlikely that a shark could even be aware of its target from eighty metres, let alone begin a fully motivated assault. But the thought lingered. He wondered if he would see any movement of water at the surface. Did the charge begin with a big sweep of the tail, like the kick of a sprinter against the starter blocks? Would the ocean eighty metres out from him stir at all? Would he notice it? Or would there be nothing?

He felt the beginnings of panic and tried to focus his mind on the face of the girl, imagined Kasia in the water with him, bare legs about his waist. When the swell picked up out on the boat, or when Jake was in one of his moods, driving *Arcadia* in a rage, as though he was trying to sink them all, the image of that girl had become for Paul something like an anaesthetic. It soothed his nerves, blunted the seasickness. Out on the ocean he thought of her all the time.

He started for the beach. When he was knee deep, he made a shallow dive, eyes clenched shut, and then stood and waded to shore. He resisted the urge to look back over his shoulder.

The police station was at the far end of the main street on its own block, an island of dead lawn, trimmed hard. There was a long driveway, a squad four-wheel drive parked at the end of it. A boat, a small runner, sat on an unhooked trailer. The nose of the boat pointed skywards like a rocket.

Inside, he pressed the buzzer on the front desk. Paul had never been inside a police station before. He was struck by the bareness of it. The bare counter. The blank walls and polished concrete floor. It reminded him of a McDonald's, the hard surfaces easy to clean, designed to deter anyone from getting comfortable enough to linger.

He walked over to a small collection of posters on a far wall, expecting to find Elliot. There were pictures of three missing persons, profiles underneath each image; none of them Elliot. On the left was Chris 'Camel' Paolino. Thirty-two. He had fisherman's eyes, shining red. Sore. He had been missing fifteen years, last seen in the Stark inlet car park. In the middle was a woman named Dixie Hill. Forty-four. Looked twenty years older, mouth sunk back into her face like there weren't teeth behind it, the skin around her brown eyes swollen and scarred. Last seen hitchhiking the North West Coastal Highway a year earlier, fifty kilometres north of Kalbarri. And last there was a small boy. An eight-year-old French tourist: Nicolas Peret. Missing two years, last seen on Cable Beach, Broome. Police held concerns for his safety.

Paul studied a large poster on sexually transmitted diseases, photographs of bacteria and viruses taken through microscope lenses. They were bright, blooming figures, like galaxies, fluorescent-lit against black backgrounds. HIV was a neon planet, towers reaching from its surface. Chlamydia something like a meteor shower. The interstellar images were hard to relate to one's own body. They seemed less repulsive this way, Paul thought. Even the long, snaking form of syphilis looked almost graceful.

Not sure I can help you with that.

He turned. A woman stood behind the counter, studying him through her glasses.

You look lost, she said. The nursing post is back towards town.

I don't have . . . he began, glancing at gonorrhoea. He turned back to her. I'm looking for Officer Gunston.

You are lost. He left a couple months back.

Who's in charge?

Senior Sergeant Freda Harvey, she said. Call me Fred. What can I do for you?

She pulled on a thin fluoro-yellow vest.

Officer Gunston filed a report on my brother, Paul said. Elliot Darling. He went missing.

She nodded. Paul eyed the revolver on her belt, at her right hip.

Do you know about Elliot? he asked.

85

The Missing Persons Unit would be looking after that now. You'd be better off talking to them. She picked up a duffel bag and walked around the counter, heading to the door. I've got to get to the dunes, join the circus up there. Fred shook her head. Who puts a seven-year-old on a quad bike? she asked, speaking more to herself than to him.

She held the door open and waited for him. Paul stepped past her and out into the sunlight.

Sorry, mate, Fred said after him, through the open driver door of the squad vehicle. I just can't help you. MPU. Give them a call.

Paul watched her leave the island of dead grass and drive off down the street, without sirens.

The town centre was busy with weekend surfers and families from out of town, up for the long weekend. Their cars filled the gravel car park in front of the bakery. The small skate park in the centre of town, unused by local kids, was now crowded with agitated children who had endured the drive from Perth.

It was a long way to come for a weekend, but Stark wasn't the sort of place you stayed long. Three or four days at most. Maybe that was the idea, Paul figured. To get in and out. Swim in the inlet, surf at the point, take photos from the cliffs south of town, then head home. See what you wanted but not stay long enough to have to see everything else, the way things might really be.

That's all Paul himself had ever known of Stark: glimpses. He had been there a few times with his family when he was much younger. His memories of those holidays were limited to the Stark caravan park and the two-man tent he had to share with Elliot. There was the sea, of course. The cliffs. The point. He had some recollections of visiting Aunty Ruth and the cousins but they were distant. His parents hadn't brought them here in a long time, and he knew it had something to do with the trouble with Jake. His parents had been coming to Stark for years, since before Elliot and he were born. They had honeymooned there. And then one year, when Paul was about ten, they just stopped coming. They no longer even talked about it. Maybe by avoiding visiting they were able to keep the town the same, untarnished. Maybe the memory of the town, the idea of it, was all they needed, was all anyone needed. It made him wonder if a memory, or an idea, was all Stark ever really was.

Twenty-one

IF THERE IS ANY REASON TO BELIEVE in god then a girl has to be that reason. Michael squinted into the sea wind from the cabin doorway, a transcendent grin on his face. Making love, he mused. Now that is intelligent design. It is a genius concept to hinge existence on. Do you not think so?

Paul had been half listening, thinking instead about Elliot and the police officer, Fred. The lone sheriff of Stark. Paul looked towards land. It was just visible, the coast a pastel smear. He wondered too about *Deadman*. Her mooring was empty when he'd walked upriver the previous afternoon. He noticed Michael still watching him and paused at the thought that the deckhand might know he had listened to Shivani and him the day before, heard the German climaxing through the thin walls of their house.

Well I have not seen any better proof, Michael continued.

A smart, beautiful woman, looking down at you, wanting you, there cannot be anything more holy than that.

Paul avoided Michael's gaze. He had never considered sex as a means to finding God, but of course he had no idea.

Inside a woman she has you completely. She might as well have everything you own.

You make a vagina sound like a bank, Paul said.

Michael laughed. Nothing can be so terrifying but also make me feel less afraid of death. When my Shivani has her legs around me I feel like I could be a martyr. I feel like I need nothing else.

Saint Michael.

Glory be to God, he said, then winked with an exaggerated flick of his head and giant smile that made him look deranged. That was the difficult thing to work out, where exactly Michael's joking ended and madness began, if there was an overlap. Despite the weeks they had worked alongside each other, Paul still had no idea what the German was doing there in Stark. He figured Michael mightn't have a straight answer for that himself.

Do you believe there is a God? Michael asked.

I went to a Catholic school.

But do you believe in God? Do you believe this all might mean something to someone else up there?

Paul shrugged. Maybe I do.

Michael patted his jumper for his tobacco before finding the bag in the pocket of his tracksuit pants. He held the bag out to Paul who shook his head.

It is reality television, that idea to me, Michael said. Believing we are on the set of some show and someone up there is interested. You know, watching the same show for thousands and thousands of years, for whatever reason.

Jake's horn went and they slowed on a pot. Paul leant down and hooked the pot line. He caught his reflection in the sea. Paused on it, almost marvelling at it. It could have been someone else. The purpose in the face. A man's face.

A shadow formed beneath the image of himself. Before Paul could yell out the bronze whaler broke the water, a pectoral fin and then a strong tail. Paul stepped backwards. Adrenalin surged like an electric charge, hot across his chest.

Michael gave him a merry slap on the shoulder. They make you nervous? he said, less a question than a statement of surprise. The German took the gaff from Paul, wrapped the slack rope around the winch head, started ripping in the pot.

So many of them, Paul said, looking back at the water and his reflection, the shark gone, a familiar caution in the face staring back at him. Gives me the creeps, he said. It's like they're following us.

Michael hunched as he lit his cigarette, shielding the flame. They are, he said.

The pot hit the tipper and Michael slid it to Paul. Paul pulled weed from inside it, threw untouched bait into the sea, carried the pot to the back of the boat.

Paul was exhausted by the conversation, by the shifting sea. He had worn the thought of Elliot, too, ever since he woke up that morning. Paul didn't mention that it was Elliot's birthday. He had considered it; had felt the urge, like it needed to be announced, just stated and left there. But he didn't want the conversation that might follow. Michael would feel obliged to ask him questions and the risk of that was enough to make Paul keep quiet on it.

Elliot would have been twenty-one. No doubt their mother would have thrown a party. Paul had been to a twenty-first party once, for one of the cousins, Anna. The table for presents. The speeches. It was like a rehearsal for a wedding. Elliot had got out of coming to it, and he would have hated any party his mother organised. Paul felt a passing relief, as crazy as that was, that Elliot had escaped it.

He was never one for birthdays, seemingly oppressed by the performative demands of receiving gifts and responding to the obligatory attention that came with them. To Elliot it was all an elaborate harassment, a day when all the separate strands of a life choreographed to close in on him. A birthday meant fuss and noise, being singled out and made to stand up in front of people. It meant being repeatedly drawn to comment on how he felt, or what plans he had for the coming year, having to make declarative, positive statements that satisfied the enquiries of their grandmother, the neighbours or the friends of their parents, to anyone who might ask him how old he was or where in life he was going, which on a birthday seemed to be just about everyone. He knew their parents didn't understand just how his brother was tortured by it. But when that spotlight locked on Elliot it seemed like an intrusion. It came to look almost aggressive, an opportunity for others to pry, to scrutinise a life that on every other day of the year enjoyed a necessary privacy.

There are things out there that are worse than your sharks, Michael continued, as Paul returned to the shade of the cabin.

The White Whale? Paul said. UFOs?

Michael tilted his head. An airliner disappeared in the Indian Ocean. Gone, you know. Lots of people disappear. There are ghosts in the water, here.

Michael went across the deck, kicked a large ball of seaweed, like a soccer ball or a head, towards a drain gap in the boat wall. Forced it through with the toe of his boot, into the sea.

Who? Paul said. Who disappeared?

Does it matter? Michael said. No one in Stark seems so interested about history. Michael was looking west towards the haze of the horizon line.

Who are you talking about? Paul said, shivery.

Who? Michael turned to face him. You have seen all the posts in the water? All those sticks standing up in the middle of the sea?

Yeah.

Isolated danger markers. They tell you of something in the water. Maybe a coral head. Most of them are for wrecks.

Shipwrecks, Paul echoed.

Hundreds of sailors in this water drowned or cut down, Michael said. Fed to the fish and the birds. Just last month they dug up another skull.

Paul had read about it on Michael's computer. *Batavia*, and the Dutch massacres on the Abrolhos Islands three hundred years ago. A team of archaeology students from the University of Western Australia had uncovered the skull of a small girl on Beacon Island; other bone fragments and musket balls had been found in the sand around her.

And people come here to swim on beaches, said the German. No idea about all the ghosts. They should not want to look too close at the grains of sand on their feet, they might find bone.

There was silence.

Arthur's boat, Paul said. Roo Dog and Anvil.

Deadman? Michael said. What about it?

They are pretty interested in it, whatever is out there.

Michael swept his hair across his face. I do not imagine they are sightseeing, he said.

I've been going up the inlet to watch it. *Deadman*. And it'll just sit there, for days, not going out.

You should not go up there.

And now it's not there, Paul continued. I haven't seen it for a week.

Michael was silent.

You don't believe me, Paul said.

I believe you. A week. So? Michael paused. They have gone longer.

Where? Paul said. What are they catching?

Michael looked at Paul. I would forget all that. Don't go back up there. Don't go looking for them.

Aren't you curious?

Nope, Michael said, and walked back across the deck to kick more seaweed.

Pantomime

ON SATURDAY NIGHT THE BAR WAS THICK with people and noise and sweating heat. The crews and families from town. The restaurant full with older couples from the city. There were girls, hair soft, not straightened or bleached. Thin blouses and designer jeans. City girls. A couple of their boyfriends at the bar. A few of the deckhands had abandoned the TAB screens and stood circling the bar like a net. Saying nothing, gripping pints to their chests.

Michael went to the bathroom. Paul took his stool, next to Shivani. He noticed her take up her wine glass. She held it near her mouth, as if shielding her face. They hadn't spoken since he had moved in to the house. Not a real conversation. Just brief exchanges, navigating around each other in the hallways or in the kitchen. He wasn't sure what she made of him, if she liked him being there, sharing a thin wall between bedrooms. He knew he had a knack for scaring her, his timing somehow always off. Stepping out of a room the moment she was walking in, or slipping up on her when he hadn't meant to. He had taken to walking louder around the hallways to warn her of where he was, slapping down his forefoot on the tiled floors as he went, feeling like a ghost with drop foot.

He sipped his beer and watched the crowd. It was still loud but he noticed a number of the deckhands had stopped talking, concentrating instead on some action nearer the bar. Paul couldn't see clearly what it was for the bodies in front of him.

It is like watching evolution in reverse, Shivani said to him above the music and chatter, leaning towards him.

What? Paul asked, surprised at the sound of her voice.

Shivani put her wine glass down on the table. She then curled her arms in front of herself like a bodybuilder, face soldierly blank.

I don't understand, he said.

Look at them all, she said. Throw some girls in the mix and they devolve. Quicker than usual.

Oh right, Paul said. Early Man.

She smiled, briefly, then looked at the crowd. It's fucking dangerous, she said. Those tourists, they shouldn't be in here.

Probably not.

Shivani turned, watching him now. What are you doing here? she said.

What do you mean?

It is just a curious thing, after your brother and everything. That you would come up here. Live in Stark. Work on Jake's boat. Come to the place where he was lost. Be around the same people.

You think it's curious?

Yeah, I think so, she said, looking back towards the crowd for a moment. It is like swimming in the same undertow where a person was last seen. Most would stay away.

Paul didn't answer.

None of my business, Shivani said eventually, then reached for her wine.

There was a shout. Paul stood when he heard it and saw Anvil standing at the bar amid the city boys, his forehead pushed against the brow of the tallest of them. Anvil and the boy stood like that, leant into each other, arms straight at their sides, making a sort of pointed arch. The girth of Anvil made more obvious in comparison. The boy was rakish, handsome. Anvil was half a head taller. He had to pull his chin to his neck to eye his opponent. One of the girls, blouse billowing under the fan above the bar, tugged on the arm of the boy. But he didn't flinch, held the huge deckhand's stare as if he knew by instinct it would be dangerous to take his eyes off him. And all the time Roo Dog stood behind Anvil, watching. A sick look on his face, like hunger. Bottle of Jack Daniel's Whisky & Cola in his hand. Paul saw the bottle was empty. Figured the boy saw it too when he threw the punch at Anvil. His only chance. The punch hit Anvil under the cheekbone. Made a wet sound, a slap of flesh. And it rocked Anvil back onto his heels.

Then Roo Dog made a wild sound and pushed the bottle into the boy's face. The base of the bottle sheared away on the first strike. On the second swing Paul saw the jagged stump of the broken bottle catch in the boy's cheek. Roo Dog twisted it, without hurry. The girl screamed and it was only then that the boy seemed to understand the damage being done to him. His eyes widened. He pushed Roo Dog away and the bottle fell to the floor. The skin underneath his right eye hung, cut, like thick pastry. The two men held each other by the collar. Roo Dog grinned. Blood greased under their feet, streaked with dirt, spilt beer. They pushed through the doors to the beer garden. Anvil followed behind, a childlike bounce in his step.

It was all so silent beyond the glass, hair and clothes streaming in the dark, a windblown pantomime. A girl stomped a foot near them, mouth agape in horror and hopelessness, but there was no sound except for music and the call of the dog racing from the televisions. The men at the bar watched, talking in breaths. Someone, maybe Richard or Elmo, swore. And when Roo Dog stepped back from the body, and when the girl crouched next to it, you almost expected the world to fade to black.

Headwind

THROUGH THE FRACTURED PERSPEX OF the phone booth Paul saw an Aboriginal man pushing a shopping trolley, the sea breeze slowing his journey. Tornadoes of beach sand swept around him, and as he passed under the streetlight, Paul imagined an old man in a snow globe.

Hello? his father said.

Dad. It's me.

Yes.

Sorry, hope I didn't call too late.

Well, it is nearly midnight, Paul.

Paul continued to watch the man's shuffling progress along the footpath away from him, crouched against the wind, until the image broke up and dissolved into darkness.

Any news? Paul asked.

Right, his father replied. Someone did call today. They wanted to know if we could be in a study.

What kind of study?

Profiling Elliot's case in a study or report. I couldn't see the harm. If they learn some more they might get to the bottom of things.

What did Mum think?

She called them back and told them to go hang themselves. Said if these people really wanted to help missing persons, they would go looking for them.

Do you think you might come up? Paul asked him.

Well, look. It's just not a great time. It is the end of semester. He paused. We have all had a bit of a knock-around. I think it might be best if we stay down here.

Okay, Paul said.

Got something for you, though, his father said. Your mum is sending up a Chrissy present.

That's cool, Paul said. I'll be alright.

Good on you. His father coughed.

How are you, Dad?

I'm good, Paul. Good.

Mum sleeping?

His father paused. She's up at Grandma's, he said. Staying there for a bit.

What? Why?

She's just looking after her mother, that's all.

Oh. Okay.

We just all had a bit of a knock-around, that's all, his father repeated, and Paul had the sense that he was speaking as much to himself as to Paul.

Michael and Shivani were in bed by the time he got home. It was after midnight but he felt wired. Overheated in his clothes, unsettled by the events of the evening, the conversation with this father. He thought of the boy in the bar and the look on Roo Dog's face. Thought, too, about what Shivani had said. Was he really at the site of some kind of danger, being in Stark? Swimming in an undertow? He had no hope but to get thinking about what Shivani knew that he didn't. Michael, too. And the rest of the town. He felt suspicion build in himself, the compulsion that came with it.

Michael's computer was on the kitchen table. Paul sat down in front of it, scanned the search history. The Oxford University website, Department of Economics. He found a photograph of Michael standing under a dim sky in front of a world that looked ancient, buildings yellowed like old bone. His blond hair was darker. Shorter and combed. But his smile was the same. He wore a grey blazer and held a certificate. A Gibbs Prize for the best overall performance in three papers in Economics.

Paul stared at the photograph for some minutes, processed it all. It was always wounding, in a way, to uncover the secrets of people, however small they were. There was pain to confirming that things were not as they seemed.

Paul listened to the wind. He glanced up at the hallway.

It was a shitty thing to do, Paul knew. Poring over other people's information. Like rummaging through drawers in his brother's bedroom, and that same excitement. The fear of being caught, the fear of what you might find.

With Elliot, the search history was mostly surfing destinations. Remote Indian islands in the Bay of Bengal. North Sentinel Island. There were desertscapes he'd looked up, national parks in the Northern Territory. Daydreams of isolation. Elliot was rarely on the computer but Paul wondered if he had missed something, if he could uncover the necessary clue. A name. A location. When no one spoke to each other, the computer was like a sort of oracle. The great revealer.

The Professor was brilliant with computers, of course. But he didn't seem to care enough to cover his own arse, to clear the search history and the traces left. It almost felt cruel, how easy it was to find things that his father would have thought he'd hidden well enough.

It was sometimes porn, softcore stuff. Cheerleaders. Photographs instead of videos. It was weird to come face to face with the Professor's fantasies when one could have wondered if the man was even capable of any feeling or desire at all.

Paul had found other photographs his father had searched of the first gulf war. They were mostly aftermaths of Baghdad missile strikes. Gutted government buildings, hard sunlight on mounds of debris. Bodies woven within, blood bright against the powdered rubble. The incongruent collage of hard materials and then the softness of human tissue. Concrete and iron and then a body without a face. A severed hand.

The search history was a gallery of horror. All so hideous that it was sordid. And Paul had felt the puzzling judgement in himself; knew the hypocrisy of feeling the way he did. How strangely hurt he was that his father might trawl through things so awful, when Paul knew he had done just the same.

And still he'd wondered what his father was looking for, what the destruction meant to him. He sometimes wondered if his father felt he had missed out. A Combat Systems officer who never saw combat. Paul had looked it all up. Read of the Australian clearance divers who searched for sea mines in the northern Persian Gulf. Frigates on patrols, accompanying supply vessels. But he knew that the Australian navy had never fired a shot. Did the Professor wish that he had?

~

The President says to me one day I'll be as tall as him but the President is the tallest fella I've ever seen. I'm not an old fella yet but I'm sure that I'm not getting much taller. It is in the blood and I know this cos my gran said my father was a small fella even when he was fully grown. He never had no shame about it or anything. He was a demon with a footy in his hands. A lot of fellas out Tennant Creek way were good with a football in their hands and could be quick over the grass but she said he was something that no one had seen before. So tricky he could run under a fella's legs. I was a baby when she told me that. It is strange the things that stick in your head. So much I don't remember. Whole years just cleaned out up there in my head. But I remember my gran.

We got so much tech equipment out here we could be in a war. Scanning for radar. Satellite-phoning bikes ahead for roadblocks. And the President talks to those boats far out at sea. The big ones. I tell the President that he is like that Osama fella. Hiding in the desert. Running the whole show from a laptop. He says he knows he ain't running nothing. Says you have to remember that you are never running the show and if you think you are then you will soon be running the whole shebang from a grave that you dug yourself.

~

Parachute

PAUL WOKE BEFORE SUNRISE EVEN without the alarm. The room was hot. He slid the window open. Put on board shorts, an old yellow pair of Elliot's he'd brought from home that went below his knee. He stepped out of the house without a t-shirt.

Outside it was overcast but already warm, the air thick. He walked through the caravan park. Heard the creak of the annexes in the easterly. Smelt the sour whiff of incinerator ash.

The back beach was empty. He scanned the long lonely curve of it, bending three kilometres south of the town around to the bluff which jutted out, red and barren, like a quarter-moon. Several hundred metres down from where he sat he felt him, like he had been there only minutes before. Elliot out on the shelf, knee deep with his rod in hand, casting into the surf.

There had been a time once when they were all down there.

103

It was years ago. His parents, Aunty Ruth and her new husband Bob. A picnic laid out on beach towels. White rolls and peppered ham. Tomato and plastic-wrapped slices of cheese. Choc milk. Jake was about ten or twelve, teaching Elliot to fish. They would run down to where the sandbanks gave way to reef, dark as blood under the surface. Paul looked down to the bunkers of rock on the shore where he had sat and watched his brother and their older cousin. Paul never liked the fishing but got some thrill out of watching. It was weird, how he liked to spectate. Be near goings-on but not involved. He had always been that way.

Paul turned and looked north and saw a woman in a dark blue bathing suit, one-piece, standing up away from the shoreline. She threw a white towel to the sand. It was the police officer. Paul got up and shook the sand from his hands.

She eyed him as he neared her, then she looked south towards the bluff. She stretched her left arm out in front of her, straightened it out, then wedged her upper arm against her chest with her right forearm. He saw the swimming goggles wrapped around her hand.

Senior Sergeant Harvey, he said when he got to her.

Fred, she replied.

She swapped arms, holding her right arm out in front. Shoulders freckled.

I'm Paul, he said. I came in to the station.

I know. Elliot Darling. I told you to talk to the Missing Persons Unit.

So you've read the report?

Fred pulled the rubber strap of her goggles over her head and pushed the goggles up to her forehead. She looked at him. They'll tell you if they find anything, she said. As soon as they've got anything solid.

She pulled the goggles down over her eyes.

Can I come? he asked.

Fred scanned him, head to toe. You swim? she said.

Yep, he said. This wasn't untrue. Both brothers had taken after their mother's gift with technique. But it had been a long time, perhaps years since he'd swum any real distance in the ocean.

You don't have goggles.

Don't need them.

Fred looked down at his yellow board shorts. Be like swimming with a parachute wearing those, she said.

Paul looked down at them. Be fine, he said.

I swim out a fair way. South towards the point, about halfway. Right down to where the reef starts. It's a good mile there and back.

Paul looked down the beach, took in the dark beyond the sandbank. Okay, he said.

I'll be going my pace. Not waiting around.

He nodded. The woman looked puzzled by him. He was puzzled by himself. What the fuck was he doing?

Fred inhaled. She stepped into the sea.

After a pause, Paul followed. Water foamed around his ankles, cool. His breath went as each churning wall hit his legs and waist, the waves small but loud, rumbling from within, whooshing and sighing as they passed.

Fred stepped through each one, comfortable. A swell above head height reared in front of them. Paul took in the green dark within it as the wave flexed on the sandbank, glimpsed the ocean beyond it, opaque, like looking through a window when the lights are off. Paul stopped where he was as the wave broke in a clean uniform arc ten metres in front of him, a blade coming down. Then the boom and thump of water, the synchronised upshot of vapour, suspended in front of them. Fred slipped under it. Paul crouched on the sandbank. Waited the half second for it, eyes closed. Gripped the sand with his fingers. When it hit him he felt the weight move over him, through him. It took his legs from the sand.

When he came up he had hoped the wave had washed him back towards the beach. He hoped Fred had continued on without him. But she was there, looking back at him, turned on her back and adjusting her goggles, the now-quiet sea smooth as fish-oil slick.

Before Paul was level with her Fred rolled over, put her face to the sea, hunched her shoulders and kicked out in one movement.

Her skin glowed in the murk. Salt hot in his nostrils. He tasted it at the back of his mouth. They were only just beyond the breakers but Paul was surprised at the depth of the sea. The sandbank fell steeply away and he ignored the trench it disappeared into and the misting dark and instead took his breath on every fourth stroke, when his head was turned towards the beach. The dunes bobbing in his vision, looking further away than he expected.

So he watched the rippled bottom beneath him and the whiting that hovered over the sand, the fish almost transparent but given away by their thin shadows. Closed his eyes on each breath.

He looked down along his pale abdomen. Saw how his board shorts glowed in the murky sea, a beacon.

Then he stopped and threw his head to the surface. Tried to settle his breath. He was aware of his dangling legs. Saw blood in the water around him. There was the overcoming surge of adrenalin and then he was all animal, crazed limbs and short breaths and a bleating sound that shamed him as he heard it but that he had no control over. He kicked out towards shore and felt the sand under foot, the water still at his neck, and began bounding towards shore.

In the shallows he felt relief and defeat. The world had been restored to normal dimensions. The surf was small and the channel beyond the sandbank no longer seemed so far out. The sun had come through the clouds and the sea was shining and green and clear. But his nerves were shot and there was no going back out.

Paul stood on the beach with his towel around his shoulders. He watched Fred go off down towards the reef, felt some opportunity go with her. He thought of waiting but then left.

Undertow

ARCADIA TRACKED SOUTH OF THE CLIFFS, along the beaches. Shallow enough you could see the bottom, light rings of limestone, weed-covered.

Onshore it was bays. Each one like the one before. You could see the gleaming heat in the sand and dirt and rock. It hurt his eyes to look at it.

Paul had read somewhere that a landscape itself has no meaning. That it was more a mirror and anything you saw in it or felt were your own thoughts or feelings being reflected back at you. But in the long dehydrated hours spent with the land there in the distance he could swear sometimes that it was saying something. Offering a kind of warning.

Ten thousand kilometres. That was the length of the state coast, from the Territory border at the north, right around the coast to the South Australian border. Ten thousand kilometres of coastline. Michael had told him that. The distance from Stark to Stuttgart. He had never considered the length of it before. What reason would you have to think about it? Until you're looking at it from some sort of distance. Until you're looking for something. Tracking it. Eyeing it, like Paul did each day. Haunting it from sea. And then? Then it seemed endless.

Locksmith

AS HE ATE, PAUL WATCHED KASIA, just like Michael and the other men. He liked to think there was something different about his staring, but he'd seen his face in the mirrored wall behind the bar, the strung-out redness of his eyes, and he would look down in shame whenever she walked by. He could sympathise with the others in some way, as ugly as they all looked lined up like that in the mirror, like the row of them had been struck simultaneously by lightning, faces drawn tight and almost expressionless with sunburn, hair stiffened by salt. At the end of a day on the boat, just the sight of the girl was medicinal.

Michael had taken to the beer garden for a cigarette when a large man took his chair, setting himself down next to Paul in a rush of exhalation.

Hey, son, he said to Paul. Name's Jungle.

Paul, he replied. Out of the corner of his eye he could see Jules smirking behind the bar.

Jungle thumped him on the shoulder and smiled. Paul had seen Jungle in the bar a number of times, overheard his long stories, but never spoken to him before. Up close the man had a huge head, and his eyes seemed to follow individual lines of sight, neither of which fell on Paul.

Who you working with? Jungle said.

Arcadia.

Ah, he said, licking his lips. Captain Jake. Poor old Jake, eh? He let out another big lot of air through his gritted teeth. Don't know why he keeps at it. If it had been me I would have left this bastard place, that's for damn sure.

Jake the snake, said Noddy, seated further down the bar. Fucking scum.

Paul almost asked Jungle what Noddy meant by that, but the deckhand had shifted his attention towards the bar, waving down the older barmaid with a big red arm.

How you going, Jules?

Good thank you, my boy, she replied. What you having?

The usuals, he said. The usual suspects.

How's the lady? Jules asked.

Spending all my money, Jungle said, giving a slow wink and elbowing Paul in the ribs. Had to get a locksmith out the other day. Now, that's a joke. And I thought strippers cost money. Was thinking I should maybe give it a go. A locksmith. Sounds fancy, too.

Jungle turned towards Richard, the veteran skipper of *Hell Cat* sitting to his left. Richard had a stubby beard, and his short dark hair was peppered white in the way of an ageing blue heeler.

Imagine being a locksmith, Richard. Imagine learning that. What would you call that? Locksmithing? Locksmithery? I mean, where does that happen? At a college? Do you do a course?

Jungle, do I look like I give a fuck? Richard said, eyes squinting with the words. The men further down the bar laughed.

We had a guy come out the other day after we got locked out, Jungle continued. Zach, the silly prick, dumber than his old man, has dropped my car keys through the jetty. So I call this bloke. Never seen him before in my life. Guess how much it cost?

Jungle looked up the bar as the men ate their food. Cost me a hundred and fifty bucks, he said, and shook his head as though reliving the shock of it. He turned again to Jules behind the bar. A hundred and fifty just to get into me own house! Isn't that a joke? But with the reno and everything, the house is all so fucking new and watertight. You'd have to break a window. Courtney made us get this big fucking front door, you know. Looks like fucking Alcatraz. You've seen it, Noddy?

At the far end of the bar, Noddy grunted confirmation, his mouth full of mashed potato.

No shit, Jungle said. It is like a door that you'd have in a police station, in an interrogation room or something. Heavy as hell. Big stainless-steel handle, not a door knob. One of those sleek lever things. And this guy comes. I've never seen him before in my life. In a minute he's jimmied the fucker open. I mean, just imagine that.

Mind-blowing, Jungle, Jules said, smiling.

Seriously, picture it in your head, you're a budding locksmith. Imagine the very first time you do that, out in the real world. Instructor is with you, and you proper open a locked door to someone's house. You are suddenly standing in someone's lounge room, looking at all their things. That has to do something to you. No shit, it would be like sorcery or something. It's fucking Harry Potter, that kind of thing. Seriously, how many locksmiths do you reckon would turn criminal?

The men laughed. Jungle seemed to enjoy the moment.

You still talking? said Richard.

The power of it, Jungle continued. Any door. Not just house—shops too, even banks. Car doors. Imagine if there wasn't a lock in the world you couldn't crack.

That's not possible, mate, someone said.

And not everyone is a cunt like you, Jungle, Richard grumbled.

Yeah, laughed Jules, placing Jungle's pint in front of him. Remind me never to hire you as a locksmith.

Human nature, said Jungle. Everyone has their limit. Their price, you know, so to speak. I'm just saying, learning to unlock doors could be it for some people.

Jules laughed and made her way to the side of the bar where Arthur and his crew were sprawled, lounging over the bar and across the tables beneath the TAB televisions with all the casual menace of pack animals. There was a ripple through them as the woman drew closer. Elbows on the bar were replaced by hands as Roo Dog and Anvil and the others leant forward. Often, when he watched Jules and Kasia at work behind the bar, Paul thought of divers in a cage, the men like sharks in orbit. Some pressed hard up against the counter, others hung back in the gloomy corners of the bar, but they were all watching. Paul couldn't understand why Jules would run such a place. Michael had told him that Jules had worked there for twenty years, since she was seventeen. Grew up in Stark, got a job in the family tavern and never left. You could see it in her face, too, as though she had been surrounded by ugliness too long, ugly talk and ugly looks, her beauty stalked and circled by men for two decades. But in that place, amid the ghoulish faces and unhinged laughter, she was almost angelic.

Kasia was something else completely. She'd become for him like a possession. It was likely the boredom of working a boat, but when he wasn't thinking about Elliot and his parents, he was thinking of her.

So what brings you to Stark, Paul? Jungle said, turning back to him. If you don't mind me saying, you stood out like an upturned turtle's boner when you first showed up.

Jules smiled, back behind the taps nearest them.

Gee whiz, Jungle cried. Never seen a less likely fisherman. He hit Paul across the back hard enough to wind him. But I hear you're doing alright.

I'm Jake's cousin, Paul said.

You're Elliot's brother?

Yeah.

He was dating Tess, Jungle said. My niece. She's a tough kid, Tess. Had her battles, too. Got caught up in that horrible crystal meth shit. Jungle considered Paul for a few seconds. You look like him, he said. You got that look he always had, like a train's coming.

Jungle shuffled on his stool, and Paul could see the man turning something over in his head. So, what you think of this fishing business? Jungle said eventually.

Paul shrugged. It's alright.

It's not for everyone. You've got it in your blood or you don't. My boy, Zach, he's got it in his blood. I can see that. He's only just hit twelve, but first thing in the morning he's down the beach with one of my rods or his surfboard. After school he'll surf till it's dark, then he fishes all night from the jetty. Poor old Courtney is always trying to whistle him back to her. He turned to Jules and winked. He's like a fucking fish.

Jules nodded. Like his old man, she said. More brains, hopefully.

More brains than a fish or more brains than his old man? Jungle said, setting himself up, mouth open with anticipation.

Not sure there's a difference, Jules replied cooperatively.

Jungle whooped at the joke and slapped his thigh. Richard, slumped half asleep next to him, flinched with the commotion.

Jungle turned to Paul with a huge-eyed expression of consternation. But I'm serious, mate. Even when there's a fucking storm going Zach will be running around in it all. Scares Courtney shitless. But there's nothing I can do about it. Not a thing.

Paul laughed. The man seemed pleased. Paul wanted to say that Elliot was just the same, that Jungle might as well have been describing his brother when they were younger, the way he talked of Zach. There was always somewhere else he wanted to be, at the edge of a jetty or the end of a beach or a bush track. Outside, away from things. He wanted to tell Jungle how the city beaches bored and depressed Elliot unless there was a storm up, when the water shed its crowds and traffic. Paul wanted to tell Jungle all that. But the pain in the thought kept the words docked in his mouth.

You, though, Jungle said, you strike me more as your indoor recreation type. You know, on a computer. The man working an invisible joystick.

Gamer, Jules said.

Yeah, Jungle replied. That's it.

Paul heard Noddy's laughter down the bar. Jungle seemed annoyed by it. What I'm saying is, it's dangerous work, all this. Even worse if you don't care much for it. You be careful, son.

Paul saw the concern in the man's red face. He didn't know how to respond to it.

If you're bored or scared, Jungle said, or just don't want to be there, the boat will take care of that for you. If you want off, it will help you out. That's what I'm saying. You have to have a reason to be out there, not to get lazy. You've got to have something to focus on. Me, it's Courtney and Zach. It's probably the same for everything. You've got to have a reason.

Jungle, Richard said angrily, sliding off his stool onto unsteady legs. What the fuck are you talking about?

Meaning of life and all that, Jungle replied.

Fuck's sake, the old man muttered as he shuffled in the direction of the toilet.

Jungle beamed at Jules and took a triumphant scull of his beer.

Life after God

THE SCENT OF DEATH WAS SO FOUL, so choking, that he woke to the echo of his own yell in the bedroom. He had seen Elliot, naked in a shallow grave, uncovered, his body shrunken and bent like a spider's corpse. Paul lay there in the wake of the dream waiting for Michael's footsteps in the hall but the German didn't stir.

After a time of attempting to fall asleep he thought of praying, but he didn't put his hands together. There was a danger in doing that, the risk of feeling nothing at all.

When Paul was younger he prayed. He prayed when the dark got to him at night. And it made him feel better. He didn't need to keep his eyes on the cupboards in his bedroom or the window.

Some nights, Paul would instead pluck the figurine of Hulk Hogan, the wrestler, out of his box of toys and take him to bed. Just like when he prayed, clutching the figurine he knew he was not alone. The rubber Hulk, deeply tanned with knee-high red boots and white underpants, had his eyes open permanently. He could keep lookout. In a way, Paul was suspicious about that then, that God could be interchangeable with Hulk Hogan, that both gave him the same comfort. Even before he hit high school he'd figured that maybe God was just something to cling to when your nerves were rattled about something.

Elliot might have believed in God. It was hard to work out what Elliot thought about anything. His father never talked about God either, though he hadn't ever missed a Sunday mass as far as Paul knew. A man just didn't talk about his beliefs, Paul gathered, and no one asked him about them. You just turned up to church, crossed your name off the divine checklist, and went home.

And the whole religion thing bored Paul. It had bored him for years. But when he thought of Elliot dead, he found himself thinking about all that stuff again. When you grow out of Hulk Hogan, grow out of God, what else do you believe in?

Fever

JAKE DROVE *ARCADIA* HARD AT THE HORIZON. Paul could almost feel his cousin's anger in the deck. With each drop of the bow over the wind swell he felt the jarring in his bones. For half an hour he braced his legs for each impact, every time holding his breath. He closed his eyes and saw the boat breaking apart, disintegrating, like one of those videos he had seen of a space shuttle burning up on re-entry.

What did you do back in the city? Michael asked, almost yelling above the wind and noise of the deck.

I worked in a supermarket. I thought about going to university. I don't know.

You do not know what you want to do?

My marks weren't the best, Paul said. My mum wanted me to go to a college, do all my exams again. Reckons I should have done better.

Is she right?

Paul shrugged.

You know my father, Michael said, my father is a money guy. That is his life. He was always saying to me, Get a degree. Get a house. He wanted to send me to the same university he went to.

Oxford, Paul said without thinking.

How do you know? Michael said, his smile fading.

Shivani. She said something about it.

Shivani? Michael replied. He reached for the tobacco in the pocket of his tracksuit pants. Paul looked to sea.

He wanted me to work at his firm, Michael continued. He thought I would be a property developer, like him. Michael raised his arms as he said the words, outstretched like an opera singer. A property developer, he declared again. Can you imagine it?

No, Paul said.

Exactly, Michael said. It makes him very angry that I am here. He gets red in the cheeks, like he has a fever.

Paul laughed.

I am serious, Michael said. I swear I will make my father ill. And it is not just him. Everyone at home in Stuttgart, all the rich friends of my parents, they are so worried about that stuff. It is all they talk about. What are you studying? Which university? What are your grades? What will you do? They ask all these questions like it matters. Michael smiled. So I tell them I want to be an elephant trainer.

Will you ever go back?

To Oxford? No sir.

Ruth was waiting in the car park when they arrived at the inlet. Paul and Michael approached the open driver-side window.

Here. She held a phone out to Paul through the car window.

120

Seeing as you are too brain dead and dumb to look after your phone, you can have this one.

He took the phone from her hand. It was no longer in its packaging but it looked new. Thanks, he said.

Call your parents. Your mum says she hasn't heard a word.

Okay.

I can't have her calling me every bloody day wondering what the fuck is going on.

Ruth reached over to the passenger seat for a neatly folded piece of paper. Your new number is on that. She cleared her throat, leant her head out of the window and spat at the ground near their boots. Michael put his hand over his face as if to hide a smile. I've put my number on there, too.

Paul nodded.

Right, I've got shit to do, she said, starting the car. And you'd better not be causing my Jake any trouble. Enough on his mind as it is.

Thank you, Ruth, Paul said.

She drove off.

~

Me and the President talk some fair amount of shit because his generals don't say much of anything.

The President once said I remind him of one of those clever Swiss knives. Not just good for one trick. He gave me one and I keep it in my pocket. It is a fancy one too. Still small enough to fit in your pocket but only just. Stainless steel. You can gut a roo with the blade on it, easy.

I told the President he calls me Swiss because he thinks he has me in his pocket. He denies it but I know it's what he thinks.

He reckons I'm too quick and clever to be cooking meth. Which is good, cos all that business is in my bones now. I feel like an old fella some mornings. Knees and elbows give me shit. My teeth hurt and I got blood coming up from my lungs.

The President has me shooting. Whenever we stop, which is all the time. Every hour just about. On the sandy desert tracks the bikes get hot real quick. We put them in any shade we can find and the generals do the navigating and run the radar while I shoot cans with the .308 and the President lies next to me with the spotting scope. Talks over my shoulder like a coach. Says you need to be as close to dead as possible cos no one is as still as a dead man. Says to hold the shot till your lungs are empty. Fire the round between heartbeats. Has me hitting whisky cans and chocolate milk bottles from three hundred metres. I shoot a roo stone dead from twice as far.

The President don't touch a gun no more. Won't lay a finger on one. He says he has earned the right to keep his prints off things.

The way he spins it, he says I'm like a son to him. Says he wants to make me a President like him so he is teaching me the ropes. The President can sound almost like one of those missionary types when he talks like that and I know he is out to right some wrong in his own head. I wonder if he has God on his mind sometimes.

There are days I almost like him. He is nicer to me than those young bikie fellas are. Some of them are sick in the head. The President isn't like that to me and maybe he does think about my situation with my parents being long under the ground.

But I know things the President has done and when you have seen a man do certain things there is just no way you can forget it.

~

Moby Dick on a handline

JULES HAD ONLY JUST PLACED HIS BURGER on the counter when the news broadcast started on the television above the bar. The deckhands carried on chatting, Jungle recounting some old misbehaviour of Zach's down the bar, and Michael, next to him, explaining Hubble's theory of an expanding universe to Elmo, while Paul watched the screen.

The story was being broadcast live from a street in the south-east border town of Eucla. Paul became aware of the men going quiet around him. Perhaps it was the hyperventilating tone of it all, the large bold headings and details scrolling on repeat at the bottom of the screen, like it was CNN. Or maybe it was the tight pink blouse of the reporter. But soon they were all watching.

The reporter stood in front of a rural police station, lights flashing silently in the darkness beside her. She explained how, several hours earlier, detectives had pulled over four men in a

LandCruiser as they crossed the border out of Western Australia, seventy kilograms of methamphetamine and ecstasy in a hollow metal tube welded to the underside of the car. An image flashed on the screen of a four-wheel drive cordoned off by tape on the edge of a desert road.

Police had launched coordinated raids across the state, the reporter continued. They seized a house in the northern suburbs of Perth and a half-million-dollar boat. A Perth woman was arrested and further drugs were discovered in an apartment in Esperance on the south coast.

A lone detective stood behind a table, turning over packages with gloved hands, answering questions with a bewildered expression.

They are not novices, he said, frowning towards the TV cameras. This is a highly sophisticated network.

These are professionals, the German mimicked aloud, stumbling over the word. Jungle laughed. This, Michael said, right here, this is the real deal.

The investigators believed the four men and one woman may have had connections to a larger organised crime network, though a link was yet to be established. The methamphetamine was most likely produced overseas, but they were as yet unable to determine how such a volume could have entered the country, or where it might have come from.

The detective was out of his depth. That was obvious. Michael said he was like an angler who had hooked a creature that his gear couldn't take, a species he couldn't identify or comprehend. Jungle declared it was like he had Moby Dick on a handline, and smiled in the wake of the words, pleased with himself.

Paul said nothing.

In the dark

TWO BOYS STAND AT THE EDGE OF THE REEF. The night ocean is warm around their legs. The sun is an hour from rising and the city is in shadow behind them, strange in its quietness. The older brother stares purposefully out into the dark. He eyes the tip of his rod. Feels each tremble of the line on his fingertip. Reads it. The younger boy watches the water, trying to settle his thoughts. He has just seen a giant octopus emerge from the darkness, the tentacles reaching into the night air and gripping each boy around the waist, thrashing them about in the dark victoriously while the world is asleep.

He draws in a deep breath and focuses on the catch bag in his hands, how he *must* make sure any fish his brother hooks gets in that bag. Paul has lost one already, the herring bucking in his hands as he pulled the hook from its mouth. Elliot isn't talking to him now. And it is still so dark, the sea. Almost black. Paul peers over his shoulder in hope that he will see the sun peering back at him above the vast silhouettes of the houses on West Coast Drive. But there is no sign of it.

And it is then that the shark surprises them in a scream of white water, a great white shark, as big as the bus they take to school, even bigger, surging over the shelf and on them before either has a chance to yell. And in a moment they are gone, deep into the animal's gullet, in one horrific crush of its jaws.

Elliot hoots as the rod comes to life, jittering and arching down towards the water. Get the bag ready, he says.

But Paul can see their blood in the water. He imagines their mother and father tracing the shoreline for pieces of them. A newspaper headline appears in his mind as real as anything.

And he turns, without offering an explanation. He steps as quickly as he can over the shelf of reef, navigating the holes and trenches, stumbling over heads of coral, kicking his toes. Elliot shouts out after him, pleads for him to come back, but Paul keeps going, hopping over the shelf until he reaches the shoreline. And then he breaks into a sprint, tearing away from the night sea and the giant octopus and the shark, and away from his brother standing alone in the dark at the edge of the reef.

Containment

PAUL SWAM BREASTSTROKE IN THE SHALLOWS, his knees grazing the sandbank with each circular kick, glancing over his shoulder every now and again as if he were walking down a dodgy alley. The sky was cloudless, the water clear. He looked for Fred. But the beach was empty.

Two swallows flew in hard arcs near him, wheeling above the water. The birds came closer, untroubled by his presence. He knew their metallic blue, their grey breasts. They saw them often on the water when they were working. And he couldn't take his eyes off them.

Elliot had always told him that the birds meant danger. He had said so since they were little. Particularly the swallows and martins that buzzed low across the water in the summer months. They were scanning for sharks, Elliot had said. He told Paul the sailors called the swallows warning birds. It meant a boat was being shadowed, that they should keep their limbs clear of the water. A swallow was death itself.

Paul suspected warning birds had the ring of bullshit, and his mother said it wasn't true. Sailors had given them the name welcome swallows, she said. The sight of welcome swallows meant a ship was near to land. But he had given way too much thought to them over the years. That was Elliot's point all along, understanding how it played into Paul's weakness for superstition.

Late-night searches on the internet only confirmed Elliot's half-truth, as it confirmed all half-truths. A swallow flying through your house was a sign of imminent death. Of course everything was a symbol of bad luck in some place or other. An audible fart in Ecuador was the sound of your soul leaving your body.

He knew a fart was just a fart, and a swallow was just another fucking bird. But with the water to himself, it was hard to not think of them as some kind of omen, to sense the shadow of something in deeper water.

On the beach he lay back on his towel and felt the sharp grip of the sun on his skin. He closed his eyes and saw Kasia next to him. The heat flash-drying her skin. The easterly coaxing goosebumps down the length of her body. When he thought of leaning over her and kissing her the image disappeared, and he felt something like sadness. There was such an impossibility to his daydreams. He was gutless with girls. It was in his DNA. For all of Elliot's bravado in the sea, his brother was the same. And girls threw themselves at Elliot. It was the moths-to-a-flame deal with him. But whenever Paul saw his older brother talking to a girl, there was the same hesitancy and timidity that he recognised in himself. The brothers had never spoken about it, why love and sex were such perplexing frontiers for both of them.

Elliot did have Tess, of course, but he never talked about her to Paul.

And Paul never told him of his one experience, a couple of years before, when he found himself alone in a pantry at a house party with a short, square-shouldered girl named Claire. She was from a state school east of the freeway. Claire had dragged him in to the kitchen for a supposed joke that only she seemed to know and he remembered being aware of her yellowish teeth under the counter light and a sarcastic laugh that rounded off everything she said. But in the pantry it was dark and once she had closed the door her laughter subsided until all he heard was her breathing. He remembered the sour, rich taste of McDonald's on her lips and on her tongue and the wine on her breath and the scent of their bodies in the heat, and the smell of flour and stale bread and honey from the shelves. He had felt for her breasts and only seemed to find the barrier of her bra that was either too large or had come loose, the cup folding in his hand. They were in there for all of twenty minutes. Later Claire vomited in one of the bedrooms of the house and fell asleep there. He never saw her again, but when he was alone he had sometimes thought of her. It was the only memory like that he had. And it was better than porn or one of the girls in Elliot's surfing magazines if just for the realness of it. At night, alone his bed and with the lights off, Claire transformed into something close to perfection, the smell of her saliva, slicked above his lip, became a perfume.

You're getting burnt, said a voice behind him.

He turned to see the bar manager, Jules, standing with her towel in her arms and a calico bag over her shoulder.

Am I? he replied.

Yep.

Paul pulled the towel over his groin.

Paul, right? she said. You're Jake's cousin. Ruth's nephew.

Yeah, he replied, not intending to sound as suspicious as he did.

You know, Stark being how it is, she said, half apologetically. No secrets. You'll learn that soon enough.

He stared at his hand in the sand deliberately, focusing hard on the thin, even coat of white over his wrists, fine as icing sugar.

Jules, she said.

Yeah, I know.

Jules lifted the thin dress over her body. In the harsh light he saw the fine markings on her skin, the squiggled lines on her hip bones, and a large red scar on her arm. He took in the tattoo below the left breast of her bikini, a small black bird, like a swallow, with its head tucked behind its wings as if it were covering its eyes.

So where's he gone, your brother? she said, crouching to reach for a pack of cigarettes and a lighter in her bag.

He's missing, Paul said, hearing the defensiveness in the words.

What do you think's happened to him?

No one knows. That's the point.

Jules stood and gave him a long look, sizing him up. She plucked a cigarette and dropped the packet on to her towel.

Sorry, he said. Everyone asks that. If we knew where he is, he wouldn't be missing.

Fair enough, she said. You know, I didn't think you'd stick it out, all this crayfishing business. You're in the pull now, though.

Paul stared into his towel, unsure what she meant.

Stark has its own gravitational pull for sad cases, Jules explained.

Sad cases?

That's obvious, isn't it? She cradled the flame of the lighter against the hot breeze. You're not alone. Don't you worry about that. Everyone has got some issues here. Not that it's a retreat or anything. There's no healing. It's more a containment kind of thing. She laughed.

You're a sad case?

Shit, she said. You are nosy.

So are you, he said.

I'm a bartender, mate. Isn't that the whole routine? She smiled and blew smoke, considering the curve of the bay. All those screwy boys at the bar, I should open a clinic.

An asylum more like it, he said.

Jules laughed.

Fuck it's hot, she said. I'm going in.

He watched her walk towards the water.

Rear-vision syndrome, she said, turning back to him. That's what my father called it. Here, everyone is always looking backwards. It's a sad as fuck thing. You'd do well to move on.

Runner

HIS CHEEK SWEATED WITH THE PHONE AGAINST IT. He was sitting on the kerb, the night air dense and warm. The sound of the sea was amplified by the absence of the wind. Surf clamoured on the reef beyond the inlet, intervals of silence punctuated by the orchestral percussion of collapsing water several hundred metres off in the dark. Other than the waves the town was noiseless. Michael had said to him once that wind was all Stark was. It was all people spoke about in the morning, he had said, that it was easy to find yourself in a conversation about it, obliging an old-timer with a guess about the exact time when the wind might turn from the south, usually just before or just after midday. There was some local pride in that wind. Flags flew in most streets, and every other shop had a windsock erected above it. When the wind was truly up the town danced violently with multicoloured fabric. The breeze roused even the toughest, tiredest, lowest tree or bush into movement. And the sound almost replaced the absence of traffic, of people. The wind gave the illusion of life.

His mother answered the phone.

Mum, he said.

Paul? Where have you been? I have been trying to get hold of you.

Sorry. It's been busy.

There's news. The police called.

When? Paul asked.

This morning.

What did they say?

His girlfriend. She was trouble. I knew that.

Tess?

The police won't ever tell us much about her, but you could just see she was tangled up in things and she was going to drag Elliot down with her.

Paul remembered what Jungle had said about his niece. His mother was right.

What did the police say? Paul said.

They wanted to know if we ever saw things. If we noticed anything in his room, or in the Pajero.

Like what?

Unusual things. Different bags. Packages.

Drugs?

Did you ever see cash on him?

They think he was a drug dealer?

Maybe he was just moving it for them.

What the fuck, Mum?

Don't talk to me like that.

But moving drugs for who, Mum? What do they know?

They can't tell us much. But it's not good, Paul. There was trouble in Stark. Bad people.

Bad people?

Something to do with a network, he said. Bikies or something. I don't really know. The detective said they've been watching some blokes transporting drugs across the border into South Australia. They think it's coming from somewhere up north, maybe Stark.

I don't understand what this all means.

The line distorted as his mother exhaled. What if Elliot got caught up in it? He might have had to make a run for it, if he had wanted out. But what if they got him . . .? His mother trailed off, then went silent.

Mum, it's not true. Elliot wouldn't have got caught up in anything. He's too smart for that. It's not like him.

Yeah, she whispered. I'll call you if I hear anything more.

They've got this wrong, Mum. This drug thing. It's not Elliot.

The living dead

THEY ARRIVED AT THE INLET AROUND three in the afternoon.

Paul left his backpack with Michael and walked straight from the inlet to the main street, all the way to its end where the police station crouched on its island of dead lawn. Fred was out front, wind in her greyish hair, hosing down the boat. She raised her eyebrows when she saw Paul and scanned him, rubber boots to the cap on his head that he had taken from Elliot's room. It was only then Paul figured the image he must have been standing there in the bright haze of afternoon, his board shorts and white t-shirt browned by fish blood, face ghosted with sunscreen, eyes bloodshot.

If you weren't on your two feet I would think you were a dead person, Fred said. She turned the water off and dropped the hose. Come through.

Inside her office were three desks. Fred lifted a stack of bulldog-clipped documents from a chair.

Have a seat, she said.

Paul sat down.

Elliot Darling, she said. I read the report.

The police in Perth. They told my parents there was trouble in Stark. Drugs.

Fred nodded. It's why Gunston left, she said. He was like me, a city cop. From Sydney. Don't think he suspected how hard it could get. Didn't have the stomach for it.

For what?

This place is bubbling with junkies. Probably keeping this town going, really. All the glass.

Glass?

Methamphetamine, she said. Ice. Stark is crawling with the stuff, like everywhere else. Probably worse here, though. It feasts on a town like Stark.

Fred lifted another stack of documents from the chair behind the desk.

Tell you what, she said. This office is like quicksand. Bloody drowning in Gunston's stuff. He'd probably prefer I torched the lot of it.

Fred carried the papers to the furthest of the three desks and dropped it with a theatrical giving way of her hands.

I'm supposed to be getting some help, she said as she moved a cardboard box from in front of him. She placed it near a stack of half a dozen or so other boxes near the door. Stood straight again, arched her back, grimaced. I'll be getting another copper, they tell me. Some Stark kid. Only twenty-four and he's a war veteran, if you can believe that. Afghanistan.

The drugs, Paul said. Why Stark?

Fred stepped back behind her desk. Pointed to the framed photograph against the wall nearest to him. A tall man gazed back at Paul. Kind eyes. White-haired.

My husband Robert, Fred said. Rob worked the courts in Sydney. Show him a town in population decline, he would show you a methamphetamine problem.

She sat down.

Rob thought meth was like the bacteria that flushes a corpse, she said. Bloats and colours it and twitches its limbs. Keeps it moving after it's dead, he'd say. You understand? A corpse isn't alive but it teems with the barely living. The opportunists. The ceaselessly hungry. Dealers and junkies. Junkie dealers.

Paul nodded.

You know the type, she continued. See them outside the deli or the bakery.

Paul had seen the men who were far too gone even for working a boat. They hovered in town in the mornings, grinning like whaler sharks. Dead-eyed. Despite the ravaging effect on a face, the drugs gave even the oldest of them a child's twitchiness. They watched everything like they were remaking sense of it.

And Tess? Paul said. She was trouble?

Tess Hopkins? Fred asked, then shrugged. Your brother's girlfriend. Police spoke to her back when the investigation began. She was known to police, had some history in town. A user. Wasn't in the mood for talking, but Gunston decided there was nothing there.

What about Elliot? Paul said.

I don't know everything the police in Perth know but I don't necessarily see any link. Unlike his girlfriend your brother had no history, no use or possession. There wasn't much on him at all.

But someone might have hurt him.

I doubt that, she said. I mean, most of them out there, the small operators, they're more a harm to themselves. It's not murders that keep me busy. Fred slapped the pile of papers in front of her. She looked up at Paul. Petty theft, she said. It is unbelievable. Stark has, what, eight hundred people? But you can't leave a door unlocked.

The police told my parents that they think the drugs could be coming from Stark.

Fred shook her head. You don't get that volume out of someone's kitchen. It's coming from somewhere else.

Where? Paul asked.

Fred shrugged. Africa. The Middle East. Asia. Even South America. Could be coming from anywhere; it doesn't really matter. The question is how.

Paul gazed at the papers. How do you stop it?

She gave a sort of smile. According to my husband there is no stopping it. I told you, it's just like the bacteria that raids a corpse. Fred laughed wearily. At least you can torch a corpse.

~

From up on a ridge we see a town. Glints and white dots in the shimmering farness like boats on a red sea. Yulara. And below us a line of vehicles on the highway, not moving, a hundred metres long. Hire vans. Caravans and motorhomes. Two squad cars at the head of it. The President says they're federal police. They're looking for us. I lie down on the rock with the .308. The President adjusts the rifle scope for me. Has me glass one of the coppers. Even at four hundred metres I can see the pulse and flex of his throat as he speaks. See him laughing with the lady copper he is talking to. So close in the telescopic sight you can almost hear them.

~

Spinning over and over, like a plane going down

JAKE TURNED INTO THE STREET EARLY, the headlights travelling through the morning dark at a greater than normal speed. The deckhands gave each other a look before the ute pulled up. Paul jumped into the skiff without daring to utter a word, and when Michael had to run back into the house to get his gloves Jake shook the steering wheel with such a rage that the boat trailer shook. When he was in this mood, every delay was enough to make him scream aloud. Any obstruction, like a stubborn door or stray cray pot, received a full-blown strike with a fist or a boot. On those mornings even Michael would put his grin away. Michael had said before that the more sober Jake was the worse his mood. It was as if he could see all of his problems more clearly, see all the shit in his world in greater detail. And Paul figured Michael was right. Jake was almost better when in the fog of a hangover or even still half drunk; at least then he was some way towards being tranquilised, deadened to things.

They went hard for the first four hours of the morning, propelled by Jake's fury. They were on their sixth run before lunch. Michael manned the winch and Paul emptied and baited the pots. They spoke less to each other, worn out by fighting the roll of the deck.

Jake gave a blast of the horn and Michael gaffed the line. He looped the wet rope around the winch head.

The pot slammed into the tipper and Michael swore.

What? Paul said to him. You okay?

You have a guest, Michael said and slid the pot along the tipper to Paul.

Paul noticed in an instant the lifelessness of the trap, the absence of sound or movement. There were no feelers poking through the slats. There wasn't a single crayfish, just a lone sleek muscular shape that took up the entire pot.

What is it? he said.

That is a Port Jackson, Michael replied.

It looks like a shark.

It is a shark.

What do I do?

Well, it cannot stay in there.

I have to pull it out? Paul asked. With my hands?

I have not heard of any better way.

Paul looked at the shark curled up at the base of the pot, on its side. It was no longer than his arm, but its diamond head looked almost reptilian, like the head of a giant snake. It was marked almost like a snake too, the cream skin patterned into triangles of different shades. He could see its strange mouth, unlike any shark he had seen before. Rows of pointed teeth were clustered together in a ball. The shark's gills pulsed.

Grab the tail. Go on.

Paul put his gloved hand through the entrance of the trap, half expecting the shark to twist on itself and tear his fingers clean off.

We cannot take so long, Michael said. You have to get its tail.

Paul hooked his arm to the top corner of the pot where the shark's tail fin was caught between the slats. He held his breath and clamped his hand down on it.

Hold it right there, Michael said. At the base.

Paul could feel the wrenching muscle against his grip. The shark rolled itself upright.

It will bite me.

Not if you keep away from the teeth.

The shark kicked and its head butted the wooden slats of the pot.

It will fucking bite me, Paul said again.

It does not think you are dinner, Michael reassured him. It just thinks you are an arsehole.

Shit, Paul muttered as he began to draw the fish back through the entrance of the trap, tail first.

Look at you, Michael chuckled. Shark man.

Do I just throw it?

But you are friends now, Michael said.

What do I do?

Put it in the sea, Michael said, and laughed. It is best to do it slow.

Paul held the shark out over the water. He leant as far over the side as he could, arm extended, lowering it until its head and most of the trunk were submerged, only its tail free of the water. The animal arched its head back toward the surface. Paul weakened his grip and the shark seemed to sense it, freeing itself with a strong kick of its tail. It darted down into the green sea and they watched until it disappeared into the clouds of silt and sand.

I shall call you the shark man, Michael said. He lifted the pot from the tipper and carried it to the back of the deck.

It was only then that Paul noticed he had been shaking. He felt the throb of his heart.

That shark was lucky it found this boat, Michael said, reaching for the bag of tobacco and pack of rollies in his shorts pocket. I tell you what. All the others, they would kill it. Michael stepped near the cabin doors and out of the wind to roll the cigarette. Except for Jake, maybe, he said.

He wouldn't kill it?

No, I do not think so. Maybe our Jake knows what it is like.

To be a shark?

Michael laughed and shook his head. To be despised, he said. Hated. Even a little feared. Maybe he knows that.

Why does everyone hate Jake? Paul asked, realising it was true. I've heard the way people talk about him. Say he's scum.

Michael shrugged, put the cigarette to his mouth, lit it. That is not my point. My point is that men always hate the shark, even more than they hate octopus or stingrays, or any other scavenger that finds its way into the pot of a fisherman. I am telling you, they would always kill the shark.

Michael blew a stream of smoke that disintegrated in the sea breeze beyond the cover of the cabin.

I once saw Noddy cut bits from a shark while it was still alive, the pectoral and dorsal fin, the end of the tail. That is how he sent it back into the water off the jetty, very much still a living shark. I watched it spiralling down into the depths, spinning over and over, like a plane going down. Michael shook his head, the smile gone. Do you know what it is? he said. Why they hate the sharks?

Paul shook his head.

Because they have convinced themselves that a shark might be the cause of all the trouble for them. It is the reason why there is no lobster, they think. The reason there is no fish. It is responsible for everything. The shark is their shit luck. The shark has made them poor. It has made their wives not want to fuck them. So when they get hold of a shark, they finally have all of the shit things in life right there in their hands, in their control.

Michael drew on his cigarette then exhaled.

And you know, he said, there is nothing more hereditary than fear. Nothing. A man passes it on like the colour of his hair. You have seen the boys at the jetty? They are worse than their old men. It has been handed down. They throw those little sharks alive on to fires. Stab their eyes. They will saw the heads off them. Not to eat—just to extinguish it, the fear.

It was true. Paul had seen the severed heads on the beach near the jetty, the coarse skin sun-wrinkled.

That is why we are all doomed. And there is no use worrying. Nothing can be done. Fear is in our design, a virus planted in every one of us. And we cannot rid ourselves of it.

Paul waited for a smile but there was none.

The dam's broken

PAUL WATCHED THE GERMAN'S EMPTY pint glass dry on the counter. Michael had sculled it when his phone rang and in minutes the mist had cleared and thin rings of froth were streaked around the inside. He studied its changing atmosphere and thought of Kasia, waiting for her to return. He heard Roo Dog's screeching laughter at the other end of the bar, Arthur's coughing, and ignored it.

Kasia appeared to collect the glass and Paul looked down at himself and inhaled as if he might just say the line he'd been putting together in his head, a question about Christmas, if it snowed where she was from, but he didn't say a word, and by the time he raised his head she had already disappeared into the kitchen.

Michael stood outside the bar doors with his phone to his ear. He looked almost divine, facing the darkness, straight-backed, with the sea breeze in his hair and his silhouette lit orange under the veranda lights. Shivani sat on the brick wall in front of him and cupped his arse with her hands.

A stunning reek grew around the bar.

Ha! Roo Dog laughed. Merry Christmas, you fucks.

Kasia returned from the kitchen balancing three plates of lamb shanks. The men down the bar from Paul shifted in their chairs and Arthur lifted his eyes from the counter. Someone made a sound of delight as she placed the meals in front of them and there was no question that it wasn't because of the food.

Order? she said to Paul as she neared him.

Steak sandwich, he said after a pause.

Kasia gave him a curt nod then returned to the kitchen.

Fuck! shouted a deckhand they called Tea Cup, the curse directed at Arthur but summoning the attention of every ear in the building. The entire tavern turned towards him, the locals and the dozens of tourists seated in the tavern restaurant.

You see all those arseholes today? Tea Cup continued, volume elevated once more, buoyed by the attention. Town's blocked up like a shitter.

What? Arthur said from the side of his mouth, the word sounding like a curse.

In town, Tea Cup replied. Fucking circus. You seen it?

No, the older man grumbled.

Oh Jesus, Arthur. You've never seen so many useless cunts in one place. Can't drive or park for shit.

Arthur muttered something, the words inaudible. His red eyes were locked on Kasia's arse.

Saw a four-by so bright yellow it could have been radioactive. Some Toyota piece of shit. Gutless as all fuck but dressed up with kit like it was a bloody Hummer. Fuck me. What a waste of plastic. I mean, why would you make a car that big? No shit, it's like they're planning on hitting a roadside bomb.

Arthur rolled his food over in his mouth, no longer listening.

Swear to God, Tea Cup said. It's like a fucking dam has broken.

You've been asleep, Roo Dog muttered. The dam busted years ago.

Good thing too, Jules said, squaring her body up with Roo Dog's. Wash all of you out of here.

Come on, Jules, Roo Dog said, unsmiling. I know you want it. I can smell your pussy from here.

Arthur grunted in amusement, eyes pointed gleefully into the trench of the bar where Kasia was refilling a fridge. Paul wanted to ditch his glass at him.

It was after ten when Paul sat in front of Michael and Shivani's place and called home, buttocks warm against the street kerb, the concrete still hot from the day's sun.

Dad.

Yes, his father answered.

Were you asleep?

No. Working.

Can I talk to Mum?

She's looking after your gran.

Okay, Paul said.

There was a pause.

How's the dog? Paul asked.

The dog is still a dog.

Paul managed a polite laugh at the old line.

Ringo is good, his father said. Think he misses you kids. Doesn't get enough of a run with just me around, poor bastard.

How long have you been on your own, Dad?

There was a pause. Your gran, Paul. She's not well. Your mum is good to go look after her. She's staying with her for a while.

Then why aren't you staying there, too?

She's not my mum, Paul, he said with something like a laugh. And who is going to look after Ringo? You're up in the middle of nowhere.

Gran could stay with you guys. My room's free.

Paul, he said gently.

What is going on with you and Mum?

His father sighed. Please Paul, he said again. This is not easy, mate. We're doing our best.

You shouldn't be alone.

I'm okay. Don't you worry about me.

Elliot wouldn't want this, whatever this is with you and Mum, Paul said. He wouldn't want Mum up at Grandma's. It's crazy.

Paul, his father said, sterner. We're doing our best, he repeated.

Yeah, Paul said. Alright.

Atomos

PAUL STOOD WITH HIS FACE TURNED INTO the stream of the shower. The cold water found the cracks in his lips, like water to scorched earth. He gazed down at Shivani's bathers looped around the shower handle. It was enough to make him feel like he was losing his mind, the urge just to touch them. He turned his back on them and scrubbed hard at his fingers with the pumice stone, digging the sharper edge into his palm until it hurt, as if he might also scrape away the thought of Shivani scrunching her bathers in her hand and standing free-breasted and bare-arsed right where he was. But it was hopeless on both counts. His fingers reeked proudly of fish guts and his cock had become as hard as the shower rock. He muttered to himself and cut the shower.

At the bathroom sink he noticed the reflection of flesh in the mirror wedged behind the taps. The frame was only the size of the rear-vision mirror in a car but he saw the line across his lower

148

abdomen, a ridge of muscle that began at the point of his hip, on both sides, and ran towards his groin. He stared at it. He heard Michael and Shivani laughing at the TV, looked back instinctively to check no one could see him. He shuffled backwards some more and saw his chest. Then he dropped the towel and moved further back until he was standing on the low wall of the shower. He crouched down, abdomen tensed, curled like a Greek statue. In the small frame of the mirror it was all new visual information. Ropes of muscle ran across the back of his arms and along his shoulders. He didn't yet have the bulk of Elliot's body but at least now there was some definition. He squared himself to the sink and studied his cock.

He stepped down from the wall and leant towards the mirror to stare at his face. His eyes peered back at him, alert but steely, like a man's eyes. And for the first time he saw Elliot in the mirror. He and Elliot had always been so different, as close to opposites as family could get. But there he was, his brother, looking back at him. Not anywhere near a replication, of course. But in that odd, passing moment he knew he saw Elliot. There was no doubting it.

Outpost

JAKE LOOKED AT NEITHER OF THEM as they skipped along the windy inlet. His right cheek was marbled purple and his eye was blood red, and there was a graze down his right forearm, as if he had fallen somewhere. Even with the stink of the river around them Paul could smell the alcohol on the skipper's breath, the sweat in his clothes. There was a persistent turmoil in Jake's face even then, tranquilised as he was underneath a hangover, his face slackened by what Paul guessed was nausea. Something like anger drifted just below the surface of any expression, never leaving.

That look always reminded him of a dog that stalked the front yard of a dilapidated house down the street when he was little. Paul had seen the men who lived there kick and hit the dog, and whenever the dog saw Paul and Elliot walk by its teeth were bared. It growled at any sound, at any stimulus at all, always feeling itself under threat. Even if the boys spoke softly to it, it would rage at them through the gate, ears flat, spitting with an anger that was hard to comprehend.

Aside from Richard's busted boat, *Hell Cat*, which had a broken steering cable, *Arcadia* was again the last to leave the inlet. An hour south, the sea was a dull green. Sediment rippled the water and surf bristled and growled on the bomboras.

Michael had once described working the deck during a swell as like working in a zoo, with the sea calling and howling, and the groans and chattering of the pots. Paul decided that it was more like a jungle, how each individual noise spoke of its own threat. The shriek of the wind in his ears. The whine of the rope, almost in frustration, desperate to pull you into the sea.

Paul's nostrils were hot with the smell of bourbon, rising like fumes from his gut, and the relentless energy on deck made him feel a sort of mania. The white glare of marine paint. The hard edges and hard sounds of the deck. The German's whistling. It all made him want to yell out, to scream like a mental case. All morning he had seen himself slipping and smashing teeth out on a railing or on the glistening rungs of the bridge ladder, the thought repeating in his head like it was on a loop. He cursed himself for having again let Michael keep him out late. He spoke to his stomach out loud, warning off sickness. It had been weeks since he'd last vomited at sea. But even the dinghy ride in the inlet had made him want to spew.

Michael pointed out two or three four-wheel drives huddled together on the shore. They were difficult to make out, tucked up at the base of the ridge, the white paint grey under the shadow of the dunes. It was an unremarkable place they had found themselves, the ridgeline above them prickled with brownish vegetation. Fishers or surfers, Paul guessed. They were too far to tell for certain. Then Jake powered the boat towards another bombie and they lost sight of them.

For the next hour Paul saw his brother's Pajero tucked into a corner of every bay they passed. He imagined him waking in the driver's seat, wondered what he would be thinking.

Michael leant against the wall of the cabin and looked into his sandwich, lifting the top layer of white bread with care as if the whole thing could detonate. He spoke under his breath in German and returned the sandwich to the baking paper.

You did not have a girl back home?

Nah, Paul replied.

Really? Why then do I never see a girl in your bedroom? You are a free man.

Paul shrugged.

I am getting concerned, Michael said. You do know this? I am genuinely worried about you. No wonder you are so bottled up, always looking like you are trying not to explode into a million little pieces. You have this look on your face. Michael tensed his entire face like someone holding their breath, squinted his eyes. Paul scoffed but Michael fixed on him an expression of sincere urgency. My friend, he said, gripping Paul's shoulders with his greasy gloves, that is your cock saying to you, *Dear God, let me out.*

You are such a tosser, Paul said. He shrugged off Michael's hands.

Now tossing is a very good idea, Michael said. But tossing is only a temporary fix. It is not a long-term solution. Eventually your cock is going to be like, *This is fun and everything, but I want to meet new people.*

You're messed up.

When did you last make love?

Paul considered the truth while Michael looked at him, and then thought of a lie.

Has it been months? Michael asked, impatient. What are we talking? Six months?

Paul could only shake his head in protest.

Oh God, Michael gasped, studying Paul's face with a look of horror. How have you been holding it together?

There was a long pause. The rattle of the breeze against the cabin door.

Jesus, Michael muttered eventually. People have killed for less. Michael looked at him suspiciously, as if Paul was a hazard, opened the cabin door and stepped inside.

Talk

AT THE TAVERN THE TALK WAS ALL about the shark seen at the point that morning. It had appeared in the middle of a thick weekend crowd of surfers, teeth bared like a jack-in-the-box, and with a hellish hole on the side of its head that looked like a giant bullet wound. The huge animal swam dumbly about as the pack made for the ledge. It bumped underneath their surfboards and had knocked an older man off his longboard with an erratic tail. No one was bitten. The surfers stood hyperventilating and laughing on the point as they watched the shark swim where they had just been, circling in irregular arcs.

The local surfers had recognised the shark, a large white pointer, five metres or more in length with a gaping cavity where its right eye should have been. Circus. In the tavern that evening some men talked of that hole in the shark as though it were a doorway to the underworld. There were theories that the wound had caused significant brain injury and nearly all of the crews spoke of Circus in that way, as a joke, the brain-damaged fish, mouthing outboard motors and cray pots, slack-jawed. Paul had heard that the shark would sometimes headbutt stationary boats as if by mistake. Michael said he thought it wasn't a brain injury but that the shark was unable to judge distance with its one remaining eye.

You know what I worked out? Michael said. What makes this place so different is everyone is in a dream.

Paul rested his head against the cool timber of the bar. He could still smell the sharpness of bile on his breath. They had spent the afternoon thirty miles from shore, the water wild with the sea breeze, the white glare of the sun in their eyes. He had never been so sick. There at the bar, with the drumming chatter of the crews in his ears, he felt sleep begin to take its merciful hold on him, and it stilled the vertigo.

Everyone likes to think Stark is so far from everywhere else, the German continued, like it is a different planet. That is all of us, I think, including me. Another Euro boy, on his adventure. Michael chuckled. I come here. All the people from the city. We come because we want to think it is the edge of the world. And we know it is not, but that does not matter. We choose to see it that way. We book our flights to come and see it that way. And maybe we need to see it like that, have some place in the world that is separate. Away from all the shit. A place we can go and dream.

Paul summoned the image of Kasia, imagining her hands in his hair. He could hear Michael sawing at his steak.

But it is mad, Michael went on. Totally deranged, you know? It is like wanting to believe you are the only one in a crowded room because you have turned the lights off. But the room is full and we sit with the lights off, in the dark, pretending we are by ourselves. Pretending we are separate from everything. That is what it is like. It is not real. Nowhere is away from the shit. Not here, not anywhere. And the people in Stark, they have not worked that out yet. The locals, they worry about the world coming and messing things up for them, complicating things. But nothing was ever easy, I guarantee you that. He paused to chew on his steak. Look at Roo Dog. Tell me he did not have a fucked-up childhood. And he was born here. I mean, how does a paradise produce such a person?

Paul opened his eyes enough for the bar lights to flood in. He groaned and closed them again.

Exactly, my friend. Michael laughed. Well said. The German paused to think. Dreaming, he said. It is all in a dream. And no one questions it. It is its own religion.

Paul imagined kissing the girl, what that might be like.

Something wrong with you? He heard her voice, sharp, the words clear and real. He lifted his head to see her standing in front of him at the bar.

You never eat, Kasia said.

He saw the plate in her hand and the burger with the serviette wedged into the single bite mark. She waited for him to say something.

I feel sick, he got out.

The girl gave him a concerned look.

I mean, I get seasick, Paul said, during the day. I don't feel like eating.

You are a lobster fisherman and you get seasick?

I don't really like fishing either, he said, despite himself, hearing the words spill out of him like a confession. Or fish.

The girl laughed. Paul felt a sort of relief at the sound of it.

You are not from here, are you? she said.

He shook his head.

I could tell, she said.

Paul glanced at Michael. The German had a mouthful of mash but he was listening in.

I guess you're not from Stark either, Paul said.

She smiled. You guess right. I am from a long way away. You would not know of my town.

I want to go there, Paul said, again hearing the words before he had any real control over them.

Kasia raised her eyebrows. Michael shifted beside him. Paul couldn't believe he had said such a stupid thing. He felt like driving his forehead into the bar.

Poland, she said to him. I am from a small place in Poland. She turned to Michael. Chelm.

The German nodded. Paul looked to him as if for help.

Near Lublin, she said, turning again to Paul. Have you been to Europe?

No.

You have never been? she repeated. And you want to go to Chelm?

He nodded.

She made a puzzled face as she walked along the bar collecting plates.

Well, you should visit, Kasia said. It's very pretty.

Jules walked out from the kitchen into the bar and whispered something to her. Kasia nodded and turned for the kitchen doors but spun around before entering.

Nice to talk to you, fisherman. She grinned. And Merry Christmas.

She disappeared before he could respond.

Paul sat in silence, aware of the stagger of his heartbeat. He could sense Michael watching him but avoided meeting his eye.

I might head home, Michael said eventually. You coming?

Nah, he said.

Paul stepped out into the beer garden. The lights under the veranda were off, or broken, and the tables outside were in darkness.

Paul, eh? someone said, the voice coming from the blackness in front of him.

Yeah, Paul said. Who's that?

Noddy, mate.

Oh. Hey.

You're the brother, Noddy said. Elliot's brother, right?

Yeah, Paul replied.

This town might not be the same anymore but some things never change. Everyone here is in everyone else's pockets. You want to keep a secret, don't live in Stark. Unless you want to punish yourself.

Paul heard laughter. He recognised it as Elmo's.

Where is he? Elmo asked. Your brother? Where has he run off to?

Why would he run anywhere?

The shadows didn't respond.

You're on Jake's boat, yeah? said Noddy. Good luck to you.

Elmo laughed again. The Grim Reaper, he offered.

Paul was unsure what they meant by it. He said nothing.

You don't know about him? said Noddy.

Know what? Paul replied.

Jake, your skipper—he's a murderer. Paul could hear the

pleasure in the deckhand's voice as he said the words. He could sense both of them smiling.

Surely you knew that, Elmo said. He's your cousin, isn't he?

I don't really know him . . . Paul began. What do you mean? Who did he murder?

I think the technical term was manslaughter, hey, Elmo? Otherwise he wouldn't have ever come out of that lock-up.

He comes in one night on *Arcadia*, stupid drunk, Noddy said, and Paul could tell he'd recounted this story before in something like the same words. It was near midnight when he comes roaring through. Cleans up two boys who were having a fish in the inlet. And then . . . The deckhand hit the table hard. The two men laughed.

Young kids, mate, Noddy continued. Your age. Bit younger, maybe.

Yeah, said Elmo. Would have been about that.

And he runs straight over the top of them, Noddy said. He paused and Paul smelt the marijuana smoke breathed out towards him.

One of them survived, you know, Noddy said. Don't fucking ask me how.

Got messed up, of course, Elmo said. Don't have a boat go over your head and do okay.

Noddy cleared his throat. They got him out. Rushed him to the city. In hospital for a year, he was. That's what I heard. Learning to walk.

What about the other one? Paul said.

There was a silence. Boat just broke him, Noddy said eventually, voice deep and deliberate. Took three days before he came up, all twisted and bloated.

They waited for Paul to respond but he couldn't.

Anyway, Noddy said, I've got no idea why Jake came back here. I mean, shit—this place? I would have run off somewhere if I was him. Just taken off.

No idea, Elmo echoed.

~

I wake to gunfire and the sky pink above me and think I'm dreaming. The President and the generals' sleeping bags are empty. I crawl through the cold dirt until I see those two generals. One is lying flat out on his back. Blood in the sand underneath him so that it looks like he is lying on a blanket. The other is curled up on himself. I come up on another man and see the light-blue uniform. Face down. Somewhere off in the scrub I hear someone moaning and crawl towards the sound of it through dew-beaded spinifex. In a small clearing I see a woman leaning against the rock. Legs shot up. Seen her before. The federal police and the roadblock back near Yulara. And I see the President stand above her with the rifle. His long white hair in the desert wind like he's some sort of spirit. The police officer rolls and turns her head to the ground. Puts her arm up as he fires.

We ride hard out through the sand country. Just the President and me. Ride all day until the sun is low enough. In the dark we hear a plane. Maybe more than one. Later a helicopter. All night I listen to the sky and to the President whimpering in his sleep and try to get my head around all this business. The gunfire and the dead generals and the President standing over that woman.

~

The windy season

BY NINE O'CLOCK ON NEW YEAR'S EVE the tavern was full and hot and loud and there was mayhem at the bar. Roo Dog had tried to piss in someone's handbag. Through the crowd, from the tavern restaurant, Paul witnessed the entire ghoulish event. There was Roo Dog, perched on his toes. Skeletal arms crooked into his jeans. And the other deckies, like statues behind him, frozen in anticipation. Faces green under the lights of the bar. When the girl shrieked, the pack imploded, howling and screeching, breathless in their delight. Roo Dog had fired short, managing only to urinate on the girl's white dress and down the back of her legs. The girl spun around and saw the large tumbling bodies and purple necks, the frenzied laughter. Her pretty face creased in horror and confusion. She began to cry. Paul watched her push through the crowd, away from the bar. Roo Dog was buckled in amusement, overwhelmed, his spidery hands on his knees.

Fucking crazies, Michael yelled to Paul above the noise. Shivani lay curled up on his lap, eyes closed. Despite the heat, she was wearing one of those furry hoods that made her look like a sleeping Eskimo. An Eskimo in a miniskirt.

Nut jobs, all of them, the German said again, tugging a pack of cigarettes from his shorts pocket.

Paul nodded in reply, quietened by what he had just seen. The helpless look on the girl's face. Roo Dog's demented joy. The strange theatre of it all. He sculled the last of his beer.

All these city girls, Michael declared, shaking his head, the boys cannot handle it. They lose their minds.

From the slight terracing of the tavern's restaurant they had a good view of the crowded front bar. Even in the slam of bodies everyone was aware of the deckhands; the menace in their movement and the violence in their laughter. People skirted warily around them, fashioning any available distance in the same way baitfish do around larger predators, the crowd contracting as one away from each hazard.

Shivani stirred, lifting her head from Michael's shoulder for just a moment before closing her eyes again.

She alright? Paul asked.

She is fine, said the German, raising one of her limp hands with his. She is the dreamer. Always sleeps when she is stoned. Probably a good thing, though. Going to get fucking wild in here soon.

Through the windows Paul could see more bodies out on the square of grass at the crest of the dunes that they called the beer garden, t-shirts and summer dresses rippling in the sea breeze. There must have been several hundred people at the tavern. He couldn't believe the numbers he had seen that day in town. At lunchtime there were queues at the bakery that went out the door. The caravan park was full. The rivermouth might as well have been a beach in the city for all the people down there; big cackling groups, lolling about on beach towels, getting drunk and sunburnt.

Is it always like this? Paul asked.

Shivani says every New Year's it is big. People just come. I do not understand. Always lots of people, she says. And always some shit happens.

Like what?

Oh God, Michael said, covering his eyes with his hands. Like, last year, he said, his smile gone. Shivani said that last year there was this one girl. She came up from the city. Prettiest thing in the whole place. All those boys losing the plot, watching her dancing and stuff. She goes off in the dunes with some backpacker. American, I think. Surfer. Anyway, of course the boys followed them up there. Fucking lunatics. They scared the surfer dude off. Roo Dog was swinging a star picket around.

What about the girl?

Jesus, Michael muttered. Those boys were walking up and down that dune like ants, so I've heard.

You're not serious? Why aren't they in prison?

I do not think the girl reported it. And the American just got the hell out, apparently. Went east.

That is so fucked, Paul muttered, almost to himself.

Yeah, the German nodded. It is.

Paul watched Anvil, all red eyes and leering smile, careening through the crowd like a white shark.

Michael gently squeezed Shivani's nose. The sleeping girl didn't move.

I'd better get her home, Michael said with a sigh. One more drink, maybe. You?

Paul shrugged. They had been at the table since five o'clock. He was as drunk as he had ever been.

I shall get us another jug. Mind sleeping beauty, would you?

Michael levered her from the arm of his chair onto Paul and lurched off towards the bar. Shivani collapsed against him, out of it. She smelt of marijuana and perfume. Paul could feel the heat of her small body, her bare legs resting heavy on his lap. A sleepy finger clawed at his chest. Her breath was cool on his neck. He was instantly hard. Paul looked out across the tavern and saw Michael in the roll of the crowd. Under the green glow of the lights the place could have been underwater. The room shimmered. Everything seemed slowed down, almost graceful, as though being pulled by a tide. Shivani moaned, shifting a little, turning her head so her mouth was now on the skin of his collarbone. He had never had anyone on him like this, never taken a girl's weight on his body before.

You like the look of her, yeah? Michael said, suddenly beside the table, the jug in one hand.

What? Paul stammered, trying to sit up in the chair. Shivani roused, looking up for a moment.

That girl, the bar chick, he said, sitting down.

Paul eased back into his seat. Kasia, he said.

Kasia, Michael replied, clicking his fingers like an old man. What do you think?

She's pretty, I guess.

Yeah, yeah, Michael mused, raising his eyebrows. Could certainly do worse in Stark. That is for sure.

Shivani woke. She sat up on the arm of Paul's chair and glanced at him; a dazed, puzzled look. She pulled the hood back from her head and yawned.

Michael, take me home, she whimpered. Why is it so loud?

Come on, dreamer, Michael said. He stood and pulled Shivani up from the chair. Get in my bed.

Michael finished the rest of his schooner and put it down on the table. You coming back now? he asked.

Paul shook his head.

You are so wasted, man. The German grinned. See you in the morning, yeah?

Out in the beer garden the wind blew strong. Paul couldn't hear the sea but he could feel it, its warm salty breath already in his clothes and stiffening his hair. A covers band sweated under the stage lights. The huge crowd was packed hard, occupying a rectangle of lawn no bigger than half a tennis court. Paul stood as close to the stage as he could get, each step nearer like going deeper underwater, the pressure around him greater. A lead guitar cried out, filling the air like an alarm. A soaring distressed melody. Paul closed his eyes and felt the weight of the crowd pressing in on his body, a big, hot current, drawing him back and forth, threatening to consume him. He laughed, giddy from the force at his back and on his limbs, the danger of it. He listened to the fevered singing of the crowd around him.

Then he noticed the singing quieten. The band up front continued but Paul felt the change in the bodies around him, a ripple of unease spilling from somewhere metres behind. The crowd tightened, stepping awkwardly into each other like spooked cattle. He heard the intensifying sounds of anger and desperate voices. The people at his back scattered and suddenly there were shouts and wide eyes, faces wild as though possessed. Paul heard the slapping thud of flesh into flesh and saw someone on the ground. It was one of the bartenders, his long blond hair sprayed over the lawn like a halo, young face grimacing in fear. There was a large cut above one eye. Anvil circled over him, hysterical, ordering the boy to stand up. Then, right in front of Paul, no more than two metres away, there was a girl, screaming, trying to pull her arm free from the long bony fingers around her wrist. Another gangly hand crawled at the front of her skirt and cupped between her legs. Paul saw Roo Dog's vacant eyes and joyless smile, like a zombie in the gloom away from the lights of the stage. The girl threw her head back, her eyes pleading, her wrist still in the man's grip. Kasia.

Paul felt himself lunge forward, a stumbling run, falling into Roo Dog's ribs. He heard the hollow knock of a chin against the back of his head and when they hit the ground the deckhand gave a muted grunt and went slack underneath him. Paul rolled off and scrambled to his feet. It was then that he felt the sudden heaviness on his jaw. Everything went noiseless and dark and indistinct, as though someone had just knocked him from the beer garden out deep into the night ocean. All he could hear was Anvil, the screams faint in his ears. Paul turned away from the voice, still on his feet, and saw the blank glow of faces. There was the taste of blood in his mouth. He waited for the next hit. He closed his eyes, resigned to it. Then someone grabbed his forearm. He was being pulled away from the stage, away from Anvil, back through the writhing wall of people. He could only just make her out. The black singlet. Her light brown hair bouncing in front of him. The girl weaved and pushed and ducked through the boil of bodies, all sweat and skin and open mouths. She held his arm firm, leading him. They stepped over discarded cans and plastic beer cups. The grass was slippery under his thongs, his toes sticky. Kasia began to run and he staggered with her. It felt as though he was being drawn through a portal, the beer garden a blur. They ran to where the crowd thinned and where the tavern yard turned to bush. There were two others with them now, another girl and the long-haired guy he had seen on the ground. Blood was streaming from his brow. The four of them sped through the dark, down a thin sandy path. Dune scrub danced at Paul's feet. He heard the girls' shallow breaths and nervous laughter. The sea breeze in his ears. Music far behind him.

Paul woke to the tray of the utility shuddering against his back and the drone of bitumen passing below. Above him the sky was so bright with stars it was almost unreal, and with the warm wind tearing over the tray and through his hair he imagined for a moment he was strapped to the belly of a spaceship, looking down on the universe. The brief vertigo made his heart beat a little harder and he smiled at this. He turned and saw Kasia sitting next to him, leaning back on her hands and looking up, her hair whipping forward over her face in the breeze. She was older than him. He could tell by the way she sat there, limbs relaxed, composed. Her face calm. Serene.

The ute slowed and Paul felt the suspension lurch as the vehicle clambered onto a rougher, looser surface. The tyres scratched for grip. The tray rumbled. He could smell dust in his nostrils. He propped himself up on his elbows and watched the dark clouds trailing behind. Low walls of bush lined the wide gravel track. The vehicle slowed again and this time it stopped, the engine cut. The ute ticked and whirred as life left it. Paul could hear the crash of surf. Kasia turned to him and saw he was awake. She smiled.

He followed them down the short sandy path that led to the bluff, listening as the others talked. The blond guy was now

169

shirtless, holding his scrunched-up t-shirt to the cut above his eye. His name was Matthew. He had a British accent. Paul couldn't tell where the other girl was from but they called her Fran. She carried a plastic bag full of bottles that clinked and chimed on the walk down to the shore. From the path they could see over the long sweep of the point. Paul watched the white trains of water, thundering down the cape. The moon cast a pale slick over the sea. The tolling of breaking waves was loud in the dark around them. He couldn't tell if the breeze had backed off or whether the bluff sheltered them from it, but the air was still and warm. They walked to where the headland gave way to the bay and where the water subdued, protected by a furrow in the reef like a shielding arm. Matthew continued up the rocky point, the t-shirt still to his forehead, while the girls put down their things. Paul sat near them and watched as they both pulled their work singlets off over their heads and dropped them to the ground. And then, breathless, as they unclipped their bras. The girls joked nervously about the black water that waited for them. Their skin glowed, luminous against the dark rock. Paul couldn't believe what he was seeing. He almost said something about the danger, about him being a good swimmer but being too drunk to help if they got into trouble. But the words didn't come out. Fran shucked off her jeans and Kasia unbuttoned her khaki skirt and the two of them stepped down towards the water, two small figures in the shadow of the bluff. Soon they had dipped down from the rocks, out of view.

Matthew was now just a silhouette at the furthest end of the point, backlit by the phosphorescence of the surf. With his hand to his head he looked like a man trying to hold on to his hat. Beyond him, rising from the plateau of the reef, was the bluff.

Under the clear night sky the red walls looked almost blue, its bare, cratered slopes like something out of *Star Wars*. Paul lay flat on his back and felt the percussions of the breaking waves in the dense rock beneath him. He thought of the photos on Elliot's wall and wondered if he had ever been here. Paul could imagine him out on that point, sitting on his surfboard, eyes lit up.

Hello, Kasia said above him, drying herself with her t-shirt. And Happy New Year. She raised her arms behind her head, wringing her hair.

Oh . . . Paul stammered, sitting up.

We have not had introductions, she said in a mock-serious voice, holding out her hand, grinning. My name is Kasia.

Paul, he replied, rushing the word, trying not to look at her bare breasts. My name is Paul.

They shook hands. He looked away towards the bluff. Saw Fran and Matthew walking away in the direction of the car, slipping into the darkness of the path. Kasia sat down. He was fiercely aware of her body next to him, the sound of her breathing.

You do not like to swim? asked Kasia.

Not at night I don't. Not in the middle of nowhere.

Oh, she sighed, disappointed. It is so lovely. So warm.

No thank you.

Paul looked at the dark water. He wrapped his arms tight around himself. Kasia grinned at him.

Where did the others go? he asked.

Francesca will come back for us, Kasia said. They went back to town. Matthew is still bleeding a bit. He might need stitches.

You okay? I mean, what happened back there, at the tavern . . .

Yeah. I am good. Fucking losers, she said, shaking her head.

What were they doing?

God, I do not know what happens in their heads. We just finished at the bar and came out to see the music. And then that skinny one grabs me.

Roo Dog.

Yes, that horrible one. He tries to kiss me. I push him off but he will not let go. And then Matthew tells him, Stop. Next thing, the tall one comes and punches him. So crazy. Then you come, falling down. Like Superman, kind of. Kasia laughed.

Paul grimaced.

No, no, she said. It was very brave, Paul. Not pretty, but brave. She gave another laugh then reached over and ruffled his hair.

I can't believe them, he said. That they could do that.

I do not worry about it. I have seen guys like that before. They are in every place, not just here.

A large wave thundered far up the point, the sound of it suddenly everywhere.

Besides, she said, I have only been in this country a few months. I have got more to do, you know? They cannot scare me off.

How long will you stay? Paul asked.

In Stark? I am not sure. It is just so different from home, you know? It is kind of shit here, she said with a sigh, but it is somewhere else.

What's it like where you're from?

Cold! she gasped. In January, like around this time, it is fucking freezing. She leant back and laid her head down, closing her eyes.

No, no, she continued. It is beautiful. Like, where I am from, in Chelm, it is lovely. Old, like, really old buildings. Five hundred years or more, even. Big rivers. The woods. All the tourists love it. I have just seen enough, you know? I needed to get out.

I thought I should go to a wild place, far away. She laughed. Like everyone else does.

Paul lay back down beside the girl. He stole a look across at her and saw the water beaded on her legs and the patchy translucence of her underwear.

What about you? she asked. When will you go home?

After the summer. Think the skipper will pull the boat out around May, for the winter. I might go back to Perth then. But I don't know. At home, it's weird now.

You are the one with the brother. I heard some things.

Paul nodded.

You have not found him?

No.

And your parents send you here? she asked, puzzled.

I wanted to come.

But they let you?

I'm not a kid.

No, she said. It is just, I cannot understand. I would have thought they would want you with them.

Paul shrugged.

Where do you think he is?

I don't know. It's been so long. Over four months. The police say to be prepared for bad news.

Bad news?

They think he might not be coming back. He might not be alive.

She watched him, said nothing.

I'm just not sure if I can go home yet, Paul said. I don't really know if I want to.

Kasia sat up. Come on, she said.

What?

173

You must swim.

No. Please. I can't. It's still dark. Whitetips feed at night.

White what? Kasia laughed, pushing herself to her feet.

Reef sharks.

And monsters, maybe? she said. A Loch Ness monster?

No. Just sharks. They are bad enough.

Really?

Forty-eight teeth. And that is just the exposed ones. A great white has two hundred and fifty back in its mouth.

My god, she said, with a big smile. You have a phobia.

When I was a kid I was too scared to swim in the neighbours' pool. I was convinced that a great white shark would come out of the pool light. Swim up the pipes, the wires. Break into the swimming pool through the light fixture and eat us.

Paul looked at his hands. Inhaled and hoped more words would materialise in his head. Something that sounded less unhinged.

There will be no sharks, Kasia said. I promise. She stood over his legs and grabbed his arm, trying to pull him up.

How can you promise? he said weakly. He could see the prickled skin of her thighs, the fine hairs. He felt dizzy with her there, that close to him.

There you go, she said as she pulled him to his feet. The girl lifted his shirt and he helped her drag it over his ears. Despite the warm air he began to shiver.

Good boy, she said to him.

Kasia held both his hands in hers. In the moonlight her pale blue eyes were like halogen globes. He couldn't speak.

Come on, she said.

Kasia led him over the cool plates of rock to the small keyhole in the reef. She stepped down into the darkness, still holding his hand, drawing him in. Paul thought of Circus. He thought of the hardness in his shorts.

Paul slid into the sea with her, letting his weight go. He kept one hand on the lip of the reef. His feet searched for the bottom but it was deep. The current spun around his legs in broad columns of water. His breaths were shallow. She pulled him to her, wrapping her legs tight around his waist. Her arms hard across his back. Her chest against his. She sighed into his ear. He drew a long, jagged breath.

You know this place, Stark? Kasia whispered, her chin on his shoulder. It is so harsh. It is funny this place, you know? It can be the worst thing ever. Be really shit. And then it will be beautiful. Maybe it is just like everywhere else in that way. Shit and beautiful. Or maybe it is special. That is what I don't know yet.

Paul felt the girl shift on his waist, her hand move down on him. The bluff towered above them. The surf sang out.

~

You see us going through deserts. Through the heart of everything. But before this? There's not so much I can tell you. There is not so much that I know. I never did meet my dad. Know my mother wasn't well and she was dead when I was small. Then it was just me and my gran and I was twelve when I found her stiff in her bed. She'd died in her sleep but had a look on her face like she'd tried like hell not to.

Must have been sometime after that some bikie fellas in Tennant Creek were looking after me cos I was thirteen when they got me into the business. Just dealing at first, then they taught me how to cook. Back then I swore it was the smartest thing I ever did. Like I'd been given the keys to a bank. Learning different methods, different recipes. Learning the whole shebang.

Markets. Profit margins. They would pick me up from my house and drop me at the edge of town someplace where it was safe from coppers or anyone else and then they'd leave me alone. A farmhouse or a van. A demountable shed. A shipping container. Leave me with as much ice as I could smoke. You'd OD before you got anywhere near through any of it. Cooking an ounce a day. Four or five days straight before they'd drop me home to sleep.

Then I met the President and he got me out of cooking. Said I was too smart a kid to rot in a lab. Said the chemicals were killing me and I sometimes wonder if he was too late.

And I don't expect no sympathy. Why should you give it. I never ran. I could have tried. There's a lot that I don't know but I do know there were times that I could have tried to run. And you don't know some of the things I've done. Everything's got its price. I've done things that should never be asked of anybody.

But after everything you wonder what is left. You can wonder what is underneath your skin. And you reckon there will be a time when you will see it. When it will be clear and decided like some kind of judgement. A reckoning. That is what it feels like. A wheel on a gameshow that spins and its finger rakes over the different shades of your insides. Flickers over it. The dark and the light. Good and the evil. The human and the parts of you that are not human at all. And the wheel spins and it is all the waiting to find out where the wheel will stop is what keeps you awake. The dark or the light. The good or the evil.

~

Afterglow

HIS FACE SCRATCHED AGAINST THE cracked leather of a couch. There
was the sound of dishes being put away. Daylight stormed his
eyes when he opened them and his whole body tensed. He sat
up and looked around the living room.

There you are!

Paul turned to see Matthew standing in the kitchen, a wide
smile on his face despite the wound above his eye. The skin
of his brow looked tight. The stitches bulged like upholstered
leather.

That was some night, hey? Matthew said, the words singing
off the tiles, his English accent bright and melodic.

Paul nodded.

Twenty-three stitches. Can you believe that? The bastards. It'll
look like I've got a train track on my head. My mum is going
to have a fucking freak-out. Matthew laughed. Can I get you

177

something? he said. Would you like a cup of tea? Or we've got coffee.

Water? Paul asked.

Matthew reached for the cupboard above the fridge and removed a glass. Kasia just went to the shops, he said. She'll be back soon.

I might go see if I can find her.

Suit yourself, Matthew said. He walked around the kitchen counter and handed Paul the tumbler of water. Here, get that into you. You look like shit.

The air outside was windless and hot. The sun bit his arms and the nape of his neck, a sharp burning, like the heat from a flame. As he walked Paul inspected his chin with his fingers. He could feel the bruising. He opened his mouth and closed it again and could hear a clicking within the hinge of his jaw, near his ear.

You going home? a voice said from behind.

Kasia stopped her bike next to him, putting a bare foot down to the pavement.

Paul shrugged.

Somewhere you have to be? she said.

No.

I have lunch if you want some.

Okay, he said.

She hopped off her bike and he followed her, the two of them walking without speaking.

Inside, Matthew and Francesca lay on the couch, looking at each other. Francesca was touching Matthew's eyebrow with her fingertips. Kasia stood behind the counter of the kitchen, scooping ice-cream into the jug of milk and coffee. Paul sat on the kitchen stool, racking his brain for something to say. The blender relieved the silence. Paul cleared his throat.

Kasia pushed a glass of iced coffee towards him. Paul thanked her, the words catching in his throat and arriving somewhere between a whisper and speech. She looked at him, eyes serious as she sipped from her own glass, remaining stern when she drew the cup away, melted ice-cream across her upper lip. Paul laughed and she smiled.

When they'd finished their drinks, Kasia took his hand and led him to her room. Once through the door she kissed him, and he tasted the sweet and sour of sugar and coffee. She pulled her phone from the pocket of her shorts and put it on the bedside table then sat down on the bed, a brown leg tucked under her.

Come here, she whispered.

They lay down and watched each other, not touching; the girl sizing him up, and Paul waiting for the moment to abandon him, as if she might see the error in what she was doing and who she was doing it with.

She smiled.

What? he said defensively.

I do not know, Kasia said. She leant in and kissed him, in a confident, deliberate way that seemed worldly. Slow and purposeful. He did his best to follow her. She kissed the smooth membrane inside his lip, and when he reached for her tongue with his she pulled away and he could sense the smile on her mouth. She kissed him softly, then hard, and he laboured behind, like a toddler imitating adult movements, each action a second late. But he heard the soft intonation of her voice, the hum and murmur that he read ecstatically as pleasure, and he knew that, even if it were just for the present moment, she wanted this. Wanted him there.

Then they held each other, still clothed. He sensed the weariness from the night before returning like a tide. He listened to Kasia's breathing deepen. Felt the slight spasm of her legs as she fell asleep.

It could have been hours that they lay there. Paul wasn't sure. He had noticed the colours changing in the room. The light that knifed between the curtains had softened, and the sharp lines of sun on her bedroom wall that had glowed like molten glass were now redder and less defined. However long it had been, it mattered little. Sometime later he opened his eyes and there was no more sunlight on the walls, the room cast in a pinkish light that was almost dreamlike and that made the sleeping girl look beautiful in a way that was frightening. He knew he should leave before she woke and came to her senses, but he couldn't move. So he just watched her. He played with the string bracelets on her wrist, feeling so much like the curious boy in Elliot's room. He traced the words of a tattoo on her hip. He didn't understand what it meant, didn't recognise the language or the script. There was so much to Kasia he didn't understand and didn't know.

Elliot would have known what it was to feel the heat of another body against his. Paul imagined telling Elliot about Kasia, about the way she looked right at that moment, and how happy and afraid and sad he felt, how all those feelings had swirled in him at once.

Paul was tired but he resisted sleep for as long as he could. He couldn't shake the feeling that this was the last time he would be this close to Kasia, as if this proximity were a licence that would soon expire. In a few hours he wouldn't be permitted to hold her waist in his palm. He kissed her cheek and savoured the warmth of her skin on his lips. He hung on to consciousness, watched her like she was the last thing he would ever see.

When he woke the room was dark. Kasia was still there, asleep, under her sheets with her back to him. He checked her phone on the table next to the bed: 11 pm. She didn't stir as he put on his shoes. He thought for a moment about waking her but he didn't.

The swimming speed
of sharks

PAUL AND ELLIOT HAD SHARED A BEDROOM right up until Elliot finished high school and the family moved to the newer, bigger house in Cottesloe with a third bedroom. Elliot had found their proximity frustrating, of course. He was neater than Paul, and he hated Paul going through his things. Even when they moved and Elliot gained his cherished room at the end of the hall, there was no lock on the door, and Paul would often go in there when his brother wasn't home. But it was a lie to say Paul knew everything about him. He knew some things, but not the details, not the indecencies, the secrets. Although Elliot and Paul talked a lot, there was a line they never crossed.

The closest Paul ever felt to him was at night, in the room they shared before the move. In the dark his brother would emerge. His voice became clearer. Paul would ask him questions just to revel in the sound of him speaking. But eventually Elliot tired of Paul's questioning, and then he would talk about sharks. Remind Paul of how a great white shark has forty-eight exposed teeth, two hundred and fifty set back in its mouth, hidden by tissue, like knives sheathed. Or how a fully motivated great white shark could reach speeds of up to fifty kilometres an hour. As fast as a car on the road. There was no outswimming it. No chance. And you wouldn't be seeing it anyway, Elliot would tell him. The preferred attack trajectory of a great white shark was near vertical, two tonnes of animal striking from underneath, and hard enough to make you leave the water with it, arcing through the sky in a violent rainbow of fish and boy. The impact of a bite at that velocity could break a person clean in two, and the last sight you would ever see would be the great fish swimming off with your lower half. That's if you were lucky. If you were really lucky it would try to finish you with the one bite. A less hungry shark, or a more cautious shark, well, that might just take a lower leg, or a foot, or gouge you in the thigh. After that it would wait until you bled out, disappearing to a depth at the edge of your vision, like a spider in the shadowed corner of a web.

And no matter how hard you look you will never see it coming, Elliot would say. There is always something you cannot see.

Arm in arm with a hippy

THE WIND CAME IN JUST BEFORE lunchtime but it felt different. It blew from the north-west, thick and warm. The horizon blue-black. He had scanned it throughout the morning, and held his breath each time he saw the tell-tale silhouette of a cray boat; the tall cabin perched at the bow, the over-long flat deck. But none of the boats he saw were *Deadman*. Paul thought of Kasia, too, and it made his body tremble with nerves. He wanted her so much but couldn't bear the idea of her changing her mind on him. For three days he had avoided the tavern, despite Michael's urging. He tried to imagine the right words to speak to her. For hours on deck he rehearsed what he might say. But even in his mind the sentences fell apart and he could picture the doubt on her face. He could hear her gentle voice letting him down. The politeness of it cut through him like a fishing knife.

The German was edgy too. Paul could tell he had spoken to

his father again; he muttered to himself as if replaying a difficult conversation, forehead furrowed.

He thinks I am avoiding my responsibility, Michael said. Not to him. To God. Can you fucking believe that?

What would God want you to be doing in Stuttgart? Paul said.

That is a good question, Michael said. I do not know. Friedrich, he knows. He and God have been speaking lately, and God is not happy with me.

Paul nodded his head, solemnly. You don't want that, he said.

There are just two things you need to know about my old man. He worships money, and he worships God. In that order. And he talks a great deal about Jesus. He talks about him all the time, as if he is his business partner.

How do you mean?

Jesus gave us our big houses. Jesus blessed Friedrich with Lamborghinis and boats. He is always telling me that I should be thankful, that I must thank Jesus. He gave you your place at Oxford, Michael, he says to me. Jesus gave you your business smarts. Michael's eyes bulged. Friedrich is a big fan.

Jesus Christ, Paul said.

Michael grinned. The thing is, Michael continued, if Jesus were alive I cannot imagine my father inviting him over for dinner. I have read the book. I know what it is in it. I do not think Friedrich would like Jesus very much if he met him in person. Imagine the conversation. *So, Friedrich, do you know that a rich man has as much hope of getting into heaven as a camel does passing through the eye of a needle? What do you think of that? Would you like some more wine? I'll make it run from the fucking taps.*

Paul laughed.

But still he always has that Bible with him, my father. It is there in his briefcase. It goes where he goes.

A cyclone was passing a thousand or so kilometres north-west of the town but the deckhands had seen its swell in the ocean that afternoon. The sea became bloated as the sun lowered and by the time they reached the jetty and the waiting freezer truck the tide was pressed hungrily at the foot of the dunes.

There was just enough light once they were done loading crates for Paul to navigate the flooded beach of the inlet and pick his way along the path in the bush to *Deadman's* mooring.

The boat wasn't there, but he sat on the bank and stared at the black water. Heard thunder somewhere far-off. He couldn't help but feel he had tripped some wire with Roo Dog and Anvil, started something that would find its own ends, beyond his control.

He waited until nearly all light was gone, mosquitos buzzing in the murk around him, before he got up off the riverbank and headed back towards town.

~

I lie flat in the earth and the President he doesn't lie down next to me with the spotting scope but stays on his feet somewhere at my back. My hands are greasy on the stock and I dry them on the thighs of my jeans.

You have heard some of the things I've done? the President says.

Yes, I tell him.

I've done some things, Swiss.

Yes.

I've done some things. Taken things.

You mean stolen them.

Well I'm a fucken bikie Swiss yes I've stolen things.

I know.

No you don't know. That's not what I'm saying. Not what I'm saying at all.

Well what are you saying? I turn to look at him. White sun back-lighting him so that his features are a fuzz and he looks like some sort of angel. A fattish angel in all black and heavy boots.

Take your shot, the President says. He gestures with a thick finger for me to turn around.

What am I shooting?

Just shoot the fucking rifle Swiss.

I fire. Swear under my breath at the roaring call of it out across the desert. Wonder how far the sound carries beyond our vision and who might be there to hear it. I pull back the bolt and the casing spins into the air.

You heard of San Pietro in Vincoli, he says.

I shake my head.

You probably did hear of it. There is not a soul out there that doesn't know about it.

San Pietro? I ask him.

St Peter in Chains. It's a school Swiss.

Okay.

It's a primary school.

Yes.

Take your shot, the President says.

At what?

Take it.

I close my eyes and the gun roars and I grip the fore-end as if it could strangle the sound.

You don't know it, the President says quiet. You going to ask me why I am talking about San Pietro in Vincoli, Swiss?

I turn to look at him again.

He flicks his head for me to turn back.

It was all a big bloody mess Swiss. His name was Jamie. Jamie was a good worker. Had been with us since he was about your age. I'd taken care of him. Like I have taken care of you Swiss. Take your shot.

I curse. Fire. Hear the President breathe out behind me.

Got a big house on the Pacific, the President says. Manly Beach. Fuck's sake. Got himself a wife on the outside. Catholic. And they had a little boy and Jamie wanted out. For years he asked me if there was a way out and I warned him there was no going anywhere. It wasn't clean to have men on the outside and I couldn't have it. It was his problem, you understand. His wife and his little boy. He had complicated things for himself. It was not my problem. Take your shot.

I fire the round. Reload. My eyes are closed now.

And then Jamie fucking left, the President says. Said he was out. Just like that. You know what I did?

I shake my head.

I went to San Pietro in Vincoli. Mid-morning when all those kids were running about on that school oval. I walked on that oval through all those kids. Walked up to Jamie's little boy and I shot him in the face.

There is silence between us when the President says that. Just his breathing quick in and out of his nose. Then the President says, take your shot.

I don't know what you want me to shoot. The President doesn't seem to hear.

Why would I do something like that? he asks.

But I can't speak. I listen to the shuffle of the President's boots on the hard ground behind me.

I didn't have to do it, he says. Didn't have to shoot a little boy, Swiss. Take your fucking shot, the President says.

I breathe in. Fire.

When I turn he has gone.

~

Angela

PAUL SAT HUNCHED OVER A TABLE IN the beer garden, watching Kasia through the window while Michael smoked, standing square to the sea, considering the windblown inlet and the starless sky above them. In the beer garden the sea air around them was dense and warm, the atmosphere carrying the weight of the storm behind it. Thick raindrops tapped intermittently on the wooden table and beaded their pint glasses.

It is not all that nice out here, Michael said, grimacing as a swollen droplet struck his face.

I don't know what to say to her, Paul said.

She kissed you, my friend. What are you so worried about?

Paul glanced at the window, saw Kasia looking out at him.

Shit, he muttered, dropping his eyes to his feet.

A beautiful girl is a good problem to have, Michael said. He looked up at the sky, peering into the blackness. I think there is a dog up there, a big dog in a hot-air balloon, and he is holding his dick over the edge of the basket and he is pissing on my face.

I've made a mistake, Paul said. She's too beautiful for me.

Michael blew smoke and turned towards the tavern. He nodded in agreement. I can assure you, he said, if anyone has made the mistake it is her.

Paul gave him a sick look.

You know, Michael said, looking back out to sea, I have a feeling we will not be going back out for a few days. Cyclone *An-ge-la*. He drew out the name, mimicking the whined vowels they had heard on the TV. She feels like she is still coming south.

Paul shuddered, despite the sweating heat.

Michael fingered the stubble on his chin. *An-ge-la*, he moaned again. Coming to visit Stark. Now, that is a very strange thing. Strange world we are in now.

Paul gazed hopelessly through the window.

Oh, come on, Michael said. You look like a man watching his house go up in flames.

Paul grimaced.

Or are you worried about that evil, skinny fucker?

Roo Dog? Paul said. He shook his head.

You probably should be.

They're not in town. Think they're still at sea.

Michael cursed. You shouldn't be going up there, he said. I told you not to go upriver looking for them.

Yeah, Paul said. I know.

There was a pause. Okay, Michael said, that's enough. The German held a palm out to the rain. Squinted skyward. Go in there, he instructed. Smile. Stop looking like you need to shit.

And then what? Paul said.

The way I see it, the thing you have got going for you is that she is human. You are human. It is a handy thing.

Paul tried to imagine himself in conversation with her, tried to picture her laughing at something he would say. He couldn't.

You have a mouth, Michael continued. She has got ears. You say things, she will understand them. It is not so difficult.

Paul groaned and took a large scull of his beer.

This is crazy, Michael said. The tavern has a roof. Why are you allowing the horrible dog to piss on my face?

And then Kasia was coming through the door.

Paul sat straight-backed at the table. Michael rushed his cigarette to his mouth as though plugging a hole.

You are hiding from me? she said to Paul, less a question than a statement.

Michael gave her a sympathetic look and examined his diminished cigarette with deliberate care. My bedtime, he said, and stepped by her and into the tavern. Kasia didn't take her eyes off Paul.

Why are you out here? she asked. Is it raining?

Yeah, he admitted.

Her eyebrows were raised, commanding an explanation from him. It was a look his mother had given him before.

I'm sorry, he got out, and failed to put more words together. His throat strained, reaching for words that weren't there.

It is okay, she said, and produced a forgiving smile that Paul knew was the death blow. Do not worry so much. It is cool.

Kasia began to collect the empty glasses from the table.

No, it's not like that, he said.

I hope your head feels better, she said, her back turned to him, wiping down the benchtops. I am so sorry that happened to your face. The punch, you know.

191

I think about it, he said.

Kasia paused near the doors. She stared at him, waiting for him to continue. He didn't.

She sighed and cocked her head. What is it that you think about, Paul? she asked.

What happened. You and me. I think about that all the time.

She gave him a puzzled look and gestured for his empty pint glass. Paul gave it to her.

I think about you, he said weakly. I always have.

When? she asked, as if trying to disprove the point. You never speak to me.

Paul rummaged for words, looked towards the inlet.

Kasia followed his eyes and peered into the dark, puzzled. You think about me while you are lobster fishing? she said, frowning in mock dismay. You see a crayfish and you think of me?

Paul shook his head miserably. The girl laughed. She put the tray on a table and sat down next to him.

A crayfish isn't such an ugly thing, Paul said.

Kasia gave him a bemused look.

To another crayfish, he said, finishing one of Michael's lines.

Kasia laughed. That is a terrible joke, she said. Tell me another.

I don't think I've got one.

Come on, Paul. She took his face in her hands. Her fingers were cool on his cheeks. When she looked him in the eye like that he wondered if she knew the power she had over him.

Tell me a funny lobster joke, she said, and I will forgive you for hiding from me in the rain.

Okay, he said. I have one. Not a crayfish joke but Michael told me a fish joke. I don't know if you will like it.

If that is all you have got.

I'm not even sure I can remember it.

Kasia groaned and rolled her eyes.

There are these two fish, Paul said. I think they're in a fishbowl.

Does not sound like a promising start, said the girl, shaking her head.

Wait a sec, Paul said. Give me a chance. So, there's two fish in this fishbowl. One says, *Wow, it's a little bit wet in here.*

Oh my god, she gasped. You lose. That was very shit, Paul.

Wait for it, Paul said. That's not it. So one fish goes, *It's a little wet in here*, and the other one says, *Holy shit, a talking fish!*

The girl left a pause and then laughed hard. Paul soaked up the sound of it.

That was bad, Paul. I am sorry, I cannot forgive you.

Fair enough, he replied.

Kasia smiled. I better go; I need to get some sleep.

I meant it, Paul said. What I told you.

You think about me? That is nice. She ruffled his hair like a mother and he shrugged her off. While you are out catching your lobster. She smiled.

I hate it on the boat, Paul said, looking back to the dark of the inlet. So much. You'd think I might be used to it by now, the seasickness. But I don't think I ever will be. And then there's Jake losing his mind. I sometimes think he's trying to sink us. It's like he forgets Michael and I are there too. He sits up there and you can feel it, you can honestly sense it in the deck, just how angry he is, as if he wants to bury the boat.

I would not like that very much, Kasia said.

I always think about being elsewhere, Paul continued. Think about so much different stuff. It's all you do. Just think, and pull pots, and think some more. That's probably the problem—with Jake, I mean. Too much thinking. It's not a good job if you've got issues.

Issues? she said.

Paul thought of telling her about Jake and the accident, remembering the way Elmo and Noddy had told it, how the broken, bloated body of the boy had drifted to the surface days after it had happened. He decided not to.

Kasia was watching him. What else do you think? she said. What else do you think about me?

He looked at her, noticed the change in her face. I think about things I want. Things I want to do.

What things?

He laughed.

Kasia held the dishcloth in her hands. What do you want to do, Paul?

Jesus, he said. He looked at her pleadingly. I can't just say it.

I am not asking you to say it.

He shifted towards her, and when his lips met hers he could almost sense the eyes at the windows, the men at the bar watching them. Without seeing them he knew the looks on their faces, some blend between disbelief and disgust, and then resignation, and even something like respect. And whatever they thought of him, he couldn't have cared less.

In her room, Kasia pulled off her black cotton shorts and her work singlet. Flicked on the ceiling fan. She put a hand under his t-shirt, cold against his chest, and pushed him to her bed with an ironic grin, conscious of the cliché. But to him all of it was perilous and new. He felt an urge to tell her he had never slept with a girl before, wanted to be truthful about all that. But speech was beyond him, and he knew she would find out, if she didn't already suspect. She straddled him, her blue underwear puckered and faded almost white. She pulled his hands to her thighs, looked at him seriously. He saw her skin prickle under his fingers, goosebumps scattering across her body and he thought of wind over water. She pulled up his t-shirt and lightly scratched his abdomen with her fingernails, down towards the elastic of his boxers, then back up again. He worried she might feel the drumming beneath his chest, his ribs shuddering like the deck of a boat. Kasia undid the buttons of his jeans and lifted herself up so he could pull them from his waist, squirming to kick them off his legs. She leant forward with an elbow on the bed to kiss his lips, her hair in his face, pulled down his boxers with one hand. Just the air on his naked body made him shudder. He reached for her underwear, soft and threadbare under his fingers, and she lifted her hips so he could pull them over her buttocks to above her knees and she hooked them with her toes and cast them from the bed to the floor, and he could faintly smell her then, could feel the warmth of her crotch against his. When she sat up he held his breath, braved a look down to where their bodies met. Skin pale and bristling under the fan. The shine of her wetness on him.

When she pulled him into her he made a short whimpering sound that he could not control, curled up as if wounded. Kasia pushed him by his shoulders back into the bed. She held his face to look at him, frowning with an expression like agony or worry, her mouth open and he thought she might say something. But she just exhaled, rolled back and forth at her hips, pushing her body against him, eyes always on his, never leaving them, like she was holding him to account.

You are perfect, he said later as they lay together in the yellowed haze of the bedside light.

She scoffed.

SAM CARMODY

You have hands of an old man, she said, tiredly, running the pads of her fingers across his palm. I wonder what the hands on the old fishermen are like. I feel sorry for Richard's wife. It must be like being felt up by a tree.

Paul laughed.

And your eyes, she said.

They remind you of Richard, too.

She sighed at his joke. That look scares me sometimes when I am working, she said. These big eyes at the bar. I wonder what they see.

Like a train's coming?

Yes. Exactly. She gave him a suspicious look. What are they seeing?

They like what they are seeing now.

Oh, Paul. She grimaced. I am serious. What are these bad things you think about?

Paul shook his head. You'll think I'm a weirdo.

I already think you are a *weirdo*, she said, voice lilting as she said the word for the first time.

He considered telling her—telling her all the mad shit. How he hated the sensation of his heartbeat, or how the patter of water sometimes became loud and dark in his ears, or the terrible ways he would see Elliot. He cursed himself, under his breath. Freed himself from the thoughts, with effort. Turned again to Kasia. Saw she was asleep.

Deluge

THE CYCLONE PUSHED ITS WAY DOWN the coast. An order came through from the city that no boats were to go out. And none would have. The sea was wild in a way that made fishers look at the ocean as though seeing it for the first time.

Paul and Kasia walked up to the sandbar where a large crowd had grown to watch the sea, locals and tourists. It had become an event. 100-YEAR STORM the headline in the local paper had read the day before, which seemed overblown. But in truth there had never been any record of a tropical storm system tracking so far south. The jetty had become fully submerged overnight and a yacht was sunk, drowned on its mooring. The power was out everywhere in town.

The sea was brown and the wind hot and damp against their skin, like the warm-blooded breath of an animal, alive. Lightning forked at the horizon line, maybe twenty kilometres out. It was hard to distinguish the sound of thunder from the noise of the wind and tremor of the ocean in the dunes. The crowd stood there, mostly not saying anything, just watching. The low light around them had the milkiness of late evening even though it was midday. Jungle's boy Zach and some other kids ran about on the lawn above the inlet, excited by the way the breeze wrestled with their limbs and resisted their movements. Paul looked across to see Richard and his wife, the old man scowling at the ocean suspiciously. The power in the storm system was unmistakable, and unfamiliar.

Kasia leant in next to Paul and he smelt her hair. She whispered something in his ear about the darkness of the clouds. He closed his eyes and tasted the sweetness of her breath as she spoke to him. He felt the surge of want for her.

The rain came in a sudden, extraordinary downpour that had people squealing in fear and laughing nervously as they ran for their cars or fled across the park to the toilet blocks or towards the town.

Kasia and Paul ran down the main street, in the middle of the road, the weather having cleared the town of traffic. For a second the abandoned street lit up as if under giant stage lights then returned to darkness. Kasia grabbed his hand and hooted. They ran even harder. Paul looked across at her, saw the whites of her eyes, her smile almost glowing in the low light. Then the thunder exploded above them and they both ducked instinctively. Paul roared and the girl laughed as they cut onto the front lawns of his street. By the time they reached the front door their clothes were wet through and their shoes squelched in the tiled hallway. Their laughter echoed through the house; they were breathless from the sprint, nerves firing.

In the hallway leading to his bedroom, Kasia pushed him

against the wall and kissed his neck. Paul groaned when she grabbed his cock through his shorts. He slid his hands under her wet shirt and felt the warmth of her stomach against his palm. He sensed the grimace of her lips against his when his fingers found her nipples and she grabbed his forearms as though to slow him down. Her breasts were cool. The soft skin roughened, her nipples stiffening. She pulled the wet shirt over her head, unclipped her bra.

They dumped their clothes in weeping piles on the carpeted floor of his bedroom. On his mattress their bare skin dried quickly. Paul lay on top of her, his wet hair in his eyes. Once more thunder detonated above them and Paul flinched.

It is okay, Kasia whispered, smiling. Her eyes watched his as she reached a hand down and pulled him into the heat of her.

The lightning storm passed but the rain continued: a constant drumming on the roof that Paul thought might never end. He listened to it while Kasia slept, the creak and groan of the gutters, twitching under the weight of the water. The sound made him think of his brother.

Elliot would drag him outside whenever there was weather. Once, when Paul was five or six, Elliot had made him come and watch him surf out in front of the house in a huge winter storm. They had snuck out the laundry door and sprinted across the road in the rain, Elliot leaning his foamie into the gale and Paul carrying a beach towel that would prove useless, wet through before they made it to the beach and then stolen from the sand by the rising tide. Elliot had run up the beach checking the current, a nine-year-old with a foam surfboard, tackling a deserted ocean all on his own. Paul had taken position up near the dunes, the sea making him retreat into the scrub as it crept over the beach.

He hated being made to watch. It felt like he was there to watch his brother die. And he quickly lost sight of Elliot. After some time, when Elliot hadn't reappeared, Paul stepped out from the relative cover of the scrub and raced down onto the beach. He called out for his brother, young voice howling into the wind. Then he had run back to the house in tears, tormented by the dilemma. Should he tell his parents, and risk getting his brother in trouble, or leave Elliot out there on his own, in danger? He was huddled in the bushes in the backyard, still crying, when Elliot found him. His older brother's eyes were big with adrenalin and he laughed at the look on Paul's face.

What are you smiling about? Kasia said sleepily. She put a warm hand to his chest.

Elliot would love this, he said. This weather.

Why? she murmured.

Listen to it, he said.

Kasia turned to face the ceiling and they both lay there. The beat of the rain against the roof had an urgent, frantic presence to it. It was as if the weather was a living thing, an animal thundering against a cage.

It is wonderful, Kasia said.

When we were little, Elliot was always out in storms, Paul said. And even now, if he was here right now, he would want to go do something in it.

Like what? Kasia asked.

Anything. Surf. Fish. I think he liked the fact that you got the world to yourself when the weather was in.

That is very strange, Kasia said. I cannot imagine wanting to be alone.

I never really understood it.

Do you miss him?

I think about him. See him sometimes. He's like a ghost, almost. But then he's not. He could be out there still.

Do you think he is?

I don't know. Kasia combed the hair from his eyes with her fingers.

What's he like? she asked.

Shy, he said, and he turned to her.

Like you.

Elliot was never scared of anything, Paul heard himself say, like he had heard himself say before.

Kasia nodded. How are your parents?

Dad's himself. Acts like nothing's even happened. I think Mum feels alone with everything, Now she's at Grandma's, staying there.

She ran a hand through his hair. They listened again to the rain, hearing the building music of it.

What does that mean? he said, touching the tattoo on her hip bone. Is it Polish?

Ah, my tattoo, she said. You have seen it.

I don't know what it means.

Have you always been so nosy? She laughed.

Sorry, I was just curious.

I know that, she said. For a boy who never tells very much of himself, you are very curious. She ran her finger along the words. It says: *Im yesh l'adam menora, eyno pohed m'hosheh.*

What does it mean?

It is Hebrew. It says that if you carry your own lantern you will endure the dark. It was something my grandmother used to tell me, like a saying.

She was Jewish, your grandmother?

Yes. Like me. Kasia pointed to the last word inscribed. *Katarzyna.* That is my grandmother. I got my name from her. She is no longer with us though.

Katarzyna, he repeated. Did you ever meet her?

Only when I was very little. But I remember her. And I can remember her saying that. She used to tell me that I have to always be positive, no matter how terrible things can be.

I like it, he said.

She would say it when I was sad about something. My father said she would always say it to him, too. It was like the thing she lived by; it was what got her through so much pain.

What kind of pain? Did something happen to her?

Yes, Kasia said, a melancholy smile on her lips. A war happened.

~

Mid-morning we pull into a farmhouse. It's still some distance from the coast but I see the ocean west of us, big and dark blue, and it makes me feel uneasy, like I'm looking at something I shouldn't be.

The farmhouse belongs to an old lobster-boat skipper. We sit out on the veranda and I listen to them all talk.

The President says his bit about cleaning things up. If something went wrong out there he says we are all in the ground. The old skipper promised there was no trouble out at sea. The President leans back in his chair and watches the old skipper. The old man looks in his hands like he is looking for a ditch to jump in and finally says that there were some things in town to clean up. A fella who knew things he shouldn't know.

Not a gang fella. Lovesick. Soft. Protecting his girl who owed money. The skipper says this city fella had walked right up the jetty to their boat in the inlet, told them that he knew about the ships and told them he would tip off the coppers if they didn't leave his girl alone. It was almost sweet the skipper says.

The President doesn't find anything sweet about it and tells the old boy as much. The skipper goes looking for his ditch to jump into again and then the President turns to me. He doesn't say it but I know in the way the President looks at me that this city fella is now my business.

I wonder about this fella, if he knew he'd signed his own death warrant then and there when he walked up that jetty and spoke to these men. Got his name on a list that there is no getting off without ending up in the ground.

~

Wake

IN THE DAYS AFTER THE CYCLONE PASSED the sea was as flat and still as Paul had seen it. The surface was strewn with junk that the storm had ingested from the beaches and drawn up from the sea floor. But the swell had disappeared and there seemed to be no movement in the ocean, not the slightest current. Things just sat in the sea where the storm had left them, inert on the surface, suspended like space junk. Michael and Paul were amazed at the things they saw floating in between runs, and Jake slowed the boat alongside any sizeable object so they could get a good look at what it was. They found a couch, possibly from a roadside collection. Michael's highlight was the kangaroo they came across eighteen miles from shore. The carcass was dark and swollen. Michael posed with the marsupial, leaning back over the water as Paul took a photo of it with the German's phone. After lunch they came across an upturned catamaran. Jake had circled it, sounding his horn in case there were people clinging to it. Then he called the Maritime Safety Authority and reported it. That was as much as they could do. They were too far out to try to tow it; it would be too much for *Arcadia*. A hundred-thousand-dollar boat and they had to leave it behind.

As he worked, Paul found himself smiling, just like the German. The memory of Kasia relaxed him. It didn't stop him feeling sick, but it took the dread and melancholy out of the seasickness. He was vomiting and feeling incredible happiness. He even thought of Elliot less, he realised guiltily. When he did think of his brother, he found himself resisting the thought. It was almost as if he was back under the bedsheets again, pretending not to hear Elliot calling his name. But then Kasia would come back to him and Elliot would disappear, and he had to admit to himself that there was a relief in that, in forgetting it all, at least for a little while.

Paul knew by the way she kissed and the way she touched him that Kasia was experienced. He presumed his inexperience was equally apparent, but she seemed to tolerate his efforts. Mostly he simply watched and she guided him along. He observed the change in her face as he entered her, how her eyes closed and forehead creased. Her groans resembled both pain and relief. He would look down and watch the pattern of his body disappearing and reappearing, at one moment visible and then hidden. The simple visual subtraction, his cock erased from view, concealed inside her, was almost too much to take. After a moment watching he would close his eyes and grit his teeth and try to withdraw his thoughts before he lost his grasp on them. And he never did in time. Orgasm would sweep heavily over his body, a crushing, plunging feeling, like being driven deep down into the sea. Kasia would kiss him hard, and then she would watch him as he drifted slowly back to her from the depths, as though he was swimming up to the surface.

Big room

AT THE BEACH PAUL KISSED HER SHOULDER. Kasia's skin was hot against his lips. She lay face down on the towel, head turned away from him.

Have you seen the shark with the eye missing? Kasia asked, voice muffled by the towel.

Circus? No one has for a while. He's probably washed up somewhere.

The easterly was strong and desert-warm. He watched gusts run out across the sea in individual lines, prickling the surface, and he imagined the downdraught of invisible flocks of birds.

Maybe we could do it, you know, in there. Paul nodded towards the ocean.

Fuck?

He shrugged, tried to not look injured by the sharpness of the word and how she delivered it.

Ha, she said. No thanks.

Paul said nothing.

Kasia sighed. It is one of those things that are better in the mind than it is in life, she said. Would you like me to flush the ocean up your pee-hole?

Paul shook his head.

Exactly.

He watched the fine silver hairs of her back. He imagined her in the sea with her hands linked around the shoulders of someone else.

You know, Paul said, Michael says we are all doomed.

Michael says a lot of stuff.

He says we are designed to fail. People. All of us. It is in our design.

That's honestly what you guys talk about?

He reckons we are a faulty product.

We are not so bad. We went to the moon, didn't we?

A long time ago.

She shrugged. But we still did it. How can anything be impossible after that?

What do you think? Paul asked.

What do I think is the point of it all? she said, amused.

Paul shrugged.

Kasia rubbed her nose on her towel and looked back at him. Love, maybe, she said. Trying to be good. I believe that the future can have good things in it. Is that enough?

Paul rolled back over and sat up. For a moment his eyes were overwhelmed with light.

What is it with boys and questions like this? she said. Get them alone and it is always these *big* questions, like children thinking about dinosaurs or aliens or monsters under the bed.

Women, she said, they worry about the world they live in but men are always worrying about some different one that does not exist. They are incapable of talking about anything real.

That's not true.

It is, she said. Does Michael ever talk about his father, or why he is here?

All the time.

How does his father make him feel? Why is Michael hiding on the other side of the world, on a fucking lobster boat? I mean, you said he was studying at Oxford?

Paul laughed her questions off. I don't know, he said.

Kasia turned onto her back and exhaled, as if the weight of the sun had pushed the air from her lungs.

Paul watched her.

Why here? he said. Why did you come to Stark?

I saw it in a travel shop.

You saw Stark in a travel agency? He laughed.

No, she said. There was a shitty little travel shop next to the restaurant where I worked when I was in London. I walked in there on my break, crying like a loser. The man even made me tea because I was crying so much.

Why were you crying?

A boy. It was dumb. Just some boy who turned out to be an arsehole. And I was telling this old man all about it. He was as old as my grandfather, in his stupid little shop. I mean, who even goes into a travel agency anymore? And I told him about this arsehole, the full story. He sat down with me and we started going through all the places I could go, what I might find there. I do not even know if there was a computer in his shop. She laughed. But he was helping me to plan my escape from London.

But why here?

There was a poster of people swimming with a huge shark. It was as big as my apartment. Bigger even. A big shark with white spots.

A whale shark.

Yes. I did not know there could be such a thing. But it was so peaceful. Even in the picture I could see that it meant no harm, and I decided I wanted to do that. I did not have the money, but I needed to come here. I needed to swim with that big shark. We worked out where it was, me and the old man, we worked out that it was in the west of Australia, all the way up where the continent bulges into the sea. Right at the tip of the bulge.

Ningaloo Reef, he said.

The plan was to work my way up the coast, try to earn some money until I got to Exmouth and the reef and the shark.

And you got stuck here.

I got stuck. I ran out of money. This place, where I thought everything would be easier. A simple time. That is how I imagined it would be. And then I find this. Stark. At the end of the rainbow. And it is as fucked as anywhere I have ever been.

Paul snorted.

It really is. That tavern, it is like a black hole. Everything tumbles towards it, all these angry men and their problems. The pressure is so intense. That woke me up. I realised that everywhere is just the same. You do not find peace, you know, like it is some kind of destination. It is not something that you can search for and visit. It is not in London. And it is not at the edge of the earth. My grandmother said it: you carry your own light with you. She was smart, my grandmother. Again, she was right.

So much for the whale shark then, he said.

No, she said. I just need more money and I will be out of here.

Paul pulled a face at this, felt like a child for doing so. Kasia stood up and raced barefoot across the hot sand, swearing loudly. A mother pulled her toddler towards her legs and glared at Paul as he got up to follow.

Come on, fisherman, Kasia yelled.

Before he had really had time to think about it they were out beyond the bank. He dived down towards the seabed. Sunlight crisscrossed the sand. He looked up and saw Kasia's legs dangling, the sun blazing above her, could tell by the way her arms circled close and quick by her side that she was unsure what he was doing, awaiting the moment he might grab her leg to spook her. Paul let himself drift, totally numb to any thought of a stalking white shark, staring off into the decline of the sand into the sea and uncaring about what might be gliding at the limit of his vision.

Off-the-boat

AT THE TAVERN THAT NIGHT MICHAEL was drunk. Even at his most intoxicated he always maintained a remarkable level of outward composure. His skin didn't blot or become flushed like Elmo or Jungle, or like Paul, too. Michael didn't sweat, and his eyes never became bloodshot. It was his choice of discussion topics that gave him away, the lines of argument becoming more and more obtuse and hard to follow.

It was Richard's birthday. The cook, Jolix, had prepared him crayfish as a special gesture, against the man's wishes. Richard was predictably disgusted by the fuss made over him. Paul had been surprised to discover the skipper was only fifty. He looked at least two decades older. He sat at the bar, hunched over his food, looking every bit the old dog guarding its bowl. Despite himself he had drawn the amused attention of the intoxicated

German, and therefore every other deckhand at the bar. Michael leant over Richard's shoulder and peered at the birthday meal.

I feel uncomfortable eating a crayfish or a crab or anything like that, Michael told his audience gravely. In front of people, I mean. Some people do not seem to mind putting their face into a crab. Sucking the meat out of its legs. They will even do it in public. Does that not strike you as an intimate thing to do to an animal?

Shivani giggled. The men at the bar were stumped by the question.

Michael turned to the unmoving Richard. Richard stared at the crayfish, its two halves lying upturned on the plate, the white flesh shining under the counter lights. Richard never took much notice of Michael's talk, and seemed too tired now to utter a word anyway. But for a moment he let the lobster sit there, cutlery bound in a serviette next to it.

Ignore them, Jules said. Happy birthday, you grumpy old shit.

Happy birthday, alright, Richard muttered. Fucking fishing net took out three of my pots this afternoon. Cut right through the lines. Now I've got a thousand dollars of pots sitting on the bank in one hundred metres of water. Fuck's sake.

A fishing net? Elmo asked. How big? Must have been a smoker to cut lines like that.

Should have seen the fucker, Jungle said. Size of a football oval. Even bigger.

Three times that, Richard said. Six hundred metres long, I reckon. Easy.

Get fucked, Noddy said.

Super trawler, Richard said. Sure it was. Nothing else drags something that big. They would have cut their net loose in the cyclone.

I thought it was a spill at first, Jungle said. This giant shadow. Black as night. But there were birds going fucking mad above it all. More birds than I ever seen in one place in my whole life. Then we went closer.

What did you see? Paul asked.

This net, Jungle began, it moved liked it was alive. Turning big and slow, shimmering with fish of all sorts. Think I saw a hundred sharks around it. Maybe more. Reefies and tigers and god knows what else. And all this life and death and pot floats and coral like the whole ocean was being sucked into this thing. Honestly sent chills right through me fucking soul.

Jesus Christ, Elmo said.

It gave me the creeps, Richard grumbled. It was as bad as that bloody mutant fish.

Circus, Michael said. So, you've got the shark with its eye, this portal into the underworld. Now there is a black hole coming to visit us. You know what this probably means?

What? Jungle asked.

I think all evidence suggests that Stark might actually be the centre of the cosmos.

Jungle scoffed. Fuck me.

Scary, isn't it? Michael said. The universe spinning on an axis of cigarette butts and crackheads.

Michael elbowed Richard, who managed a rare smirk, and the men laughed. But Paul saw Arthur and his crew skulk through the front doors, looking tired and mangier than ever. Roo Dog, Anvil and Arthur took stools at the adjoining bar, eyes so dark and bloodshot there was no white in them. It was too late to get up and leave. Tea Cup walked over.

What are you fuckers on about? Tea Cup said, approaching from behind them. He slapped Elmo on the shoulder with a fat palm.

The German figures that we're the centre of all things earthly and intergalactic, Elmo said. They all laughed again.

Tea Cup gave a tense smile and raised his arm to Jules.

You hear that news about Carnarvon? Tea Cup said, looking at Elmo but with his voice raised to ensure everyone heard him. Boat rocked up on the town beach, he said, just today. All the way from Indo, packed full of Afghans.

No shit, said Elmo. I can't believe they got so far south. From Indonesia?

Yep. Java.

That's incredible, Elmo said.

No it's not, Tea Cup spat. It's a fucking disgrace.

The group went quiet again, as if already bored with where Tea Cup was headed.

Paul glanced at Shivani, who was peering unconvincingly at her phone. Michael stared at the counter. He was smiling.

We are being invaded, Tea Cup said. He placed his pile of coins on the bar and took up his pint of beer like a weapon. I told you. The dam is busted. Mark my words.

What would you do if you saw one of those boats? Elmo asked Tea Cup, throwing the scenario to him like a clay disc to a shooter. You know, out there?

Sink it, Tea Cup shot. No joke. Fucking tear a hole in it and watch the fucker sink.

Some of the men laughed in agreement. Tea Cup looked around at them, drinking in their approval. His eyes settled on Shivani.

Boat full of gooks, he muttered, like the words were bitter in his mouth. Sink them and then use them for cray bait. Off-the-boat pieces of trash.

Paul watched the faces of the men in the bar mirror, their awkward reflections, how they both avoided each other's eyes and tried to find them, each individual attempting to detect the mood of the whole. He saw Michael, noticed that punchline grin on him. He could sense something was coming and he had to stop it.

You still talking? Paul said.

The men at the bar turned at the sound of his voice. Paul thought he might have heard a gasp. He wondered if it had been his own.

What? Tea Cup grunted.

Are you still talking? Paul repeated.

Tea Cup looked around at the other deckhands as if in bemusement. Would you listen here? I think he is trying to tell me something. What are you trying to tell me?

Just saying I heard you, Paul said. I heard you the first time.

You heard what?

There is a boat in Carnarvon. You want to shoot everyone in it. I got that. Now you're just repeating yourself.

Paul returned to his food while Tea Cup stared at the side of his head, apparently unsure what to say or how to proceed. Elmo gave a short laugh that convinced no one.

Think you are the big man now, Tea Cup said. Think you're a fucking man now with your Polish slut.

It was then Paul noticed Kasia had stepped out from the bar kitchen. He saw the worry in her. She held the doorframe like her legs might give out. He felt a flash of heat right through his body.

You lonely, Tea Cup? Paul said, turning to look him square in his reddish face, seeing the spittle in the corner of Tea Cup's mouth. I bet you beat your dick like it owes you money.

The bar seemed to fall into an even deeper quiet, a crushing absence of sound that felt to Paul as if they were all in that moment in a vacuum, the tavern drifting, listless, in outer space.

Outside, Tea Cup said, the anger in his voice weakening it, the words barely a wheeze.

Give it a rest, Tim, Richard said.

I fucking said outside, Tea Cup said again.

You going to show us how much of a hero you are? Roo Dog said from the other side of the bar. He stood up.

Reece, Arthur said. Leave it.

But Roo Dog ignored his skipper and rounded the bar.

You going to show us what you got inside, mate? Roo Dog said, grinning at Paul. Just like your brother did?

For god's sake, Reece, Arthur said with a cackling laugh that Paul read as nervousness.

Jungle stood. You'll have to deal with Jake, he warned.

Fuck Jake, Tea Cup hissed.

Jungle is right, Tea Cup, Michael said. Jake will be looking for you. I do not know if you want that.

What would a Nazi know? Tea Cup said, finding his voice again. The words reverberated through the restaurant.

Michael shrugged. Sounds to me like you have learnt plenty enough from the Nazis.

Michael, Roo Dog said, unsmiling. You got a death wish too?

That's enough, Jules said.

It is enough, Jules, Michael said earnestly. You are right. Sorry. He pointed to his glass. He smiled at Shivani and then Paul. We should be going, he said.

Michael stood up and shuffled out into the beer garden, searching his pockets for his cigarettes. Shivani and Kasia followed, and then Paul, hearing the low, smouldering talk of the men at his back, like a fire lit.

In the void

BEYOND THE BLEARY GLOW OF THE JETTY and the lights along the inlet, the footpath ducked into bush and into unbelievable blackness. Kasia gave a mock squeal. Paul felt his eyes widen and his breath grow shallow. The thick scrub around them blocked the cool of the sea and shrouded the path in sour, musty fumes. The leafy pong of insects and decomposing reptiles. In the dark they slowed, laughed in whispers, moved hesitantly, walked the path from memory. Kasia grabbed Paul's arm with both of her hands and leant against him. Her breath was hot against his cheek, sweetened with wine.

This is how it must be to be blind, she said, giggling, as they edged forward. Or dead.

Paul imagined a black hole. Depthless. Dimensionless. He noticed how his knees had become bent.

In the void, Kasia whispered about travel and the drugs she

had taken. It hadn't been much. Ecstasy a handful of times. Acid in Florence. Cocaine in Brazil. She told him how with cocaine, when you were up, even just someone touching your arm, raking their fingernails across your skin, was enough to make you crazy. A kiss was something else again. She said she wanted so much to have sex with someone while on cocaine. She had never done that before. Paul hoped she'd say she wanted to do it with him but she didn't.

The bush tapered as the path returned to the roadside, within range of the streetlights. The sudden chill of the sea breeze made him shiver. Kasia let go of his arm and ran ahead. Paul pissed on the gravelly fringe of the path. The loose ground shifted underneath the stream. He briefly imagined her in Brazil, being held by other men, and felt the thought sweep bitterly over him.

Jack-in-the-box

ARCADIA WAS THE FIRST BOAT TO LEAVE the heads; Jake said they needed to make up time. He avoided Michael's and Paul's eyes as he said this and took his coffee with him up the ladder without another word.

They were in for it. They both knew that. The German was already into the bream with his knife, whistling a jaunty tune in which Paul detected uneasiness as much as the deckhand's typical irony.

Paul was nervous too. There was a bad feeling every time they set off with Jake primed like a fighter. Whatever it was the skipper was dealing with, he would take it all out on the boat. They would feel the skipper's mood in the deck. He'd drive even harder at the swells and the ship would heave with the violence of it. And it would go like that all day. Jake punishing himself, punishing the boat, punishing them.

They pulled and rebaited pots on the sand-bottomed grounds thirty kilometres out, the sea dark with the trench beneath them, one hundred and forty metres of water deep. By noon they could barely hear the sound of the skipper's horn for the wind in their ears, and the large swells had begun to whitecap.

Sometimes I think a mine wouldn't be so bad, Paul yelled to the German as he pushed a pot into the water. The departing rope snarled against the gunwale. A billionaire's sandpit, he said.

Michael grimaced, nodded his head. The deckhands took a moment to scan the ocean around them. The swells stood above the horizon line. But Paul felt a sort of calmness, resignation.

I could think of more fun things, Michael shouted. His face was so different without the smile in place.

The cray boat lurched down and white water surged over them. Both deckhands had to drop to their knees on the deck as they were pitched into the side of the boat. Traps clattered around them.

Holy shit, Paul gasped, and laughed.

Michael's expression was blank, humourless, and as close to fear as Paul had ever seen it. I want this to be over now, he declared matter-of-factly. I want a beer and a smoke. I want them now. I want to be home. I want to be on top of my Shivani.

Paul nodded.

This place, Michael yelled. Stark. It is not so much fun now. It is dangerous for you here. You should go back to school.

I don't mind it, Paul said. On a fishing boat at the centre of the universe.

Michael shook his head, unsmiling. He reached for a cigarette.

You really think if you hang around here your brother will show up?

What do you mean by that? Paul said.

Michael shrugged. Smoke scattered the moment it left his lips, broken by the gale.

I'll keep moving, Paul continued. I'll see things. Travel. Like you.

Like me, Michael echoed. Friedrich says I am lost.

Your father knows where you are.

My soul is lost. That is what he means. He worries I cannot be saved.

What does it matter? Shit, Michael. Your soul is lost?

It is my father telling me these things, Michael said.

You worry too much about what your father thinks.

I am not worried about my father. He paused. It is the world that is the problem.

The world?

Yes. The people like my father, they are the ones with their hand on the wheel, and they are driving us all into hell.

Paul sighed.

There is no stopping it.

I don't think it has to be like that, Paul said.

You do not know what you are talking about. Michael breathed hard out his nostrils. Joseph Tainter, he said.

What?

Complexity theory. Civilisations rise and then they fall. It is in the design. There is no hope.

So you are Nostradamus now?

It has been like that from the beginning, Michael said. Why are we any different?

Maybe we're smarter. Jeez. There's always hope.

I guess there is prayer, too. And lucky charms.

What's wrong with you?

I know, Michael said. Maybe we can see off the fiery end to the industrial age with some garlic and a crucifix.

Paul swore.

Michael glared at him. There really is no place in this world for hope.

I think there is.

Tell me, then, what is your hope? Why are we any better than the Mayans or the Romans?

I don't know, Michael. We went to the moon?

Michael laughed. We did not go to the moon. The US military went to the moon.

Even so, we are capable of it.

Capable of what?

Of anything. We could run cities off solar power.

Jesus, Paul.

We could harness wave power. The wind.

You really believe that shit?

I do.

Because the US military went to the moon? Buzz Aldrin was a fighter pilot.

So what?

So they were all in the air force. It was about power, Paul. It was flexing muscle and PR and shock and awe.

It wasn't just that.

Neanderthals made weapons, too. It is not such an advanced idea. A rocket and a spear is the same thing.

It was about discovery.

It is never about discovery. That is not the way people work. It is always about making money or making war. Profit or perfecting destroying people. Dollars or disintegrating flesh and bone. That is all it is ever about.

That's bullshit, Paul said. How can you not believe in the future?

Because no one cares for the future, Michael spat. Not my father, no one. Most of us do not even see it. We are blind to it. We share our blindness with the apes.

Paul sighed. So don't go home to your father, then. Just don't.

Why should I care for the future? Why should I not make money, enjoy the end of times like every other cunt?

Oh great, you sound like a true dickhead.

It is not so easy. Michael shook his head. My father said he is running out of patience with me. He said that I am running out of time to make things good with him.

Screw it. Who cares what he says?

He will cut me off.

So?

You are forgetting, Michael said. It is my family. He removed his gloves. It is not so easy.

Paul met Circus that afternoon, the shark emerging from the featureless depths and thudding hard against the hull right where Paul had vomited just moments before. It leant back in the water, mouth open in a slack, toothy grin. Paul yelled a garbled sentence to Michael, who was in the cabin making coffee. His words were swept away in the breeze.

The shark dropped its head to the water, sinking into the shadow of the bow, and was gone.

Ruth was in the car park when they returned to the inlet.

You need to watch yourself, she said through the driver-side window.

Why, he said, doing his best to sound nonchalant.

People say they've seen you looking around, she said. Poking your nose up the river. Talking to that copper. God's sake, Paul. People see shit like that around here. There are—

No secrets, he finished for her.

She looked past him to the sea, breathed out. She looked afraid. There is bad shit in this town, she said. Things you don't want any part of, I swear it.

Was that what happened to Elliot? he said. Bad shit?

Paul, she said. I don't know what happened to your brother. But I don't want anything happening to you. You understand?

Memories for ghosts

MICHAEL WAS ASLEEP, FLAT ON HIS back on the seats in the cabin. It was an hour journey back to shore after they had set the last of the pots. Paul stood out on deck in the glare and screaming wind, watching the sea to the west, thinking about what Ruth had said, thinking about Elliot.

He opened the box of gear on the outside cabin wall. Took up the Buck fillet knife, drew it from its sheath. It had a red rubber handle, the thin steel blade curved slightly upwards. The blade was longer than his palm, sharper than the others. He slid it under his damp t-shirt.

When they reached the inlet Kasia was waiting. She was leaning against a wooden upright near the jetty's edge, striking a Hollywood pose with her left leg kicked upwards and her hair in her face. Michael wolf-whistled and she burst into laughter.

The two of them walked home along the footpath. He was grateful she was in a talkative mood because he felt almost too tired to speak. She talked about Poland, and about her grandmother. Katarzyna had been one of only a handful of Jewish survivors of the war who had returned to live in the town. Kasia described how, in the winter of 1939, after the Soviet army withdrew and the Nazis had come, they gathered all of the young men in Chelm, including Katarzyna's father. Two thousand men forced onto death marches. She told Paul about the Ghetto, about the round-ups of 1942. How nearly all of the Chelmer Jews were taken or shot in the street. Katarzyna's entire family; her sisters, her parents. They all went to the camps and she never saw them again. But she escaped.

She was my age, you know, Kasia told him. Twenty-three. She hid in a cupboard when the soldiers came to do the final round-up and miraculously they did not find her. A few of them in her street made it into the tunnels under Chelm, the chalk tunnels. They hid there before escaping to Warsaw. There she met my grandfather.

Why did she return?

Most Jews that survived the camps left Poland, almost all of them. They went to America, Israel—anywhere else. They just wanted to forget. But Katarzyna said she needed to stay in Chelm. It was where her memories were. She was very tough. Stubborn, my grandfather said.

If you carry your own lantern, right? Paul muttered.

Yes, Kasia said, pleased he had remembered. Exactly.

Katarzyna had told Kasia that after the war she lived surrounded by the dead. All of her memories were of people who no longer existed. She lived with ghosts.

Later, in his bed, Kasia read while he slept. He dreamt he was swimming after Elliot. But he never saw him. There were bubbles always within sight, the fizzing wake of flippers, but the further he swam out, the darker and colder the water became and quickly his brother's trail of bubbles dispersed and then vanished.

~

It's hard to account for the importance of what goes on in a person's head at night when they close their eyes. Brain still fizzing and ticking like a dirt bike engine just shut down. People who talk about their dreams like they are important always sound dumb-headed and kind of religious. The way they recite fictions as if they really happened. Trying to make sense of it all like scripture.

But of course I dream too. Every night in that desert. And here at the farmhouse. And I've thought some bit about what they all mean. And I've come to think it's just the way of the brain to discharge the things that don't come out of a person's mouth. That maybe all the silences got to get spoken somehow. People groaning or screaming out in their sleep. Save it all up during the day so it comes out like an awful song in the darkness.

There is a lot that don't get said by fellas. A different kind of detail they register but don't mention. They'll take on facts but save the information on how it makes them feel. A fella will see somebody get hit by a truck and the fella will talk about the sound the body made and the colour of the truck and the speed they guess the truck was going but if any of it made him think about god or his own beating heart you wouldn't know. And it's all got to get out somehow. Like bullets sitting in the chamber of a rifle. Unspent. Clogging things up. So it makes sense the mind would keep firing while you're knocked out. All those things not said and not entertained while the sun is still up. The brain uncasing every unspent thought while you're asleep and trying to fire them into the night.

I dream about my grandmother. See her lying in her bed. And that look she had. Eyes still open. Like she was trying to call out to me.

And I dream about this job I've got to do. Don't think so much about it during the days but I dream it nearly every bloody night. Hear that .308 going off. The roaring call of it. See the surprise on his face. See the moment he knows he's dying. See him looking at me.

~

Snagged

PAUL HAD SEEN THE BOAT EMERGE OUT of the whiteout of the horizon, disembodied by the distance at first, its shape stretched and almost unreal, disappearing for seconds at a time behind the swells, as though it were only ever in his imagination. But as *Arcadia* motored towards the boat he quickly knew it was them.

Deadman sat low in the water. Engines off, or dead. There were a couple of figures standing at the rear of the deck, leaning over the stern railing. As *Arcadia* neared them, Paul could make out Anvil peering into the sea. Arthur, too. Thought of the fillet knife. It was in the cabin, inside his backpack.

Jake slowed, cut the engines. Paul heard him call out. Arthur waved him off, one hard swipe at the sky. Jake yelled again, asked if they were snagged, if they needed help.

It was then that Roo Dog stepped out from the cabin. He stood shirtless. A smiling corpse, so pale Paul had the impression he could see through him. Sun catching the round edges of ribs, his collarbones. Long hair in his eyes, stiff like wheatgrass, twisting in the sea breeze. He reached behind him, into the cabin, and drew out a large gun, cradling it in his arms. Michael swore without moving his lips. Up on the bridge Jake said nothing. Roo Dog raised the gun towards them. Two barrels. Michael and Paul stood only a foot or two from each other on the deck but Paul knew the gun was trained on him, he was sure. Could almost feel it. And it was so quiet with no engine noise. Paul heard the flap of his t-shirt against his chest. Wash against *Arcadia's* hull, like a crowd shushing itself. Arthur called out to the deckhand. Roo Dog ignored him. Lowered the gun toward the sea. Gun blast, and then silence. He laughed, walked back into the cabin.

Arcadia's engines growled and they turned shorewards.

Filthy ugg

WHEN KASIA FINISHED HER SHIFT SHE wanted them to walk to the jetty. She was excited to see him, eager to talk.

In the dark of the path, as he listened to Kasia, he thought about what happened that afternoon as if it were on a loop, repeatedly playing out in his mind. Roo Dog drawing the rifle from behind the cabin door, pointing it towards him.

But even if Paul had wanted to he doubted he could have found the words to speak of it in a way that made any sense.

At the jetty two boys were fishing, twelve or thirteen years old. Both snapped wary looks over their shoulders at the sound of Paul and Kasia's feet on the boards. Paul recognised one of them as Jungle's boy, Zach. Had seen him at the inlet with Jungle during the storm, running about in it on the lawn.

Zach nodded at Paul when they neared, wearing the sharp expression of a boy who Jungle reckoned had prematurely aged him.

Paul peered into the bucket and saw whiting, most undersized, turning over on themselves, tails arched skywards.

Kasia screwed up her face. They need more water, she said.

They aren't going back, Zach scoffed, a look of disgust on his face. He walked over to them and inspected the bucket himself before squinting up at Kasia, as if trying to fathom the tortured look on her face. Zach looked much smarter than his dad.

Are they dying? Kasia said. The other boy wheezed a laugh from the jetty's edge, his back to them. Zach looked at Paul with eyebrows raised then turned and walked back to his friend.

Paul put his arms around Kasia while she stared into the bucket.

It is such a strange place, she said.

Paul breathed in the warm scent of her scalp and the soapy perfume of her hair. He thumbed the strip of bared skin between her singlet and her jeans. The skin rose in bumps under his touch.

Zach stepped away from the edge of the jetty, carrying his jumping line over towards the bucket. He dropped the blowfish from the hook and clamped the spiny fish under a filthy ugg boot. Kasia stiffened. Paul knew what was coming. Zach raised his boot above the bloated fish. They would have done this a hundred times before, but they seemed excited, as if aware of the girl watching them.

The executioner stomped his foot down hard on the fish. There was a cartoonish expulsion of air and clear fluid. Zach bellowed in delight. Kasia put her head in her hands.

They lay in the dune scrub, the wind whipping over them.

Would you ever come to Poland one time?

Of course.

233

I would like to take you there. You can meet my friends, and my crazy cat. Kasia made a wounded sound and clasped her hands to her chest. I miss my crazy cat.

What is crazy about it?

Kotku, she said. He is an unwell cat. He has a sickness in the head.

What kind of sickness?

Kasia groaned. Kotku likes vehicles, she said. He likes moving things. She began to laugh. He jumps on buses, or tries to jump into our neighbours' cars when they are leaving for work.

Your cat gets on buses? he asked, attempting to sound amused.

Paul! she cried, reading his mood as suspicion about her story. You have not met Kotku. I am so serious. My mother has had to pick him up from the station. She has had to get Kotku out of the bus herself. Once he gets in, he will not listen to anyone but my mother or me. Kotku is a very fat, very nasty cat.

Paul shook his head.

Why would I lie about this? She unravelled into laughter. It is true. My cat is really crazy. Fuck, I miss my cat.

Paul slid his hand underneath her singlet. He circled his palm on the warm, soft skin of her belly.

I think you would like Poland, Kasia said.

Paul noticed the breeze go quiet, finally giving up on its rage. It was near midnight, he guessed.

Paul kissed her mouth and rolled on top of her.

Have you done it like this before? he said. On a beach?

Not with you, she whispered. She held his face in her hands.

He felt a sort of restlessness. He wanted her touch and resented it.

When did you do it?

What?

Who did you do it with, on a beach? Who was it with?

234

Don't be silly, Paul, Kasia said. She sat up and he rolled off her. What's wrong?

Where have you gone? she said, looking in his eyes. It is like you're not even here.

That doesn't make sense.

You don't talk, you're keeping things in. I can see it. And now these questions about someone I've slept with?

I was joking.

She sighed. It is late, Kasia said. I might go home, okay? I need sleep.

Falling through a building turned on its side

PAUL SAT ON MICHAEL'S COMPUTER long after he and Shivani had gone to bed. In the still night he could hear surf breaking on the reefs. He read the feed of news stories, just skimming them. Atrocities and absurdities. A warlord posing with the bodies of three hundred dead men. A blue whale washed up on the beach of a Thai tourist resort. Quickly he felt himself dragged down by the weight of it all, the news like an undertow. But he knew if he slept there would be more dreams.

So he sat there, skimming. Searching.

He found an email from the University of Oxford's Admissions office confirming Michael's re-enrolment in the following semester. Paul caught his own face in the computer screen, how strangely alert he looked. There was that feeling that came with the discovery of something he wasn't meant to know, the excitement and a sort of sadness, too, like grief or maybe even guilt. But he already felt too far gone to pull back or turn the computer off.

Soon he was looking at the breasts of an English actress he'd never heard of, a girl not much older than him. She stood alone at a sink in a cramped London bathroom, peering into the reflected image of the phone in her hand with an expression on her face that Paul recognised. Kasia had looked at him in that way before. He wondered whether she had ever taken a photo of herself, and if she had, who might have it. He wondered whether, if he spent long enough searching, if he dug deep enough into the digital silt, he might uncover an image of her, wearing the same tender, trustful expression, unaware that she was gazing into the abyss, a hundred million eyes watching without care or affection. His eyes, too.

Another click and Paul was watching the low-definition sex tape of a US college student, surrounded by the naked arses of older men, dangling their limp cocks desperately towards her busy mouth, and he thought of wilting plants leaning towards water. There was another video, this time with some sort of production values, garish stage lighting and multiple cameras. A man was throttling a girl with such conviction that Paul wondered if the fear in her eyes might be real. He examined the sheen of tears on her cheeks.

It was a feeling like plummeting, being in the grip of information. Like falling through a building turned on its side, descending through windows, doors and passageways, portal through portal.

He watched as a drugged Mexican girl had her throat cut by a man in a balaclava, the executioner wearing a Nike t-shirt, struggling to remove her head with the studied attention of a carpenter working through the rough grain of cheap timber.

Paul spent a moment trying to decipher the feeling it gave him, simultaneously adrenalised and fatigued. At once heavy and empty.

He pulled himself away from the computer, stood in the kitchen like a stranger to himself. He heard the sea, breathing in the dark.

The sea. It struck him then.

He sat back in the chair and in seconds he had brought up a report. The United Nations Office on Drugs and Crime. Transnational organised crime. Bulk carriers and fishing vessels.

Drugs found stuffed in twenty frozen shark carcasses. A tonne of cocaine. Intercepted by Mexican naval officers in the port of Yucatan.

He read of payloads of methamphetamine dropped from bulk carriers in the Bahamas, GPS attached, later collected by fishing boats. The United Kingdom navy found two hundred and forty million pounds' worth in the hull of a forty-two-metre fishing boat. The floor had to be broken and unbolted to uncover the methamphetamine, then the boat was sunk.

In each case study or news item he imagined Elliot. Involved in each story, implicated somehow. A mule, a runner. Pulling up cargo from the sea. The feeling it gave him, the feeling like an excision, a filleting knife through the softness of his belly and up to his neckline, and taking everything with it, hollowing him out.

He turned the computer off, sat back. Pinkish light in the windows. Fred would soon be at the station.

Scavengers

THE EASTERLY OFF THE DESERT WAS colder than he'd anticipated. He'd wished he'd put on trackies. The town was monochrome in the low light.

When he reached the station, Fred's four-wheel drive was not out front. The boat was gone too.

Paul ran to the harbour and when he got to the end of the jetty Fred was still there, standing in her boat.

You look like hell, she said, cheerful.

I haven't slept.

She gave him a puzzled look, shrugged.

Where are you going? he said.

Fred crouched towards the compartment underneath the centre console. Fishing, she replied, voice echoing in the hull. You know, Paul, we need the tonic of wildness. Fred looked up at him. Thoreau. *We must be refreshed by the sight of inexhaustible vigor.*

I think you're right, he said.

She groaned, head down again towards the floor of the boat. Not you, too. I thought it was just the old and the dying who bought all that bullshit. Yearning for the meadow. You're just like my husband.

You said a town like Stark is waiting to be picked clean.

I did? Her voice was muffled.

Bacteria and all that. You said crystal meth, it was like the bacteria that raids a corpse.

Yes, Fred replied. She stood up and looked at him. I did say that.

And then there would be the larger scavengers, too, right? I don't know. Sharks?

What are you saying?

How do you know there's not something bigger out there? Paul looked beyond the inlet. Fred's eyes followed.

Like what? she said, her eyes sharp at the horizon.

Arthur's boat. *Deadman*. We saw them, west of the banks. In two hundred metres of water. Roo Dog had a gun.

She sighed. I could check his permit.

He shook his head. No, it was like they were looking for something.

Might have snagged a pot.

Not that deep. And there was no line in. They're not fishing, there's no way. They never offload nothing from the jetty.

But they go out so deep?

Paul nodded his head. Further, maybe. A lot further. No one sees them for three or four days at a time. And then there's nothing in their crates when they come in.

Smuggling, she said.

He nodded.

~

Not hard to turn fishermen to smuggling the President says. Not hard when all they are pulling up are empty traps. Staring into the water wondering how they are going to pay mortgages. Get worrying about their kids and the car and the doubtful look on the faces of their women. Worrying long enough that a fisherman gets thinking about creative opportunities on the open sea. Gets thinking about treasure. Beyond imagining.

And that big bloody Indian Ocean, the President says. Coral heads that could tear the heart out of boats. Swells that step up out of the southern ocean like they've come straight from a hell. Hardest thing to control that line between land and sea, the President says. Impossible. Ten thousand kilometres of deadly coast. Most of it unpatrolled, of course. Because you can police the internet. Spy on every word written. Lock down airports and have a camera on every street. But the sea? No one controls it. No one owns it. Always been that way and always will.

~

A sun that never comes up

THE GERMAN LEANT AGAINST THE CABIN wall, his jumper pulled up around his chin, the breeze sweeping the smoke from his smiling mouth. The south in the wind had blown the sea a greenish-brown. Paul shivered at the gunwale, drenched t-shirt stuck to his abdomen. He hadn't seen Fred for four days. Her boat wasn't at the station or harbour. He puzzled over where she could have gone. The thought of Kasia lingered with him, too. When he brought his face to his shoulder to wipe the sea spray from his nose he could smell her, her perfume on his collar, and it didn't comfort him. Instead, it took to his mind like a toxin. His thoughts became necrotic, blackening, each thought feeding on the one before it.

Michael gaffed the floats and Paul took the line around the winch. He could feel the chill of the rope under his gloves, cold from the deep water current. It ran through his body. The

German emptied the pots and Paul rebaited them, pushing the traps back into the sea.

That morning the rope menaced his legs, uncoiling in strange, reaching arcs, twisting and snapping across the deck, angry with the immense weight at its end. At times Paul had to jump to avoid it. Every time he sent a pot into the water the German turned his whole body to watch on, take it all in, entertained by Paul's efforts to keep from being ripped overboard.

At mid-morning Jake turned the boat to sea. Paul picked at the feathered crust of a bread roll, tearing slivers of ham from its sides. The German emerged from the cabin with a coffee, tranquil. He had the unhurried tread of a holy man.

How many girls you reckon you've been with? Paul asked him.

Fucked? Michael clarified.

Paul shrugged.

Not enough. The German smiled, shaking his head. Never enough.

What number? Ten? Twenty?

No, no. Michael squinted. He scratched his beard. More. Have to be more than that.

Same for Kasia, I bet.

Good for her, Michael said.

Paul didn't meet the German's eyes but he could feel them. He put his face down into his roll and took a reluctant bite. Michael sipped his coffee and continued to the bow, kicking clumps of seaweed through the drain gaps as he went.

You are a ray of sunshine today, are you not? Michael said, turning towards Paul.

Get fucked.

The German made a sound, as though he was considering the words seriously. She is a beautiful one, Kasia, he said. You cannot keep that to yourself. You cannot have her history, her future. You do not own her.

Paul didn't look at him.

She must have had dick after her all the time, Michael said. He left a philosophical pause. Of course she has had some fun. It would be very sad if not. Like a bird not in the air. Terrible, sad thing for that not to happen.

You're a tosser.

Like a sun that never comes up, Michael continued. Sad thing.

With a grunt Paul threw his roll high into the air. The German stood straight-backed to watch it break up mid-air, tomato slices and cold meat scattering into the sea. He scratched at his chin again but didn't look back towards the cabin. Instead he returned to cleaning the deck.

On the next run, the deckhands didn't talk. The German whistled, mimicking the dissonant call of the winch, trying to follow its wavering melody. He whistled a more jaunty melody as he emptied the traps of lobster, and a happier one still as he watched the departing line stalk Paul's feet. Paul shuffled away from it. He kicked at the coil with his shin. Then the rope pinched the front of his boot, closing over the toe like a noose. Paul yelped and swore, lifting his leg high until the rope slipped away, buzzing and grunting over the gunwale as it ran into the sea. Paul kicked the wall hard, swearing again.

Lord of the dance, Michael said, nodding.

Paul glared at him, shaken and pale.

It is very pretty. The way you move, very pretty.

~

Before midday the wind swung, gusting in from the west.

His mind felt slippery, as if each track of thought was in a constant descent. The crash of a cray pot against the tipper became the blast of Roo Dog's rifle. And he saw *Deadman* in the shifting distance, in the shadow of every swell. Saw his brother's bloodless face in the gloom of the trench below them, read blame and fear in it.

And when he reached for an image of Kasia, something to soothe it all, the vision would plunge into a perverse, vivid spectacle that he was unsure if he could stop, unsure if he was even trying to. He imagined other men, their hands rough over her thighs, kisses blunt and thoughtless but somehow enough to please her. He saw their bodies smother her, faces stern with pleasure. Blank.

By the time they began the twenty-mile journey back to Stark, the sun low and wastefully beautiful over an ugly sea, he had pictured the German sliding his cock into her. He imagined Jake, too, the skipper masturbating feverishly over her cooperative, unclothed body. Each thought gathered heavy in Paul's veins, setting like concrete in his limbs. With every image came the very real feeling of weight in his gut. He imagined it might drive him through the boards of the deck, down into the hot atmosphere of the engine cavity and then straight through the hull, bolting towards the seabed.

And he longed for her, then. He had never wanted anything so much.

Stripped

WHEN *ARCADIA* REACHED THE INLET Paul saw the messages on his phone. It was his mother. He let Jake and Michael head off without him. He watched them go, and when the car park was empty and he was alone, he called her.

Paul, she said. Where have you been? You are worrying your father. He keeps calling Ruth.

Yeah, sorry. It's just that we're out of range on the boat.

You've got to call us. You and your brother, you never talked to me. Why doesn't anyone talk in this family?

I hear you and Dad aren't talking.

You have no idea what it's like, she said.

Elliot is my family too, Mum. He's my brother.

There was silence on the line. Just answer your phone, she said finally. Talk to us. She paused.

What is it, Mum?

The police came. A detective. He said they had searched a house here in Perth. They found more cash. A few hundred thousand dollars.

What's that got to do with Elliot? Paul demanded.

They also found two loaded pistols, his mother continued, and a silencer. He came here and told me that, Paul.

Paul watched the shadows of the boats in the inlet, like a silent crowd, listening in.

They're certain there's a link, his mother continued. The police took some more things from his room.

What did they take?

I don't know. I haven't been back to the house. Not that your brother had much left in that room. They said they're trying to put together a picture or something.

They're not going to find anything, said Paul. What do they think he is? A junkie? A fucking mule?

Don't talk like that.

Elliot didn't know drug dealers, Paul said forcefully.

Maybe not, his mother said. But Tess did. I'll bet she knows what happened to him.

Paul took a big, shuddering breath. The thought of people in Elliot's room, strangers going through his things, took the air out of him. Elliot would hate anyone in there.

I almost wish they *would* find something, Paul heard his mother say. I'm so tired of guessing. She sighed.

They're not going to find anything, Paul said again.

~

From the farmhouse we drive south to the town of Notting. On the way the President talks a lot. He says that we are the same me and him. We both have lost everything. And he reckons that a fella is smarter not being tied to things. He says life is like that sea near the farmhouse. That most people don't have the imagination for just how rough it can get. How deep and dark and full of nightmares, worse than any the mind can summon. And when it comes in and the water bloats you don't want to be anchored to anything or you will sink. Boats that are tied down will sink on their ropes, he says. The world is far too fucked to have ties to anything or anyone in it.

But him and me we are free he says. Set to do the best out of this business. Fellas with things they love don't do well. Love isn't a clean thing, he says. And I wonder if he is still talking about St Pietro in Vincoli and the boy on the school oval. Or whether he is talking about other people. Other places. And then I think that maybe it doesn't matter.

At Notting we stop on the thin dark road where the city fella and the girl with the debt lives, a small white cottage that is the only house for miles. Park on the verge in the cover of trees. We find a line of sight to the front door and windows.

This is where we'll find the city fella, the President says. The President says he will make a good start for me.

~

Like letting a glass fall from a counter

IN HIS BEDROOM THEY KISSED AND SHE told him to let himself go. He imagined her kissing other men in that way. He tried to rid the image from his mind but couldn't. There was a weight to those thoughts that he struggled to resist. When they poured in they stayed there, setting hard around his brain like tar, gripping every thought, weighing down each sensation. When that heaviness got hold of him it almost felt like he was only a spectator, watching himself and Kasia from afar. He could see her touch on him, the tenderness in it, hear their murmured sounds of pleasure, but he was disconnected from the scene. It all seemed so temporary, fleeting, when set against the images of the men she had loved before and done those things with. Even at the moment she came, and when she dropped her head to his ear and gathered her breath enough to tell him she loved him, her affection seemed pointless. Even worse. It felt fraudulent.

You are nice, Kasia said, wedging herself up against him.

Why do you say that? he said, hearing the defensiveness in his voice. He had wondered briefly if she'd sensed what he was thinking.

You are gentle. Good to me.

Paul lay on his back and thought of another man lying on his back. He tried to discard the thought as much as he indulged in it. He had noticed he did that. As much as he hated to imagine Kasia with someone else, he was drawn to each terrible visual his mind conjured, almost mesmerised by the violence that took place inside of him when he thought those things, the terror and anger and sadness.

You are, Paul, she said. She traced a finger through the film of sweat on his breastbone.

He moved in behind her, pressed his chest against her back. In the dark he found her cheek and swept the few strands of hair on her face back to her ear.

I had this guy treat me so bad once.

Paul put his lips to her neck and kissed it.

So bad, Kasia repeated, and shook her head. She reached up with her right hand, her arm brushing his face, and she cupped her palm behind his neck, raking her fingers across his scalp.

What? Paul asked. What did he do to you?

Kasia straightened her body and breathed out hard. Just bad shit, she said.

You know, she said abruptly, turning to face the ceiling as though the thought had jolted her awake, one time he tried to have sex with me while I was sleeping. I woke up and he had put himself inside me. Can you believe that?

She rolled over again, and he felt her relax against him once more. He waited for her to continue speaking but she didn't.

Who? he said. Who are you talking about?

A guy I was seeing. Last year.

Was he your boyfriend? Paul asked, trying his best to sound indifferent, detached.

No, not at all. Kasia sighed. We were not really going out. It was just a fling. Two or three weeks.

Paul could hear her breath slowing but he was alert. His thoughts stirred and gathered speed as though his brain was rebooting, and as he lay there, limbs tightening, his eyes adjusted to the darkness.

I had fallen asleep, she whispered. We were out at a bar with his friend. I was very drunk. We went back to his place and I must have passed out. I woke up and he was inside me. I did not move. I do not know why. I have no idea why I did not stop it, say something. But I just did not believe it, that he was doing this to me, thinking that I was still asleep.

She pulled his slackened arm from her waist across her body, tangling his fingers in hers.

He finished himself off, she continued. Got up and, you know, cleaned himself. He asked me to leave afterwards. He did not want his housemate to know I had been there. Like he was ashamed of me.

That's shit, Paul muttered. He drew his hand away and rested it, unmoving, on her hip. And he imagined another hand, someone else's, where his was.

Yes, she said, sounding more awake. It was shit. Kasia rolled her head towards him. In the dark Paul wasn't sure if her eyes were open. She turned her face back to the pillow.

I found out later that he was hooking up with other girls that night, at the bar. He would tell me to go get him a drink and he would be hooking up while I was gone. I had no idea it was all happening. I was so drunk. So stupid.

How did you meet him?

He worked with my brother and me at a restaurant in London. I guess he must have come over for a drink one time. It was not like this went on forever. I only saw him for a bit after it happened. Maybe two or three times. He stopped calling me. He moved on. It was not this huge relationship or something.

Why did you put up with that? Paul asked, and allowed himself to wonder if she would have been so passive if it had been him, whether she would have allowed him to be that way.

I do not know why I let him treat me like that. I never would before, or now. Why for him? I do not really know.

How old was he?

He was not that old. My age, maybe a year or two older.

And you liked him?

He was handsome, yes. He was travelling as well, like my brother and me. French. Maybe it was the accent, she said, with a laugh that was a brief exhalation of breath.

She traced his forearm with a fingernail and he didn't move.

Are you okay?

I'm just tired, he responded, aware of the contradictory energy of his voice, the force in it.

You seem unhappy, she said. Is it Elliot?

I don't really care anymore.

You do not care?

I'm sick of talking about it.

Okay.

Everyone treading all over him, going through all his shit like they're welcome to it. It's like it's a fucking puzzle, like it's some game to them.

I am sorry, Paul. I do not think it is a game.

He didn't reply.

I am sorry, she said again, now wide awake.

Forget about it.

Are you okay with me?

How many people have you slept with? he asked.

What? What are you talking about?

Nothing, he muttered. Just a question.

Where did that even come from?

It's just a question. Why can't you tell me? How many people?

I would never tell you that, Paul. It is not a big number, but it is none of your business.

Five? More than that?

God, she sighed.

Ten? he said, attempting a laugh. Fifty?

What is this about?

I just want to know, he said, hearing how weak the words were. I don't give a shit, really.

What does this have to do with anything? I told you about some creep and you want to know how many people I have hooked up with?

Paul didn't say anything.

I should not have told you that. You did not need to know. I was just trying to say how much that I thought you . . . She trailed off, giving up on the sentence.

They lay together in silence, his hand inert on her waist. A part of him knew he should hold her, apologise. But in that moment he was convinced of his right to those questions. He turned towards the wall and heard her sigh again.

You think I am a slut? she said. It was dark, and she was silent, but he knew she was crying.

Paul rolled over onto his back, saying nothing, leaving her words to fall into silence, like letting a glass fall from a counter.

In the morning Kasia was gone. He went out into the living room, expecting to find her sitting on the couch, angry but wanting to talk, but she wasn't there. He called her phone and knew somehow she wouldn't answer. He felt the panic rising in him, fear surging cold in his limbs. He felt like screaming, felt like crying too, but he couldn't.

USS *San Jacinto*

ELLIOT AND PAUL HAD FISHED FOR TWO hours alone under the lamp on the Cottesloe groyne, caught nothing. Used nearly two whole bags of bait, the mulies thawing and falling apart in the wind current, pecked by blowies. It was midnight when Elliot decided they should head home.

Up above the dunes there was music, boozy chatter from the bars and restaurants. Easter long weekend. Elliot suggested they walk the beach.

So where you staying up there, in Stark? Paul asked. The sand beneath his bare feet looked almost blue, agleam under the floodlight of the surf club.

I'm sharing a house, a little way out of town.

With a girl?

Yeah.

What's her name?

Tess.

She your girlfriend?

Fuck's sake, Paul. Yeah, I guess.

Paul laughed uncertainly, knowing he was forcing the topic.

Why didn't Tess come down here with you? Paul asked, breathy in the soft sand, carrying gear, the rod and bucket.

She didn't think Mum and Dad would approve of her. She's probably right.

Is there something wrong with her?

Nothing's wrong.

Okay.

They stepped into shadow, beyond the lights of the strip.

Elliot sighed. There are things she needed to get free from. She was having trouble in Stark. I didn't see it at first. He paused. There's always something you cannot see.

What do you mean?

It is never simple, his brother said. It is never how it looks.

I know, he said, trying to sound like he did.

You don't, Paul. His brother had stopped walking, a motionless silhouette against the dark of the dune.

There are things you don't get, Elliot said. About our family.

You mean about Dad?

Elliot went silent.

I know about the Gulf War, Paul said. Operation Desert Storm.

How?

I found some things, on his computer. A photograph. He was a combat systems officer.

So you know he bombed people?

He didn't, Paul said.

Guided missiles, his brother replied. Tomahawks.

That's not right, Paul insisted. Australians didn't bomb shit. I read it all.

He was an exchange officer. He was on an American ship. The *San Jacinto*.

Paul's eyes were tiring, trying to focus on Elliot in the blackout of the beach. He turned to the sea, to the flashing of the reef markers and freighters, the lights of the island. He thought of the images he's seen, the ones his father had searched. Blackened rubble. Corpses burnt to bone.

The Professor killed people? Paul asked, but it wasn't really a question. He knew now that his father had.

They were the first ship to fire at Baghdad, his brother said.

How do you know all this? he said, turning back to Elliot.

I remember Mum telling me, years ago. I was a kid, don't know why she did but she told me, all of it. Think she had no one else.

Paul heard Elliot drop his gear to the sand. His brother sat down.

And last year, Elliot continued, they were in the garden, didn't think I could hear them. Mum was crying. Dad was trying to talk her out of leaving him. Promised her he'd get treatment.

For what?

Dissociative disorder. Post-traumatic stress. He was discharged from the navy because of it, years back. Same year I was born.

Paul set down his rod and bucket, sat next to him. He couldn't see Elliot's face.

You never said anything.

What could I have said?

That the Professor was fucked up?

That's not how it was, Paul. And you were young. You didn't need to know.

Know what?

That nothing is ever how it seems. That you can never really know a person. There is always a secret.

For some moments they didn't speak.

But he should have told us, Elliot said eventually. I wish he'd told us.

It's Dad, Paul said. He doesn't talk about things.

Why? Elliot asked.

Paul thought about how strange it was to hear his older brother ask him a question in that way, like he really needed an answer.

Don't know, he muttered. It was all Paul had, all he could offer his brother, and he wished he could say more. He listened to the shadow sitting beside him, wondered if Elliot was crying. Then Elliot stood, picked up both of their rods from the beach.

Can you bring the bucket? he said, in a cooler tone and Paul knew the subject was done. That they'd never speak of it again. And then Elliot walked towards the stairs that rose out of the dark to the gaudy brightness of a car park. Paul watched him go, saw his brother's shape dissolve into light.

Land of children

THE DULL SLICK OF THE INLET CHURNED under the engines, an eruption of black sediment, like cold coffee disturbed. They went noisily along the riverbank. Paul looked at the town and hated it, dreary in the morning dark, lightless except for the miserable glow of the toilet block above the inlet car park. They were the last boat out of the mouth. Jake had arrived late again, setting them back an hour.

Paul wondered if Michael knew Kasia had left Stark, if he had heard anything, if he might even know where she had gone. Jules had been tight-lipped when he had gone to the tavern to look for her. She confirmed that Kasia had left town, adding only that she had said she did not want to be contacted.

It was afternoon before Paul could speak of it.

She's left, Michael, he said. She took off. I don't know where.

The German looked at him without surprise. Yes, I heard. Jules told you.

There are no secrets in this place, Michael said. You should know that by now.

Where is she?

She said she is from Poland, did she not?

You think she's gone home?

Michael shrugged.

How could she?

I think it is a good thing.

What? Why?

It is her life. If she needed to go, I think it is good she went.

Paul stared at him. But I love her.

Do you?

I do.

What did you give her?

What did I give her?

Why should she stay? Michael said. What did you give her? Respect?

Respect? You don't know anything. You don't know about her and me.

What did I say about secrets, my friend? There are no secrets in Stark.

Bullshit. It's all there is. Everyone has a fucking secret. Including you.

Me?

When were you going to say you're running back to Oxford?

You have been going through my shit.

You're enrolled next semester. What happened to seeing the world, Michael?

Is that what you do? the German said. Creep around like some pervert, pry on other people's lives?

Paul exhaled.

Is that what you did to Kasia? Did you dig around a bit too much?

None of this is your business.

Ha. Now you want privacy? Michael laughed bitterly. I mean, what the hell did you do? Jules told me Kasia was upset. You were unhappy with her? Angry?

No, Paul replied. I wasn't.

You get what you give. Treat the world like shit, you will have shit raining down on you.

What are you talking about?

You have been such a little boy, Michael said, his teeth gritted. A scared little boy. Such a brat.

Fuck off.

You do not own her, Paul.

I said fuck off.

I thought you were better than that, Michael said. Better than them. Michael pointed in the direction of land. All the scared little men in this place, trying to own everything. Trying to rid the town of anything that makes them uneasy. Scared of their women. Scared of sharks. Scared of foreigners. Terrified of the past. The future, too. Always scared and trying to act so fucking tough. Michael yelled something in German, looking skywards. And I thought you were bigger than that, he continued, returning his gaze to Paul. You need to grow up. You all do. This whole place, Stark. It is a land of children.

As *Arcadia* grunted into the inlet at dusk Paul noticed flashing police lights in the car park and a crowd gathered at the foot of the jetty. Standing beside him on the deck, Michael stiffened, eyes wide as he stared at the scene. But all Paul could think of was Kasia, and how ugly Stark was without her.

Zach

WHEN THEY REACHED THE JETTY they saw Jungle, the huge man swaying strangely as he walked away from the small crowd following him. Richard had the deckhand by his left arm and seemed to be trying to hold him back. Paul sat frozen in the skiff as the two men tumbled up the jetty. Jungle's face was twisted in a way that made Paul lose his breath. His eyes were huge and his mouth was stretched wide open, as though in a scream. But as he passed them there was no sound coming from him other than the drumming of boots on timber and Richard's hoarse pleading.

As they went by Jake yelled out to him. It looked as though the deckhand was going to throw himself off the end of the jetty and into the sea with the old man attached. But when he reached the edge, Jungle simply dropped hard onto his knees, the boards making a short, oddly musical sound. The men behind him stopped, the crowd on the jetty falling silent, and with Richard standing stiffly beside him, a hand still clenching the arm of the large man's jacket, Jungle began to cry. Michael moored the boat and they joined the crowd of deckhands.

Jungle's eldest boy, Zach, had that afternoon drowned. Fred had been waiting for Richard's boat to arrive back at the harbour to deliver the news. The boat crews stood together uttering quiet statements of disbelief as Jake and Richard knelt with the quivering shape of the man who had lost his son.

When Courtney arrived, the men left the pair alone, huddled together on the damp boards of the jetty where Zach had fished so many evenings.

In the tavern versions of the story circulated, most of it gathered from the account of his friend Dan, who had been in the water with Zach. The boys had set off to surf the back beach just a few kilometres from the centre of town, close enough to ride their bikes. The surf was small, the water clear. When they first walked over the dune and saw the super trawler's net in the surf they had thought it was a shadow from a cloud but the sky above them was big and empty and blue. The size of the net mystified them. Its long inky shape stretched several hundred metres down the beach, so vast that it hardly seemed real; stranded on the bank, shifting back and forth in the surf, as if alive.

Apart from a jetski further around nearer the point, the boys were alone. Dan had wanted to ride back to town and let people know of the net but Zach wanted the chance to see it up close.

They paddled out on their surfboards, stood on the sandbank as they neared it, waded closer. Dan was scared. Put off by its size up close. Its slow, heavy movements in the surf. The shining scales beneath the netting and the smell of rancid flesh. But Zach had wanted to touch it. He was holding on to the floatline when a wave came and the giant net distended as if breathing in and when the wave had passed Zach was gone. Never made a sound.

Two older boys were towing each other around in the beach breaks on the jetski, taking turns whipping into the small swells on surfboards. Dan had waved to them, cried out, but the older boys didn't hear him above the volume of the motor.

And Dan, just twelve years old, had paddled to the beach alone, the trawl net quiet behind him, the indifferent whine of the jetski in the distance.

Leviathan

THE FANS ON THE CEILING OF THE church worked hard. It was dim inside, airless with the crowd of men dressed in sagging suits. Jowels slick with sweat.

Father Mobu gave a homily on Jonah and the great fish. Jesus had clung to that story, the priest told them. Jonah swallowed whole and resting in the gullet of the fish for three days, taken by the sea, before being delivered back to land. It was a story Jesus returned to often, he said. It gave him faith in the possibility of renewal in the aftermath of death.

Paul looked for Tess, Jungle's niece. She wasn't in the front pews. Not where Jungle sat leaning into Courtney, the big man limp, as if all his bones had been broken. Eventually he spotted her standing at the back of the church, leaning against the white brick in a short velvet dress. Tattoos on her right shin. He recognised her face from the photograph in Elliot's room. Later, as Jungle and Richard and other men carried the coffin up the aisle towards the doors, he looked for her and she was gone.

After the service they drove to the inlet. Paul watched the younger men in their op shop suits or ill-fitted hand-me-downs. Black sunglasses. All stone-faced, hands clenched tightly in front of themselves, observing Hollywood convention.

They stood on the jetty. The wind blew the ashes back across everyone.

It was hard to look at Jungle, to witness how completely a parent could be undone by the death of a child. The rumour was that Jungle and Courtney would leave Stark for Perth. Paul tried to imagine renewal, how either of them could emerge from the guts of such a thing.

The wake was at Elmo's place. Michael, Shivani and Paul sat on the back lawn as the men drank beer to the edge of consciousness, fulfilling some apparent last stage of the process. Richard looked even more tired than normal. He grabbed Paul by the arm, told him to watch out for himself. There was talk going around, Richard said. He should avoid Roo Dog and Anvil best he could.

Witness

PAUL WALKED BACK TO THE HOUSE ALONE, in the middle of the road, limbs numb from the beers. He sweated through the suit Ruth had lent him. It belonged to her husband. Fred was crawling alongside him in her squad vehicle, head out the driver-side window, before he even heard the engine sound.

Paul, she said.

Where have you been? he asked.

Fishing, she said, and cut the engine.

Yeah, sure, Paul said. It's been days.

I want to talk to that girl of your brother's, she said. Tess. Jump in.

Why? I don't even know her.

She's not cooperating. You're Elliot's brother. She might talk to you.

Paul climbed into the passenger seat. It was a strange feeling to be sitting next to the police officer, in her car. He was suddenly aware of how drunk he was.

Fred was quiet as they took the road to the main highway, nine kilometres climbing out of Stark, the ocean growing big in the side mirror, the land low and beaten like a battlefield.

You think I'm right, he said. You think I'm right about Arthur's boat.

I don't know, she said. The girl might, though.

There was a long silence before she spoke again. *Cetus.* The bulk carrier. That's its name.

Cetus, Paul repeated.

Flag of convenience ship. Russian crew.

How did you find out?

I went out there. I saw it. It was off the shipping routes, east of the shelf, right in the maze of reefs. It was as if it was looking for something. Lost cargo, I'm thinking. Something too valuable to leave behind.

Deadman. You think they're looking for it too.

Fred nodded.

So what's happening? Can't you arrest them?

No.

But you told people? You told the authorities?

It doesn't work like that. This kind of thing takes a lot of resources. A lot of boxes need to be ticked. There's no coast guard in Western Australia. Just customs and the navy, and they're busy rounding up refugee boats for the PM. It's a political hassle to divert border patrol down here. Then you got the Organised Crime Squad. They have their hands full in the city. They want more information, more evidence, if they're going to sniff around up here, miles at sea.

Fuck.

Language, she said.

What about Elliot? *Deadman*? Roo Dog's gun?

Fred turned right at the highway.

Think about it, she said. You've got a lone copper in a town of eight hundred people calling up the feds. Customs think I'm some old nutter playing sheriff on her boat. Sounds like conspiracy theories to them. They need something solid. That's why we're speaking to Tess.

They didn't talk for the rest of the drive out to Notting, an hour's drive south and then east for another half hour. Away from the sea, out of the path of the wind, there was colour and height to everything. Peppermints and eucalypts. Dark greens and yellows. In Stark there was hardly a living thing above shoulder height, just spider orchids and smoke bush ducked behind dimples in the red sandstone as if avoiding gunfire.

Fred pulled into the thin unmarked road, shadowed by white gums. She parked in front of a fibro cottage. Fred got out and Paul walked slowly behind her on the gravel path, through the overgrown garden, wildflowers in the long grass. Bottlebrush and everlastings. Stood on the small porch. Fred knocked on the flyscreen.

They heard footsteps.

Tess opened the door, wincing as she put her face into the sunlight. Dark eyeliner. Pale. Thin-faced. Still in her dress from the funeral.

Who are you? Tess said, looking at Fred, then at the squad car on the verge.

Senior Sergeant Freda Harvey.

You're the new Stark copper.

Fred nodded.

I've already talked to another one of you. Gunston, or whatever his name was. I've talked to lots of people.

Paul looked beyond Tess to the dim, carpeted hallway. Imagined Elliot standing there.

Can we come in? Fred asked.

No.

Tess ignored her and turned to Paul. What about you? You come to sell me God or something?

No, he said.

Where did you get that suit? She looked him up and down. It's fucking awful.

I was at the funeral.

Her face flushed with suspicion.

We just want to talk, Fred said.

You don't want to talk. You want to ask questions.

Elliot, he said.

The police have already been up my arse about all that.

You told them nothing, Paul said.

Fred sighed.

I wasn't going to tell them shit, Tess said.

I'm his brother.

I figured, she said, looking him in the eye, jaw tensed.

Paul looked to Fred.

I don't know what you want from me, Tess said.

You've had contact with Reece Hopkins.

Roo Dog? Haven't bought off that horrible fucker in ages. I've kept my distance. Like I said, the police came down on me over all that. I've paid my dues.

I'm not here to bother you about whatever you've bought or not bought, Fred said. Your habit is not my concern.

Don't talk to me like that, Tess replied. She began to close the door.

You know something, Paul said.

Tess sighed. Nothing that will change anything.

But you know something. How could you not say anything?

It's not my business, Tess said, louder. I told you, I told the police everything I could. The rest, it's not my business.

She closed the door.

Paul looked at Fred. She stood a moment then turned back towards the car.

Paul watched the greenery recede on the drive back towards Stark, the bush giving way to stone. He shielded his eyes from the lowering sun and the windblown ocean west, the horizon white as hot iron.

You hungry? asked Fred.

Paul shrugged.

Well, she said. I am hungry.

They pulled into the roadhouse south of town, sat in the empty dining room. Red carpet. Chequered. Jukebox in the corner, unplugged.

Wish that girl would talk, Fred said, almost speaking to herself.

Maybe she's afraid, he said, tiredly. She's scared of Roo Dog.

You know they're related? Tess and Reece. Same mum.

Roo Dog is her brother? Paul said, sitting up.

She wouldn't be alive otherwise. The debt she is in.

Paul leant on his elbows, hands in his hair. Tried to process it all. They sat in silence. He thought about the cottage, its dark hallway. Felt already hungover from the wake earlier that afternoon.

The counter hand put down the plates. Porterhouse steak in front of Fred. Chips in front of Paul.

There you are, the girl said, and walked back to the kitchen.

Paul took a chip. Fred unwrapped the napkin from around her cutlery, placed it over her lap.

What kind of gun is it? he said, glancing around the table at her duty belt, wanting to talk about something else.

Glock 22.

Fred picked up her knife and fork.

You ever shot it?

Of course, she said.

Not during training and things. I meant, have you ever shot a person?

I know what you meant, she said. She looked at her plate. Yes, she said eventually.

Kill them?

She rolled her eyes. Can I eat?

You've killed someone, Paul said.

Two, she said. It was two people.

Fuck.

Language.

Fred sawed through the steak.

Sorry, he said. It's just—who?

Father and son back east, in Sydney. Drug family.

Paul resisted the urge to curse again. What happened?

We were doing a bust, she said. Fred shook her head. It was them or me.

Is that why you're here? Why you left Sydney?

She laughed. I'm not your sob story copper, kiddo. Nothing about that keeps me awake at night.

You thought it would be easier, Paul said. You thought it would be easier working in a small town. Like Gunston did.

Fred shook her head. Rural beats are always hard. I knew that. Police work in a fishbowl. She chewed and swallowed. It was

Robert's idea. He thought the sea air would be good for his lungs. Fred tapped her chest with the back of her hand. Sea air doesn't do it, it turns out. Oncologist was spot on. Lasted six months.

Twenty-mile crucifix

ON FRIDAY AFTERNOON THEY FISHED the coral grounds twenty miles out. The wind up. Surf foaming on the reefs around them.

Arcadia slowed on a pot, idled. Jake yelled down. Paul looked to the upper deck, saw the skipper's arm stretched over the railing, index finger pointing westward. In the middle distance he could make out the markers, like figures standing on the surface. A coral head or a shipwreck beneath them. There were three of them. The one in the middle thicker around its top half. An irregular clump. Like something had become caught on it, or was tied to it. It looked like drapes from a distance. A decoration.

Jake pulled them up closer, within fifty metres of the strange figure. Cut the engines.

Paul heard the call of the wind. High-toned and constant. An alarm. Or was it just the wind? Was there any sound at all? Next to him Michael might have said something. Cursed maybe, or sighed. Paul stared at the marker. Felt himself drawn toward it as if it were a black hole, crushing all feeling, every thought.

He saw ribs, a darkened abdomen. Tied to the metal upright with rope. The corpse hung forward. A yellowed face, exposed jaw hung in a scream.

Paul stumbled into the cabin, sat on the seats, sucked in breath. Jake came down from the bridge, straight to the radio on the cabin wall. Made the call to shore.

Marine Rescue, Geraldton. Marine Rescue, Geraldton. Marine Rescue, Geraldton. This is *Arcadia*. *Arcadia*. *Arcadia*. Over.

Arcadia, Arcadia, Arcadia. This is Marine Rescue, Geraldton. Marine Rescue, Geraldton. Marine Rescue, Geraldton. Please go to eight four. Over.

Jake changed the radio to the working channel.

We found a body, Jake told the shore station. We have found a body. Tied to an isolated danger mark. Above the *Delft* wreck. Over.

He looked reluctant as he gave the coordinates, even afraid. Michael stood in the doorway, didn't say a word. They both had the look of men who had been trapped.

And Paul struggled for air, hands on his knees. Wondered if it was Elliot on the marker, unfamiliar as the body was, spoiled by the elements. And if it was, had he been tied there alive? How long had he been there? Had it been days? Wings beating above him, shadows underneath, an ecosystem of scavengers waiting for death to come, for Elliot to leak into the water.

IV

Tornado

AT THE INLET FRED STOOD WHERE THE wooden jetty met bitumen.

She nodded to Michael then turned to Paul.

We can talk later, she said. Your aunt is back there. Go to her.

Ruth was waiting in the car park, sitting in her four-wheel drive. A few of the deckhands milled at the driver's window. Noddy. Elmo. They moved away when they saw him and Michael.

Paul, Ruth called out, her voice hoarse. She leant her head towards the open passenger window. Jump in. You've got to call your mum.

Ruth's face quivered oddly at them. Michael scratched the gravel with his boot.

I'll see you at home, Michael said.

Paul sat in the passenger seat, holding his backpack between his knees. The bag reeked of bait. He looked at his aunt, waiting for her to speak. She drove out of the car park without a word.

Ruth, he said. We don't know for sure it was him.

Her jaw tightened at the sound of his voice. Paul could see the tears gathered in her eyes. She looked away from him and to the road, gripping the steering wheel hard as if it might slip out of her fingers. She drove to the end of the street, a few hundred metres, and pulled into a small car park at the back of the dunes.

Why we stopping here?

I can't fucking drive, alright? she said, shakily.

Ruth.

You've got to call your mum, she repeated.

Paul stared at her hand trembling on the gearstick. He took his phone from his jumper pocket. The ringing tone echoed across a bad line. Paul shut his eyes and listened to it. He imagined a bird in a cave, calling out in darkness. Then he heard his mother's breath on the phone.

Mum, Paul said. We found a body.

A rush of air filled the line and then he heard his mother's sobs. Ruth stiffened in her seat and began to shake, her tears beginning as a series of pulses from somewhere deep within her. Paul listened to the diesel engine rattling the windows. He could feel its vibrations in everything, in his fingers, in the plastic of the phone against his ear, as though the whole world shook. It had ended, their search for Elliot was over, and he couldn't believe how.

Ruth let out a snort. She clasped a hand behind his neck. He looked into her face. It was all wet and patchy red and her eyes were swollen. She grabbed Paul and hugged him, pressing him hard against her chest, her face soggy against his cheek.

That night Paul found himself hovering over the night ocean, straining his eyes into the murk, calling for Elliot, swearing, curses muffled by the sea. The horizon was a flat darkness and there was no light in the water except for the gold slick of the moon against the black water.

~

The President parks on the roadside in the shadow of the white gums. A clear line of sight between the trees. I mount the .308 on the car bonnet.

From three hundred metres I watch the boy from the city carry shopping from his Pajero to the cottage. Glass over his torso with the rifle scope.

The President leans on the bonnet beside me. Talks me through it all. And with the President there I find those half-seconds where my mind is as clear as the mind of a dead fella. When I'm empty of breath and my heart is still. And I know then I'm ready.

The next morning it will be done with.

~

The Professor

IT WAS EARLY AFTERNOON WHEN PAUL'S phone rang on the carpet beside his bed.

Paul. It's Fred.

Yeah.

Your father has just landed. I'm bringing him back to the health centre, opposite the station. We'll be there in twenty minutes.

There were several police vehicles in front of the station. A small crowd standing on the brown lawn. Grey suit jackets. Duty belts. Shielding their eyes from the sun. Scanning the town around them. He saw a news reporter in front of a lone camera, trying to secure his tie in the sea breeze. Paul stood beside Fred's boat and watched it all, barefoot in the sandy grass.

Fred pulled up alongside the throng. When his father got out of the car he stood tall, as if he were approaching an audience.

He fixed his collar, combed his hand through silvery hair. His father nodded when he saw him. Paul walked over.

What are you doing here?

I called the police yesterday, said his father, turning to Fred. I said I could assist.

How, Dad?

This is something I can do.

Paul turned to Fred. What's the point?

Enough, his father said.

A woman walked up to the three of them, crisp white shirt tucked into pants.

Professor Darling?

Yes.

Deb Costello. Coroner. The office spoke to you?

They did.

And they explained the condition of the body.

He nodded.

Okay, she said. Would you come with me?

The coroner led Paul's father across the road towards the health centre.

I'll come then, too, Paul said after them.

The coroner stopped in the middle of the road, turned. His father looked at him, blank.

Paul, Fred said, held his arm. Don't.

Paul shrugged off the sergeant's arm but stayed where he was, beside her. He watched his father turn and go through the opened doors of the clinic, ambling behind the coroner, hands at his back.

After dark, Paul and his father ate at the Sri Lankan Cafe next to the deli, the small restaurant run by Shivani's parents. They sat at the wooden table outside. Paul couldn't eat. Couldn't look on while his father did. He looked at his hands, nicked calluses off his palms with a fingernail.

When you going back?

Fly tomorrow, his father said. Thinking I could stay with you?

Paul nodded.

Good curry, his father said. I hadn't expected much from Stark but there you go.

He winked at Paul. Wiped his mouth with a napkin.

You going to tell me what you saw?

His father scrunched the napkin, placed it down. Breathed in.

I couldn't say, his father replied. I didn't know if it was him.

But what did you see?

Paul. I couldn't tell if it was him.

Did you know you wouldn't be able to tell?

What are you talking about?

Did you just want to see a corpse?

I'm Elliot's father, he said forcefully. The Professor's face shook for the briefest moment. He combed his hair with his fingers. Straightened his back.

When they got back to the house, Shivani pulled a sleeping bag and pillow from the linen cabinet and put it in Paul's room, alongside his mattress. Paul offered his father the couch or his mattress but the Professor insisted that the carpeted floor and the sleeping bag would be fine.

So what now? Paul said after the lights were off, the room dark and hot.

The body will go back to the city, his father said. They'll do tests.

Paul rolled on his side. Listened to the wind outside. Closed his eyes.

Paul? his father said. Can I tell you something?

Yeah.

This afternoon, when I left the morgue, they asked me to fill out a form. Another bloody form. And I know your mother had filled something like this before. More than once. These nuisance bloody forms.

Okay.

Elliot's height. Elliot's weight. All of that. And a person can't just know this always, his father said, sounding amused. Not off the top of his head. Can they?

Paul didn't answer. The wind buffeted the thin walls.

Then they wanted to know if he had tattoos. What colour his eyes were. His hair colour.

There was a long silence. For a moment Paul thought his father had fallen asleep. But he heard the Professor inhale, as if he was trying to find the breath necessary to speak.

But I should have known those things, he said eventually. Surely I should have known that. I could see it in their faces. They couldn't believe I didn't know that.

Paul heard the staggered rhythm of his father's breathing.

I don't know why I don't know that, his father said. Then the man cried.

Paul lay with eyes open, unmoving, wondering why it was so hard to listen to his father's crying. But the sound angered him. How hopeless it was, now that it was all done, that it was all too late. And it angered him that even now, in the act of confession, there were things his father wouldn't admit to.

In the morning, on the front verge, his father hugged him, his cheek hot against Paul's. He pulled away and looked his son in the face, as if hoping for some response. But Paul didn't say a word.

He watched his father go towards Fred's waiting vehicle; shoulders hunched forward, hair blown in the sea wind.

Mirage

JAKE SUGGESTED THAT PAUL STAY ON SHORE. But he didn't want to. Didn't want the opportunity to think about what they had seen above the *Delft* shipwreck. Didn't want to dwell on what his father had said to him or how broken he had looked as they stood on the verge; the forgiveness he needed that Paul wouldn't give him.

And then there was Kasia, too.

And he recognised it in Jake's face that morning as they rode the skiff from the beach, saw in him the same guilt he felt. It was a feeling that didn't settle. As if his blood flicked and turned over on itself, like a windy sea. Thoughts rushed in at a pace that he could not slow down or even truly understand.

They picked and dropped pots on the inshore reefs, tracking south of town. They were targeting the crays the fishermen called 'residentials', the ones that had never run out to sea. Paul worked hard through the morning, emptied and stacked pots with a strange energy, something near a rage. The whole time he sensed Michael watching him warily, the German unsure what to say. But there was a mercy in punishing yourself, shelter in the regime of a day's work.

And by five in the afternoon, when they'd set the last of the pots after twelve hours at sea, and when Jake turned the boat north towards Stark, Paul felt despair.

On the way back Michael slept, laid out on a leather bench in the cabin.

Paul sat on the toilet, the seat buzzing against his naked arse. He heard the wind humming against the aluminium box. He gripped his cock in his hand. He stood up when he was about to come and turned back towards the toilet. He leant against the wall, tried to scrub the mess with a boot. And then he cried. He looked into the mirror, saw the sunscreen smudged on his cheeks, his face red and creased.

When he stepped out into the bright light the deck was empty; Michael was still sleeping. Jake drove the boat close in, parallel to the coast, only five hundred metres or so from shore. Paul looked for Elliot's Pajero within the hot white of the dunes, the coast hazy in the heat. Scanned for the flash of sun on car paint, the glint of windows. There was nothing, of course. No one. For kilometres, nothing. Nameless beaches and coves, impossibly big and endless. Paul had the urge to call out, to scream and yell shorewards. Not in the hope anyone would hear. Just to feel his own voice disappear, have it taken by the sea wind.

Paul thought of that last night with Kasia. The words he had said to her, the memory of them, ran cold through his body. Sharp. The knife from abdomen to neck. It was tempting to blame Stark, its silence, its wretched empty spaces. The distance it put between people.

And Paul thought maybe at that moment he understood how Elliot might have felt all those years, the torment of living in your own skin sometimes, alone with their father's secrets.

Whitebait

HE WAKES TO DARKNESS, FINGERS ON his shoulders, the rude smell of whitebait on them. Paul keeps his eyes shut. He stays as still as dead. Elliot hisses his name and Paul tenses at the sound of it, his brother's urges somewhere between encouragement and harassment, and a kind of pleading. But Paul can picture the night sea. He can feel the reef, cold and sharp against his heels. He grips the bedsheets with his fingertips as if they're the thing keeping him from the squishy insides of a great white shark. Elliot gives up. He says he is going without him. Paul hears him pad out into the hallway. He returns a few minutes later. Paul senses him there, watching from the doorway.

When he knows his brother is gone, Paul relaxes, the relief in him spoilt by guilt. The feeling stays with him until he falls asleep.

~

It was midnight when he woke. He reached for his phone, listened to the irregular dance of the trees outside, the day's wind in its final throes.

Kasia, he said.

There was silence.

You there?

Hey, she said eventually, her voice low and composed. The calmness in it terrified him.

Where are you, Kasia?

That is not important, is it?

I'm sorry.

Do not beat yourself up. That is not what I wanted.

What should I do?

You do not need to control everything.

I fucked up.

You cannot expect everything to be how you want it to be. You have to learn that.

Are you leaving? Are you going back to Poland?

I have to go, Paul.

Home?

No, I mean I have to go now—they need me. I have to get off the phone soon.

Where are you?

Paul, she said, in a voice that sounded like a warning.

Will I see you again?

You want to know how everything will work out. You want everything so neat and perfect. She sighed. I cannot give you an answer you want.

Please just tell me if I will see you again.

You are not listening to me.

I am. I'm listening. I just really wish you were here.

They found Elliot, she said. Jules told me.

Yeah.

He heard her draw a breath. How are your parents? You should go home, Paul.

Why?

For them. They need you.

But I need you.

You should all be together.

I'm so sorry, he said. The things I asked. I said such stupid shit. It was dumb, Kasia. It was wrong. You are perfect.

God, Paul.

You are, he said again, not caring how desperate it sounded.

I do not want perfect, she said, the warning returning to the words. There is no such thing, not on this planet anyway.

I love you, he said.

He listened to her breath fill the line. He inhaled, trying to draw it in.

They are calling me, she said. I must go now.

Okay, he said, and could hear the defeat in his own voice. She waited a few seconds before hanging up.

Poppy

AFTER A PINT PAUL'S VISION HAD GONE milky. The air filled with phantom smoke.

Hello.

The girl was standing at the end of their table in the beer garden, hands clasped and smiling like she was about to sell them something. She had belts of sunburn across her arms and thighs. Her skin glowed red.

My name is Poppy. May I sit down?

It was often possible to pick backpackers or new arrivals from their energy levels. Poppy's laughter and enthusiasm for everything said accentuated the deadness of the table.

Shit, she exclaimed, looking at Paul. You've all got eyes like the devil! She laughed.

Yeah, the sun, Paul began to explain and didn't finish.

Are you all from here? she said, and someone started

answering the question. Paul felt her thigh against his, their skin immediately slick with sweat, and his cock went hard.

So, where we going after this? she asked, nudging Paul in the ribs with her elbow.

Bed, someone said.

Oh, we'll find a club somewhere, Michael assured her.

Really? Poppy gasped.

There are no clubs, said Paul.

Oh, damn, she moaned, and laughed. When does the pub close?

Twelve, someone said.

No! she moaned again, mock whimpering. I really want to go dancing!

Later, in his room, Poppy straddled him as he sat on the edge of the bed. He struggled with the buttons of her denim shorts.

I told myself I wouldn't, she whispered.

Wouldn't do what?

I told myself I wouldn't do this.

Poppy pulled her t-shirt over her head. Kissed him as he wrenched her shorts down. He rolled her onto her back, pulled her legs up underneath him, levering her thighs up with his forearms until she locked her knees over his shoulders. He would never have done that with Kasia. He would have been too nervous. Too cautious. Kasia had occasionally urged him to let himself go, but he never could. Was it out of respect? Or fear of not pleasing her? He wasn't really sure. But he did know that with Kasia sex had always felt like a precarious thing, like he was always on the verge of being overwhelmed. Telling him to let himself go was like telling him to do a cartwheel on the edge of a tall building. Just being there, with her, occupied his mind more than enough. He didn't want anything else.

Here, with Poppy, he didn't care. She pulled him inside her. He thrust into her, hard. The sensation seemed blunted, numb. He was drunk. Drunk and indifferent. He went faster, as if trying to rush time itself. Her eyes went lazy, her face slackening with pleasure in a way that seemed melodramatic to him.

She pulled the condom off and said something about it getting in the way.

Her mouth only made things worse. Feeling her teeth through her lips, he felt himself softening. At some point the bed consumed him and he pulled the sheets up over himself.

Paul woke to hot damp on the sheets underneath him, the hair matted on his legs.

Poppy lay next to him, staring at the ceiling.

Morning, she said. You're a big sleeper.

What time is it?

Ten.

Oh, Paul replied. He had guessed it was already afternoon.

Paul held his hand over his face, as if to hide himself.

Poppy placed her palm on his back, her fingers drumming softly on his skin. Paul stayed still and she soon stopped.

You want to go for a swim?

I might need to work on the boat.

On a Sunday?

Yeah, we sometimes work Sundays, Paul replied, drawing on the half-truth to say the words with confidence. They weren't going out.

I need to drink something, he said. You want some water?

Um, yeah, thanks, she said, sounding sad. As he left the room he saw her reach for her clothes.

Who wants to go to the beach? she called out behind him. Paul's a sad arse, has to work.

In the kitchen Paul avoided the German's look.

Communion

I AM NOT GOING BACK, MICHAEL SAID above the sound of the engines. Beyond *Arcadia*'s roiling wake the town scowled, still in darkness.

Yeah? Paul said, only half listening.

I told him, last night. I told my father I will come home when it is time. I said if there is a God, and if this God has such a big interest in my career, he can tell me about it himself. Friedrich was not a happy man. Oh my goodness. Michael chuckled to himself. It is great, no?

I need to go back, Paul said. Back out there.

The wreck? Michael said. Jake is not going back to that place. And I am definitely not. Neither are you, Paul.

Once more they worked the inshore reefs south of Stark, sometimes less than fifty metres from shore.

Paul ignored the German's attempts to cheer him. Instead he worked hard, didn't slow for the twelve hours they were at sea, endlessly restless and impatient.

That afternoon when they had returned to the house Michael went into his room and closed the door behind him.

Paul lay on his bed and listened to Michael and Shivani through the wall. He heard the jaunty tone of the German, telling some story, and Shivani's laughter. Paul felt the burn in his eyes and swore at himself.

Kasia. He missed the way she had made him feel, how good it had been to be caught in the flux of her. She could shake him with a look, and she knew it. And he mourned for the peril he felt lying next to her, the feeling of being at the mercy of something, or someone. He cursed himself for ever letting himself want to resist it. How wretched the stillness felt.

Back into that void came all the familiar guilt. Elliot had been alone, tied to a marker at the edge of the earth. Paul thought of how afraid he must have been. It was beyond bearing.

At three in the morning, an hour before first light, Paul got up from the bed and slipped on his thongs. Hid the sheathed fillet knife under his jumper. He closed the front door behind him as quietly as he could.

He walked quickly down the main street. There was no wind at all, the sea hushed. It was all so quiet in the dark that the town had an apocalyptic stillness to it, as if abandoned.

At the jetty he found Richard's aluminium dinghy, tied to the dock where he sometimes left it. The skipper would be there in an hour, wondering where it was.

He climbed down into the dinghy. Eyed the level of the two fuel tanks near the outboard motor. Heard footsteps on the boards.

It is very nice of Richard to let you borrow his boat?

Paul looked up and saw Michael standing above him, backlit by the jetty lights.

And there I was thinking the old man was a miserable fucker.

Why did you follow me?

You will sink, Michael said. Twenty miles in that?

Go, Paul said. Go home.

You know you will sink, the German said. His forehead crumpled with the realisation. You do not really think you will make it.

Paul didn't answer. He threw the dock line to the jetty.

Jesus, Paul, Michael said.

Paul reached for the ripcord on the outboard engine but Michael was down off the jetty and in the small boat before Paul could turn the engine over. The tinny danced under Michael's weight. They looked at each other. Michael's eyes were wide, his chest heaved. He turned to the stern, lowered the propeller to the water.

What are you doing? Paul said.

We will need more fuel, he replied.

I've got enough.

And the GPS.

I'll be fine on my own.

Michael pulled the ripcord.

You don't have to do this, Paul said.

He pulled the cord again. The outboard cried out.

They stopped alongside *Arcadia*. Michael made Paul climb on board to fetch the handheld GPS from the cabin.

299

As they neared the mouth Michael accelerated. The four-stroke grunted and groaned in the dark. Beyond the rivermouth the black sea was calm. The sky bright with stars. At the bow, shadows sliced the water, the dolphins' hard bodies shining with moonlight on them. Paul fingered the knife under his jumper, watched the night sea. The boys didn't speak. There were no navigation lights on the tinny, nothing to warn a cray boat steaming out of the inlet they were there. And they both knew that twenty miles was too great a distance for the tender. Knew that if the weather turned they were in deep shit.

As the sky lightened the madness of what they were doing fully registered. Paul could no longer see the lights of the town. There was a hundred metres of water underneath the four millimetres of aluminium hull. A rogue swell would capsize them easily. The German looked sick. But it was too late to turn around.

After an hour the sky was a pale, washed pink. The ocean oily smooth. Swallows skipped across the surface.

About eighteen miles from shore the engine sputtered then stopped. The tender skated across the sea for a moment and sunk low in the water. Michael swore. The main tank out was of fuel. The German switched the fuel line to the spare. They exhaled with relief when the outboard moaned back to life.

When they reached the *Delft* wreck there was no sign of what had been tied to the marker. Nothing to suggest it had been a crime scene. The ropes that had tied the body to it had been removed. The centre marker was just as the two either side of it; striped black and red paintwork bubbled and peeling. The iron cradle at its peak, where the light was fitted, was rusted through.

Michael idled the motor metres from the marker, the four hundred year old Dutch wreck somewhere on the shallow coral shelf beneath them. The German said nothing, giving Paul the moment. But Paul didn't know what it was he was trying to do. Maybe he hoped he might sense him there, in some way. Commune with Elliot's spirit, or whatever people might do at the place someone had died. But he didn't sense him there. There was no communion in that moment, no presence of his brother. Just the feeling they were somewhere they shouldn't be.

They had only been idling there a couple of minutes when they felt the first hint of the breeze, the soft tug on their clothes, in their hair. They looked at each other.

Michael nodded. We should get back now, he said.

I thought I might find something, Paul said loudly, attempting an explanation over the noise of the outboard.

I know, Michael called back to him. I understand it.

I'm sorry.

Don't be. Not yet. We might actually survive this. The German grinned at him.

No, I mean how I've been. You were right. What you said. I have been a coward.

Yeah. You have.

Paul nodded. Head down.

But you are out here, Michael said. Searching for him. In the middle of the fucking ocean on a tiny boat.

Yeah, and for what?

Exactly. It is crazy shit. But it is not what a coward would do.

Soon the ocean had changed. The sea breeze was still only light but the swells had grown and begun to whitecap, standing up on the deep banks. The horizon gone. Water slapping over the bow. They held their breaths when the dinghy surfed down each ridge of water. Cursed when the boat bottomed out in the

301

trench before each swell. They were convinced they would roll, sure every time that they were done. But Richard's tender held fast, somehow. They went like that for an hour or more, the gale pursuing them, always strengthening.

They were three miles short of the inlet when the outboard finally ran out of fuel. The boat skated for a moment and then stopped, low in the sea. They looked at each other. Silent. The wind in their ears. The tink and thunk of water against the chines. Michael put his head in his hands. For a moment Paul thought he was crying, but the deckhand threw his head back and hooted before giving into lunatic laughter. On his back in the pitching tinny, making the sounds of a madman.

When Richard came up on them in *Hell Cat* and saw his stolen tender Paul thought he would be wild with rage. But the old skipper just shook his head at them and muttered things to himself that they couldn't hear over the cray boat's diesels, and when he tossed them the towrope he almost looked amused.

They're all ghosts

IT WAS THE FIRST OF FEBRUARY AND THE tavern was quiet, being a Sunday night and with most travellers from the city returned to work or school. Most of the fishing crews would be already to bed, set for 3 am starts. A couple in their fifties or sixties sat at a table over lamb shanks. Pemberton pinot noir. They had bought the bottle. Kathmandu hikers' jumpers. Paul thought he should tell them that they had been duped, that Stark was no place to find yourself. He would have told them that if he had the energy. He figured they would work it out for themselves.

Paul felt for the knife in his jumper pocket. The blade was cool against his palm. He eyed the doors, listened for the sound of boots on the tavern steps.

This doesn't look good, Jules said as she walked her way up the bar towards Paul. It's late, she continued. *Arcadia's* not going out in the morning?

Yeah, he replied. We are. Just can't sleep.

You heard from her?

Kasia? He shook his head. Got her on the phone for a few seconds. She wants to be left alone.

Backpackers, mate. Farts in the wind.

You're not going to tell me where she went, are you?

She wouldn't be happy with me if I did.

Well she *hates* me.

There are things worse than hate.

Like what?

Indifference. Not giving a shit.

Paul looked at his empty pint. Can I have another? he asked.

Go to bed.

Yeah. Okay.

How you getting home?

I'll walk.

I'm driving you, she said.

The inlet glowed under what must have been a full moon. Jules turned into his street, pulled the car up on the kerb in front of the house.

You've got to take better care of yourself, she said.

Paul felt for his seatbelt buckle.

You were waiting for them, Jules continued. Weren't you? Back there, alone. You were waiting for Roo Dog and the rest of them.

Paul shrugged.

You could have got hurt.

Maybe not.

Was that the plan? Paul, were you trying to get hurt?

He contemplated the question. He didn't know the answer.

I mean, you might have killed them, too. Jules sighed. I swore it was like looking at Jake, all crazy eyes.

Paul looked at her. How can you work in that place? he said.

Working a boat is hardly a dream job, Paul.

I know. I just mean Roo Dog. And Anvil. Arthur . . .

Those boys? They're full of shit. And they know it. They wipe themselves out. Ice, benzos, they fucking destroy themselves with that stuff. They talk all loud and hard. But they've got nothing in them. Nothing good, anyway, and they know it. It drives them crazy.

Don't tell me you feel sorry for them?

I'm just not afraid of them, Jules said. Arthur's boat, they're all ghosts. They are all scared shitless. You can see right through them, Paul. You, on the other hand, you've got something to you. You're not your average smelly Stark prick.

You coming on to me, Jules? Paul said.

You wish, you little dickhead.

There was a brief silence.

Still, Paul said. Why stay? Michael said you've always been here.

It was my father's. He built that place, ran it for forty years, almost. It was his whole world. And I grew up in it. The tavern was my first job. The only job I've ever done. She snorted a laugh. Jesus.

You stayed for him?

Everyone loved Dad, she said. He was a good man, and that was his whole world. He was a great barman. Real funny fucker. But a bloody lousy businessman. Got himself into debt, not huge, but a bit. Started gambling, trying to double backflip his way out of it, like an acrobat, you know. That's how it always was with him. It was going to be some big event. A big win. And it'd be all good. More than good. He'd leap us all out of hell and land us in heaven while he was at it. The two-for-one deal. He lost the house. The boat. Lost Mum. Poor bastard couldn't live with the shame of it.

He ran off?

She shook her head. It was me who found him, in the coolroom. Hanged himself.

Fuck.

Yep, she said. Jules put a short smile together, but Paul could see the sudden reflection of the streetlight in her eyes, like fire behind glass. Everything went underwater with him except that fucking pub. Banks didn't want a piece of it, not back then. It was worthless. There was no way Mum wanted it, so I got it. I was seventeen. I've had it ever since.

Do you regret it? Paul asked.

I wish I'd done some travelling, maybe saw some more things. I always wanted to go live in Spain, Barcelona or somewhere, look east for a change, she said, and glanced out her window in the direction of the sea. The Mediterranean seems nice, from what I've read, you know. Just warm and calm, less in the mood to sink and drown things. She laughed. I don't know.

It is as far as you can get from Stark, he said.

Yeah, she said, smiling. It probably is. Not as windy, I imagine. And better-looking men.

It's not too late, Paul said. You're not that old.

Oh, thanks. Jules laughed. Of course I'm not past it. But it is what it is.

What does that mean?

It can be tough loving someone so much. It is damaging loving damaged people. Not too late for you, though, mate. You know, being loyal to people who aren't here anymore is a fucking average idea. I can see that now. There's no point going under with them. You can waste a whole life doing that.

Yeah, he said. I just don't know where to go.

There's always the city. Go learn something other than crays.

I don't know if I want to go.

It's always easier where you are, she said. Or where you've been.

Yeah, I know. Rear-vision syndrome. I know I've got to move on. Same for Mum. Dad has got his own stuff to work through.

You're a good kid, Paul. You're an idiot, but you're a decent guy.

You sure you're not coming on to me?

She screwed up her face and pushed his upper arm. Get the fuck out of my car, she said.

Thanks, Jules.

Yeah, she replied.

~

When we near the turnoff I tell the President I need to piss and ask him to pull over. He says that I should have gone at the roadhouse. I say I'm sorry and he shrugs and says he might as well stretch his legs. He turns the ignition off and gets out, still holding his jam doughnut, and shuffles around the bonnet.

I grab the rifle and step out of the car.

When I shoot him the President stops and makes a sound like a thought has just occurred to him. Not a scream but a sort of grunt. He turns and looks at me and I can see it in his face, how puzzled he is. He has the look of an innocent man who has just been slapped. He looks at the doughnut for a second and then drops it. He puts his left hand to the bonnet of the car and sits down and coughs twice. He says, Swiss? like it is a question.

I shoot him again and the sound he gives then is a long sad noise and I think that it is the sound of the dead speaking through him.

It is the hardest thing I ever did, dragging him off the road. If there wasn't gravel all over the bitumen I never would have been able to do it. I cough up blood for five minutes. Pick up the keys from the bitumen in front of the car where the President fell down. Drive some ways before I see that turnoff to Notting.

~

Troy

FRED CAME TO THE HOUSE LATE IN THE afternoon to tell him the body wasn't Elliot. It felt like another death, the way she gave the news. The results from forensics had come back. She wanted him to know before it all came out in the media. She looked him hard in the eye until she was sure it had sunk in. And he stared back like it was sinking in, nodding as if he was feeling those things a person should feel, whatever they were.

Paul asked her what she knew and she told him.

Troy Little had been missing eight months. He was sixteen, a kid from Tennant Creek, in the Northern Territory. His only guardian, his grandmother, had died when he was twelve. He was a known meth cook, under the thumb of an outlaw motorcycle club. Moved all over the country. Town to town.

Forensics found a bullet graze on the spinal column. They were diving the wreck underneath the marker, looking for the bullet. Fred said it was hard to know if he'd been tied to the marker alive or not. She guessed he had. Looked like punishment to her. Shot in the stomach, left to bleed.

~

At the door of the cottage he doesn't say much but just looks at me seriously as I tell him that there are fellas out there who will never stop looking for him. I tell him that he should head east, right through the heart of everything, till he hits the border. I tell him it's his best chance. Avoid the highways and the towns. The girl will be okay but he won't be. If he wants to survive this, he shouldn't tell anyone where he is going. He has to disappear completely and wait till it all dies down.

I drive back to the farmhouse. I can't think of anywhere else to go.

They all look at me strangely when they see me returning alone. I tell them I killed the boy from the city. Shot him dead, just like they wanted. But they want to know what happened to the President, and I don't know why I say it, but I tell them I shot him too.

~

Abatement

THE WHALERS STALKED THE BOAT. There must have been a dozen of them, at the fish heads like yard dogs. Hard, shining snouts and saggy jowls. The German stood at the gunwale, beer in one hand, his camera in the other. The deckhand glanced over, gave a mad smile. Paul didn't get the same thrill out of seeing the sharks as Michael did, but he noticed he no longer felt the same dread when they gathered by the boat. Even the bigger sharks that emerged nearby whenever the boat slowed, the tiger sharks and the occasional white pointer, he didn't fear them like he once had. There was a polite desperation about them; it was like being approached by a beggar. Their perpetual need, the twitchiness of their hunger, was more than greed. It was survival.

It was late afternoon but the wind hadn't come. The sea was smooth and clear, as blue as Paul had seen it in three months.

There were fingers of cloud on the horizon; a storm front moving up from the south. Paul baited the last pot. The engines juddered.

They were on their way in when Paul heard the engines drop and then idle. The big boat sank into the sea. Jake stepped down into the cabin with his sunglasses still on, swearing about the broken radio. Muttering. Paul caught the word mayday. Michael must have too. He dropped his cigarette onto the deck and pressed on it with his boot. The deckhands watched the skipper from the cabin door, listened to the operator from Geraldton.

We had a mayday. Bloke gave his position and that was it. Over.

What's the issue? Jake said, running a hand through sweaty hair.

Didn't say. Sounded distressed. But no call sign, no description.

The operator gave the position. Jake tried to write it down but the pen wouldn't work.

Fuck! he screamed, so loud the metal walls of the cabin continued ringing with the word. Paul, get up there and fetch a fucking pen that fucking works.

Paul leapt up the bridge ladder. It was the first time he had ever been up there. He searched the dash, heart beating. Found a stash of lidless pens in the centre console. He grabbed them all. It was then that he saw the photo taped above the speedometer. A boy, not much younger than Paul. He knew it was him, the boy from the harbour. And it made sense, then, that Jake had strapped himself in every day to stare at that photograph, punish himself.

Back in the cabin Jake took down the coordinates on the front page of a newspaper. Instant weariness fell across his face. He signed off and then pushed past them with the newspaper in hand and was up the bridge ladder in two steps. Paul and

Michael looked at each other. The engines cried out underneath their boots. Jake turned the boat to the horizon.

The deckhands peered west. Just boiling reefs, storm clouds above in atomic blooms. Jake yelled again. Paul strained his eyes and then he saw it, dark against the fluorescence of broken water. It was *Deadman*. A wave struck *Deadman*'s bow, a huge, unhurried blow, casting a cloud of spray that hung in the air like cannon smoke. The boat reared, its chest out, indignant. Another large wave moved in from deeper water. They're caught! Jake yelled down. They're going under.

A hundred metres inside of Arthur's boat the white water ran fast over the coral, fanning out and backwashing against water drawn from the deep channel on the lee side of the reef. From a distance the action appeared to happen in a vortex, energy turning over itself, swarming and combusting across the shelf like a nebula. The surrounding ocean was depthless and dark and quiet. Miles of clear ocean and Arthur had steered them into the centre of hell.

Jake moved *Arcadia* in as close as he could and Paul couldn't believe the noise. Slow collapsing of water, like acres of earth giving way, grey hillsides unravelling in a perverse slowness. *Deadman* reared once more. The deckhands scanned the boat for Arthur, Roo Dog. But no one stood at the bridge, nor at the deck.

We've got to do this, Paul yelled. Don't we?

Michael didn't respond.

Paul pulled his t-shirt over his head. He could see terror in Michael's eyes and for a second it transformed his face.

After a pause the German nodded. He slung his thumbs under the band of his tracksuit pants and jerked them down to his ankles. His tired blue underpants feathered in the easterly.

Take them off, Michael shouted, looking down at Paul's jeans.

313

I'm not wearing jocks, Paul screamed back at him.

Get rid of those pants or you will drown. I swear it.

Paul screamed a loud curse and yanked down his jeans. His skin was luminous in the low light. The engines shuddered through him, wind in his ears, the percussion of surf through his chest. He shivered with the heightened sense of everything, so aware of his limbs, the lightness of himself. Felt already like a ghost, giddy, as if he had full knowledge and bearing of his silhouette within the sound and vibrations of the world, knew the fragility of a human body and how easily it could be erased. Wondered if this was how everyone felt before they died.

Michael placed a bare foot on the wall of the boat, swore, and pin-dropped over the gunwale. Paul followed him with a messy jump and cried out as the heavy sea took his limbs. Michael swam in front of him, wearing a crown of foaming water, his limbs coated in bubbles. Around them the sea hissed, giving up the air that had been pressed into it. And above, or below, it all was a sonorous rumbling that dizzied his thoughts and ravaged his pulse. The water suddenly drew taut and he was being pulled away from Arthur's boat, out to sea. There was the brief scream of air and water. And then he was deep underwater, gazing at the *Deadman's* ribbed hull, the shadow of reef below. He kicked to the surface.

Michael was halfway up the transom ladder when the boat bucked him off. Paul swam over and found the submerged bottom rung. The steel was slick with grime. The sea clawed at his shoulders, reluctant to give him up. He managed to get a foot onto the bottom rung and pushed himself up. Another swell kicked the stern upwards and Paul tumbled over the gunwale on to the deck. He reached overboard for Michael's wrist and pulled him up the transom ladder, both of them groaning with the effort, and the German dived on board.

Michael climbed to the bridge. Paul headed for the cabin in search of the crew.

Inside it was dark and he could hardly see through the smoke. He coughed hard. A small fire burnt on the wall of the cabin. When Paul stepped inside he felt the broken glass under his bare feet, and then the delayed burn and he knew he was bleeding. He peered at the floor and saw the glass pipes and blister packs on the carpet. Paul found the fire extinguisher and lifted it from the wall. He held it towards the fire but the lever wouldn't budge. He grappled with it like a blind man, squinting with the smoke in his eyes. Paul felt the locking pin with his fingers and ripped it free from the lever. The boat rolled with a swell and he stood with his legs apart to counter it, oddly aware of his nakedness, the slight swing of his genitals underneath him. The nudist superhero. If only Elliot could see him now. He held the extinguisher towards the wall. The foam spluttered inaccurately but it was enough.

It was then he noticed the crew around him, sprawled about the dark cabin, as still as mannequins. Anvil sat slumped against the wall, belly spilling over the waist of his pants, his swollen frame awkward when inanimate, gravity rendering his bulk almost comical, like a rotting shark sinking into a beach. Paul put his fingers to the man's neck, wedging them underneath Anvil's jowls and felt the cold of the man run through him. Tea Cup frowned, haunted by whatever he had last seen. He clutched the satellite phone in both hands. And there was Arthur, the ringmaster. Paul knelt next to him. The skipper looked old and infantile at once, lying there on the floor, body curled like a freakish foetus. Roo Dog's emaciated body was shrunken further in the smoky gloom, sat against the cupboard. His neck was greasy with blood. There was a ragged cavity under his jaw. Paul picked up Roo Dog's bony wrist and felt the beat of a pulse against his fingers. He grabbed the man's face, saw his lips rippling with each exhalation. He was alive.

The boat reared again, and Paul went low to the floor, holding Roo Dog by his right shoulder to keep him upright. The deck levelled out. Roo Dog choked briefly with his neck hung forward. Paul propped the deckhand's head up with his right hand, gripping the top of the cupboard for balance with his left as the boat climbed another swell and pitched downwards once more. He looked at the face leaning on his grip, bony cheek resting almost tenderly against the upper ridge of his palm. It was like holding a skeleton. He felt the pushing out of Roo Dog's windpipe with each breath. Paul could end him so easily. Just lean on him till he stopped. But he turned the deckhand on his side, like he remembered from the swimming classes at school, straightened Roo Dog's right arm out at ninety degrees, head arched back so his airway was open. And Paul stared at the deckhand a moment, dumbfounded by the fact that he was relieved he might live.

Pots swirled on the deck, their lines snapping about in shin-deep water, snake-like. A rifle was laid out on the marine carpet, the foaming surf passing over it.

Paul yelled out, involuntarily, when he heard the engines come to life. The boat leapt over a giant swell and Paul gripped the doorframe. The engines roared as though joyful, sensing salvation.

It was the last thing Paul heard. He felt the grip of the rope over his foot, and was aware that no one screamed his name after him as the pot line wrenched him over the gunwale, oddly conscious in that instant that there was no witness. At first it all could have been happening to someone else; that was how disconnected he felt to everything. It happened so quickly. A glimpse of sky and then the scream of bubbles. Paul watched as the squared rear of the hull shrank, growing further away as he glided feet first down into the sea. He was something like twenty metres deep before his body seemed to understand the trouble it was in, before fear rushed his veins and he roared all the air out of his lungs. It was only then that he realised he was about to die. In those peculiar seconds he had the recognition that this was an experience that others had known, sailing into depths, led into oblivion by a wooden trap, the cray pot on its kamikaze dive, captained by putrid fish. A fisherman's burial. How damn fucking stupid.

He pictured his parents and felt guilt. He saw Jake, the judgement on his face, like disappointment. He saw Father Mobu and the ramshackle church and could hear the echo of a homily. He thought of Kasia, heard once more the miraculous sound of her laughter. He imagined Circus watching, curious in the darkness. And he sensed Elliot in the water, somewhere. But each thought left Paul as quickly as it came, or perhaps he left each thought, plummeting through information as though passing through rooms, window through window, doors and passageways, like falling through a building turned on its side. Water cried in his ears. The weight on him so immense, so unreal.

And he was let go, flung to a stop. A half-cartwheel, a sudden deceleration. And then just water all around him. Heavy, almost gentle. Silent. An astronaut through a wormhole, snapped into a different universe and left to drift. He looked down at the grubbiness of his feet, naked and pale. Beyond was a misting darkness, huge shadows of rock shrouded in sediment.

Paul reclined in the water, arms out. Pale light in huge rings. Far above a whaler shark swam, backlit, swirling at the brilliant surface like a great bird.

And then a figure on fire. Strong arms reaching, kicks long and even. A grip on his wrist. Elliot. How good it was to be with him again.

He opened his eyes to see Jake watching him. The skipper had a wrenched look, beyond anger. The storm clouds all sunlit and fiery above his cousin. Paul felt the engines in the deck against his back, shuddering through his spine, screaming like they could explode. He had never felt more cold and he closed his eyes. Darkness took him mercifully. On the drive back to the inlet he fell in and out of sleep. Saw an osprey turning above the deck in a darkening sky. Wondered if it thought he was dead, or nearly. When he woke again on the jetty it was night. Lights in his eyes. Jungle's arms around him. He was wrapped in silver foil. Someone talked to him in a grim voice, demanded answers to questions that were dumb-headed and he would've laughed if he could stay awake but he couldn't and it was so fucking cold.

Big Shit

WELL, I DO NOT KNOW IF I WOULD BE doing that again. I mean, if
I were you. It cannot be good for your health.

Paul squinted at the doorway.

Lucky, Michael laughed. So lucky. I thought you were gone.
Straight to the bottom, man. Just like that. All over.

There was a drip in the crook of Paul's left arm and patches on
his chest. He felt the medicated lightness of his body and the sheets
tight over his waist, heavy on his legs. The air was clean and cold.

Michael, Paul tried to say, the word tangling on his lips.

The German smiled at him. We are in Geraldton, he said.

How long have I been out? Paul managed to ask.

You were awake on the boat, Michael said. Do you remember
that? You were in and out.

Outside his window he saw only blue sky, pale. The morning
sun shone red against the frame.

You were down there for so long, Michael said. I have never heard of anyone surviving that kind of thing.

A girl swept into the room, stepping past the deckhand and stopping alongside the bed. Michael moved to the corner of the room and watched her in silence. Paul took in the nurse's perfume as she wrapped the cuff around his bicep. He felt the constriction and then the cold of the stethoscope on the inside of his arm.

Okay, she said and unpeeled the velcro of the cuff. Paul, how are you feeling?

He shrugged.

She looked at him seriously and then gave the same look to the pad resting on her forearm, recording notes, the silver pen gripped in her small hand. She was pretty, her dark hair drawn back in a tight bun. Her young face held a careful expression that seemed to belong to someone much older.

You are in Geraldton Regional Hospital. You were brought in last night.

Yeah.

I've spoken to your mother, she said. She's on her way. We'll need to keep you in here for a few days at least. You took in a lot of water. You likely aspirated a fair bit of it. We need to keep an eye on your lungs.

Paul nodded.

We'll bring you some breakfast in half an hour or so. Alright?

Yes, he said.

Do you need to go to the toilet?

Paul shook his head.

Okay, she said. I'll be back to check on you.

The nurse strode out and Michael raised his eyebrows at Paul. You lucky arsehole! he whispered, indignant.

The German stood and approached the side of the bed where the nurse had just been, eyeing the monitors, rubbing his chin like he understood what they meant, frowning as though it was bad news. He looked at Paul and winked. Paul wheezed a laugh.

All of the boys are calling you Big Shit, Michael said. Jungle's idea. He says that you refused to be flushed down the toilet, just like a big shit. The German laughed.

Paul smiled.

Do you know how far down you went? Michael asked. Do you remember it?

No, Paul said. Not really. I knew it was happening. I thought I was dead.

They wanted to put you in decompression. It was a long way down. I don't know how your brain still works.

Is Jake pissed? Paul asked.

No. I do not think so. Shaken a bit, I think.

Really?

You nearly died, Paul. The man is not very humorous but he does have a heart. Ruth too. She was here most of the night.

Aunty Ruth?

Michael tapped a hand on the foot of the bed. It was very scary, he said. We thought you were lost.

The German looked away to the window and exhaled, like he was trying to blow something through the glass and into the sky. Paul didn't know what to say.

I should be driving back, Michael said. Shivani wants me home. Your disappearing act has made her crazy. She thinks I am going to end up at the bottom of the sea. He pulled his car keys from his pocket. I'll call you later, Big Shit.

Michael, Paul said. Thanks.

The deckhand shrugged. Don't thank me. It was the skipper who saved you. He just jumped right off the bow. Craziest thing I have seen. Flying through the air like that with his sunglasses on his head. Michael ran both hands through his hair and shook his head. Craziest thing, he repeated.

Just as Paul put the lid back on his tray of food Fred walked in.

Big Shit, Fred said.

At your service, Paul replied, tiredly.

You doing okay?

He nodded.

Be a good idea to eat some of that.

Reckon they'd do chips?

Not if that nurse out there has anything to say about it.

Fred took a seat next to his bed.

I can't stay long, she said. I thought you should know that the divers found a bullet. On the wreck.

Paul sat up.

She nodded. Positive match with casings found on *Deadman's* deck. Ballistics also have a good match to Roo Dog's gun. So I guess we know who killed Troy Little.

And Roo Dog?

He's alive. He'll be in hospital for some time.

Then jail?

I can't see him seeing the outside of one for a while.

Do you think it was *Cetus* that got them?

We might never know. I doubt Arthur knew what he was getting himself into. I'm sure he thought he was making friends.

Paul lay back in the bed. Always something you cannot see, he said.

Fred nodded. That is true. Y'know I never could have pictured you doing what you did out there, saving Reece Hopkins.

322

Told you I could swim.

Fred laughed. She stood, pushing herself up on her knees.

You going to leave Stark? he asked. Head back to the city?

I don't know, Fred shrugged. Maybe I do need the tonic of wildness.

On the way to the door she turned back. I didn't tell you. Yesterday some Stark farmer was doing his fences, found one of the most wanted blokes in the country. Bikie chief, lying cactus next to the highway, not thirty kays south of town. Would you believe it?

Paul laughed, coughed. Well, it is the centre of the universe.

Apparently.

Barcelona

WHEN HE WOKE AGAIN IT WAS DARK.

He saw the shadow in the chair beside the bed. A suit jacket folded over the arm.

Dad?

Paul. His father stood.

You're here.

Of course. Shit, Paul. The Professor kissed his forehead. Catherine, he said loudly.

Against the wall on the other side of the room Paul's mother stirred in her chair.

Cath, his father repeated. Wake up.

Mum.

He's awake, his mother said. She came to the bed. Hugged him.

You've been out to it since we got here this morning, his father explained.

When we got that fucking call, his mother said, I honestly could have drowned you myself.

His father laughed, wearily. Lucky for you it takes five hours to get here. She'd cooled off.

His parents stood on either side of his bed. They both looked ragged, like they'd been spin-dried. He could see how they'd aged in just six months, and felt guilt.

You are coming home, Paul, his mother said. With us. As soon as the doctor will let you go.

He nodded. Okay.

Good, she said.

But I'm going to Europe.

Europe?

Travelling. I was thinking about Barcelona.

Barcelona?

It's in Spain.

I know that, his mother said. Sounds expensive.

I made some money. I want to see some things.

You sound like your brother, she said.

I want to look east for a change.

His mother looked to his father concerned.

You and Dad should come too, Paul said. Go take yourselves away from here for a bit.

Barcelona? his father replied.

Why not? Paul said. We can't just look backwards, Paul said. Rear-vision syndrome.

I know, his father said.

Through the heart of
everything

TWO DAYS LATER PAUL WAS DISCHARGED from the hospital. Paul and his parents drove north to Stark.

Ruth hugged him hard when she saw him at her door. Jake walked out into the sunlight to see him go. Nodded stiffly when Paul thanked him. Offered something like a smile.

They drove to Michael and Shivani's place and packed Paul's things into the boot. Paul suggested they meet in Spain in June, when Jake had docked the boat for maintenance. Michael and Shivani stood out on the sandy lawn to watch them go. Michael's hands in his pockets, grinning, Shivani's arms around his middle.

His mother agreed to one more stop.

An hour south of Stark, in Notting, she pulled them into the quiet street.

From the porch Paul could see his parents watching the

cottage, like they both could sense Elliot there. He knocked on the door. Heard the creak of boards, footsteps up the hallway.

You always harass people like this? Tess said through the flyscreen.

I'm heading back to the city, he said.

She scanned the street. Well, don't stand out there like you're trying to sell me shit.

She opened the door. Gestured towards the couch with a thin arm.

You want tea?

I'm alright, thanks. Mum and Dad are waiting out front.

Well, I'm having a tea, she said, already in the small kitchen, partially hidden by red brick. You might as well have one too.

Okay, Paul said.

You've been busy being a hero. You and that German.

Paul attempted a laugh.

They say Arthur's boat was a goner, Tess continued. She poked her head around the wall. Roo Dog would have drowned, she said, or bled out. Captain Jake and *Arcadia* to the rescue. Who would have thought? Tess shook her head. She disappeared back behind the kitchen wall.

Paul heard the purring of the kettle.

It's good, she said, I suppose. That you rescued him and everything. I mean, I would have left him to rot. And I'm his sister. I don't know why you bothered.

Paul looked out the window at the peppermint trees and eucalypts across the road. Thought it was strange to see them so still.

You always lived out here? he asked.

Grew up in Stark. Lived there my whole life. You want to know why he was out here? With a junkie.

327

No. Just . . .

This house was your brother's idea. He thought getting out of town would be good for me.

Tess walked into the living area with a tea tray.

Elliot spent all his time worrying about me. All the glass I was using, Tess said. I was fine. She paused, looked down at her body. Well, not fine, maybe. Tess gave Paul a half-smile.

She put the tray on the coffee table, sat down opposite him.

So, she said. Your brother wasn't a criminal if that's what you were thinking. But it was him who was the worry. How dark he got on everything. Spent all his time on his own, on some beach or camping up near the cliffs, alone.

Tess looked towards the window.

I always thought that was funny about him, she said. He came to Stark to get away, then he was trying to get away from Stark all the time. There was always somewhere else.

Paul nodded.

It was almost like he wasn't made for this place, like he was from another time. Prozac didn't really help it.

Prozac, Paul repeated.

Didn't think any of you knew. Don't take it personally. He wasn't the sharing type. Neither are you, I bet. Tess gave him a hard look, unflinching, like someone with the experience of giving bad news, or receiving it.

The cliffs, Paul said.

Didn't top himself.

How do you know?

I just do.

So where is he then?

I'm sorry, Paul. I wish I could tell you. I miss him.

Yeah, he said. Paul closed his eyes, tried to order his thoughts. Heard the floorboards creak under the carpet, felt Tess standing there in front of him as if she was unsure whether or not to comfort him.

You jumped into the water? she said.

Paul looked up at her, the girl's eyes flickering like they were struggling for focus.

Arthur's boat, she said. That's what I heard. Before you got taken down by the pot. I heard it was like hell's own swimming pool and you went and jumped in.

Paul nodded. Not just me, he said. Michael, too.

Elliot told me you were like that, she said.

Paul watched her still face, her eyes gazing on him with meaning. But she didn't say anything more. He looked out the window to the car.

Mum and Dad, Paul said. I better go.

She breathed in hard through her nose. Yep, she said.

Tess didn't walk to the door with him. She stood in the corridor, looked into her kitchen.

On the winding highway from Stark to Geraldton Paul looked east and inland. Felt the land flex under the sunlight. Saw Elliot's Pajero on every farm road. Imagined him standing inside the doorway of every homestead he could see across the paddocks, or walking at the base of every scrubby ridge. He knew the risk of thinking that way, the hope that whatever forces had sent his brother away might have abated. That danger had passed, and Elliot might return.

While his mother drove, Paul's father probed for stories about the season and Paul obliged him. Told him about Circus; the missing eye that was a portal to hell. Told him about the kangaroo they had found floating eighteen miles out at sea. Explained Jungle's genius behind Big Shit.

And all of it his father seemed to savour, as if any part of the conversation had some profound element to it. Paul saw the urgency in him, the sightseer's energy to his father in the front seat. Glassy-eyed and alert, like a man returned to earth, returned to life.

But it was hard to not feel enraged by his father's sorrow, his enlightenment. After so long, after all the wasted time. It was impossible not to think of the cost of the man's distance when all Paul and his mother had left now was to look at the endless land and hope, hope that some vision of Elliot would materialise from the imagined into something real.

But Paul could see that at least, now, his father saw the world in that way, too. Understood the distance between people, the distance that had cultivated between them all, and wanted to close it.

After Dongara, when the highway hooked south-west towards the sea, Paul rested his head against the seatbelt. His parents spoke to each other in quiet voices, thinking he was asleep. He kept his eyes on the shimmering distance for much of the rest of the journey home.

ACKNOWLEDGEMENTS

This novel has had many supporters.

I would like to thank Curtin University's School of Media, Culture and Creative Arts.

Thank you to Griffith Review for sponsoring my residency at Varuna Writer's House in the Blue Mountains. Thank you also to the Eleanor Dark Foundation (the voice of Troy Little arrived – scarily late in the novel's production – in Eleanor's writing studio over one snowy week in August 2015).

To the peerless team at Allen & Unwin for their patience and guidance and, importantly, for their faith in me, especially Annette Barlow, Henrietta Ashton and Belinda Lee. Special thanks to editor Ali Lavau.

Heartfelt thanks to Julienne van Loon for her wisdom and friendship. I owe a great deal, also, to David Whish-Wilson.

As a writer, I have been fortunate to have the generous guidance of numerous mentors, with special mention of Deborah Hunn, Charlotte Wood, Liz Byrski and Georgia Richter. Thanks also to Josh Wilson and Brian Dibble.

Thank you to my writer friends and 'plot doctors', especially Brooke Davis, Jeremy Lachlan, Max Noakes and Bensen Thomas.

Thanks Mum, Jess, Betty, Holii and Nathan. And Dad and Liam, for leading me towards the sea, often against my will, and who I owe my love for it.

This book is for Sylvia who weathered its storms and got us through.

Stark is not a real town. Its inhabitants are fictional, as are the events of this novel.